DAWN
Across the Mountains

Books by J. L. Hardesty

The Lost Legend Trilogy
The Lost Legend of the First Christmas
Escape to Egypt
Dawn Across the Mountains

Coming Soon
Two new series

The Adventures of Anna and the Horses
and
The Life and Times of the Littlest Donkey

Christmas, 2009

Dawn Across the Mountains
Hardbound Collectors' Edition

A Horse for Anna Maria

The Littlest Donkey and the Christmas Blessing

Dawn Across the Mountains
Copyright © 2009 Jo Hardesty Lauter

TRADE PAPERBACK EDITION
ISBN 978-0-9701493-7-4
LCCN applied for

Cover Painting by Judith Wagner
Illustrations by J.L. Hardesty

Published by
J-Force Publishing Company
51029 Smith Creek Road
Steamboat Springs
Colorado 80487

Editor
Marlene Bagnull

Additional Proofing & Editing
Msgr. George Shroeder
Cindy Witherwax

Book Design
Images Unlimited

The characters and settings in this story are creations
of the author's imagination and may not conform
exactly to accepted assumptions about
appearances and customs of the period.
The Legend is another matter. Whether it is
truth or fiction is for the reader to decide.

DAWN
Across the Mountains

BOOK THREE
OF THE

THE LOST
LEGEND
TRILOGY

Written and
Illustrated by

J.L. Hardesty

J-FORCE
PUBLISHING COMPANY

For Jim

My husband ~ my partner ~ my best friend.

Marlene Bagnull

It has been a joy and a priviledge to be a part of this journey with Jo Hardesty. I never knew much about horses before. But editing all three books of this Trilogy, I've come to believe that this tale is true and that God has indeed blessed the horse and given it a special role in the civilization of the world. This assignment became for me a labor of love, and more.

Jo asked me to share a little bit about myself. So here's my story. I felt a call to full-time Christian service as a teenager. If anyone had told me then, however, that God was calling me to a writing and speaking ministry, I would have said, "A loving God would never do that to me!" I hated English in high school, and I was terrified of the public speaking class we were required to take.

God's plan was certainly not my plan. Instead, it is "infinitely beyond [my] highest prayers, desires, thoughts, or hopes" (Eph. 3:20 TLB)! He has given me the joy and privilege of being part of Christian publishing since 1968. I have made over 1,000 sales to Christian periodicals and have authored five books including an expanded edition of Write His Answer ~ A Bible Study for Christian Writers (Write Now Publications, 1999). I am the compiler and editor of For Better, For Worse ~ Devotional Thoughts for Married Couples (Christian Publications, 2004) and My Turn to Care ~ Encouragement for Caregivers of Aging Parents (Thomas Nelson, 1994, and Ampelos Press, 1999).

The Lord has opened so many doors, including the opportunity to serve on the faculty of over 75 Christian writers conferences and to give my one- and two-day Christian writers seminars over 50 times around the nation. And I never cease to be awed by what He does at each year's Colorado and Greater Philadelphia Christian Writers Conference that I direct. When He blessed me with an honorary Doctor of Letters in May 1999, all I could say was, "Wow!" Only God could take someone who felt as inadequate as I did (and often still do) and make all this happen.

Judith Wagner

Inspiration ~ *according to Webster's dictionary ~ "something that stimulates the human mind to creative thought or the making of art."*

On Christmas day, 2007, Judith Wagner, my friend of more than 30 years, was inspired to paint the beautiful picture that appears on the cover of this book. Some months earlier, I had asked Judith if she would consider painting something that could become a book cover. I gave her the title of the book and a very basic idea of what I had in mind. Then I started praying that she might find the time in her inordinately busy schedule to undertake this assignment.

By that particular Christmas day, I had all but decided I was asking too much, and that maybe I should just do a sketch myself and try to figure out how to paint it ~ even though painting is far beyond my artistic ability. But, thanks be to God, that wasn't necessary. I could never have produced anything half as beautiful as the work of art that graces this cover. Before the day was over, Judith called to tell me that she had awakened that Christmas morning inspired to paint the cover ~ and that she was really happy with the work. "It's not quite finished," she said, "but I like it!" Such a statement from this modest, often self-critical artist was nothing short of enormous.

A week later, we met in Scottsdale, Arizona, for a big horse event and Judith presented me with one of the most beautiful gifts I have ever received. "I was inspired," she told me again, refusing to take payment for this work of love from her hands and her heart. "It was meant to be a gift, not an assignment." I still don't know what to say in gratitude.

In addition to being a brilliant artist whose work is sought after by collectors the world over, Judith Wagner is also an internationally renowned and highly regarded equine photographer. Completely self-taught in both mediums, Judith epitomizes the kind of artist who honors the gifts she received directly from God.

Both Marlene Bagnull and Judith Wagner are far more to me than contributors to these books. They are my friends. Thank You, Lord. Thank you, Marlene and Judith.   *J.L. Hardesty*

The Horse

The horse is ~ to humankind ~ the ultimate symbol of freedom. Nobility in its purest form, the horse is a tangible image of romance, power and beauty.

In the ancient memory of our mortal souls, the horse is the vehicle by which we will return to our God at the end of the journey that is the essence of our very existence on this earth.

Who, then, once acquainted with this partner in destiny, could elude the lure of independence that has echoed through the ages in the song of the horse? And who, but one without a soul, would dare to disregard the unabridged trust fixed on us by our Lord when He placed in our hands the fate of His horse?

Surely the horse must be among God's own most beloved creatures ~ and His gift of this magnificent animal, yet another vivid reminder of His limitless love for the human race.

J.L. Hardesty

Book One

THE LOST LEGEND
OF THE FIRST CHRISTMAS

On a journey toward destiny, Michael, the son of a Magi, loses both of his parents—his mother to a terrible plague, his father to unjust persecution. For many years, the brokenhearted boy lives with his mother's people, the finest horsemen of their time. With these nomads, he becomes a great horseman.

One dark night, Michael learns in a dream that he is being called by the One God—about whom his father taught him—to embark upon a pilgrimage into the unknown. He obeys the call despite his fears.

Understanding only that danger lies ahead, the handsome teenager says another sad farewell in a life too short for so many partings. Then, accompanied by a band of unseen angels, Michael sets off aboard a loyal mare with his supplies packed carefully on the back of an aged war-horse.

Some days into the journey, when the wondrous star that his father once vowed to follow appears on the horizon, Michael's expedition becomes a passionate quest for reunion. Navigating by the light of the newly visible celestial guide, the boy and his horses continue on a miraculous odyssey toward a future that will alter the history of the world, forever.

Book Two

ESCAPE TO EGYPT

As the story opens, Michael—the young horsemen readers came to know and love in *The Lost Legend of the First Christmas*—is searching for his father in the company of the three Wise Men whom he met in Bethlehem at the birth of a Miraculous Child.

Not far into this journey, an angel visits Michael and tells him that he has been chosen to escort the Holy Family out of harm's way. "You must take Mary and Joseph and Jesus to Egypt where you will be their protector until it is safe for them to return to their homeland," the angel says. Michael obeys and lives for the next decade with this Family—the three who are the source of the most vital mystery the world has ever known.

In this continuation of THE LOST LEGEND, you'll come to know the Boy, Jesus, and the extraordinary stallion, Zabbai. You'll ride with Jesus and Michael through the early years when the Son of God began to change the world forever. And, in this segment of the Legend that has been handed down for generations by the keepers of faith and wisdom, you'll begin to understand the origin of the mystical bond between horses and humans.

The Human Characters

To help you become acquainted with and/or recall those who play the most important roles in *The Legend*, we offer a brief key. Common pronunciation applies unless otherwise noted.

THE HOLY FAMILY
Jesus: *The Son of God, The Savior, The Christ, The Messiah.*
Mary: *The Mother of Jesus.*
Joseph: *Husband of Mary, foster father of Jesus.*

THE HORSEMAN AND HIS FAMILY
Michael: *Named for the Archangel, Michael is the horseman chosen by God as the source of the dynasty upon which was founded the mystical bond between horses and humans.*

Adrianna: (ah-dree-ah-nah) *Beloved wife and life partner of Michael.*

Archanus: (are-can-us) *A Magi ~ ancient Wise Man ~ and father of Michael.*

Junia: (june-ee-ah) *Deceased mother of Michael. She was a lover of horses, the very best of her tribe, the finest horsemen of their time.*

Junias: (june-ee-us) *Eldest son of Michael and Adrianna.*

Matthias: (muth-eye-us) *Second son of Michael and Adrianna.*

Neeka: (knee-kah) *Youngest child and daughter of Michael and Adrianna. Her given name is Veronica, which means Icon.*

The Essential Horses & Others

THE HORSES

Zabbai: (zah-by) *The progenitor of the line of horses that first formed the mystical bond between these creatures beloved of God and the humans graced to know them. Through the heritage of Zabbai, the horse became partners with man in the civilization of the world.*

Lalaynia: (lah-lay-nyah) *Dam (mother) of Zabbai, recipient of what may have been the Christ's first blessing.*

Ghadar: (gah-dar) *Brother of Lalaynia, faithful companion on a perilous journey.*

Corban: (core-ban) *The great son of Zabbai chosen to succeed his father as herd sire.*

THE SOLDIER AND HIS FAMILY

Zadoc: (zay-dock) *A Tribune of the Roman Army and dear friend to Archanus and Michael.*

Marcus: (mark-us) *Eldest son of Zadoc.*

Joel: *Middle son of Zadoc.*

Phillip: *Youngest son of Zadoc. His name means horse lover.*

OTHER IMPORTANT CHARACTERS

Luke: Author of the Gospel of Luke in the New Testament of the Holy Bible.

Simon: Companion to Luke and Archanus.

Joseph of Arimathea: The faithful follower who provided his tomb for Jesus following the crucifixion and prior to the resurrection.

Marvelius: (mar-vel-ee-us) An evil Roman soldier who vows to destroy Michael and his family.

PROLOGUE
Prologue

From the days of long ago, a story of immense consequence has been handed down, generation to generation. It is the account of a man of great courage and a horse of great heart who knew and loved the Son of God, and with Him took part in history's most enduring mystery, indeed the greatest story ever told.

This is a tale shared for centuries around night fires all across the land, from Marrakesh to Ceylon, from Rome to South Africa, from the mountaintops of Peru to the grassy plains of the brave land to the North—and beyond.

Throughout the ages, no culture in which there were horsemen was without its carrier of this Legend that makes known the origin of the everlasting alliance between the horses and the humans who have journeyed together through time.

PROLOGUE
Prologue

Recorded by the trembling hand of a dying elder of a Native North American people, who valued the horse above all other earthly treasures, this tale of truth was hidden away to be found many generations later by a child of the Americas who would understand and once again pass the Legend on. The child grew old, as children do, and entrusted to me this tale it is now my responsibility to tell.

Ride along now, won't you, aboard God's beloved horse, as the adventure that began in *The Lost Legend of the First Christmas* and continued in *Escape to Egypt* reaches its climax and heralds the dawning of the age of grace and forgiveness, wherein the Son of God made all things new.

MEMORIES & Dreams

Around The Year of Our Lord
30 A.D. (Anno Domini)

Echoing down the canyons of time,
eternity beckons . . .

And the waters of life flow toward reunion
in the everlasting sea of God's merciful love.

J.L. Hardesty

JESUS

A fresh breeze drifts across the land, suggesting the nearness of dawn. Grass sways and frothy whitecaps appear on the ridges of water that migrate in small waves toward the shore of the awakening lake. On a nearby mountain, in the blue-gray allusion to night's farewell, a man kneels in prayer.

A tattered garment hangs loosely over the supplicant's emaciated body. Golden-brown hair falls in tangles to His shoulders, and an unkempt beard hides the bony angles of His jaw. His chest heaves and His clasped hands tremble. But His eyes, gazing heavenward, are clear, His expression, resolute.

He watches the freshening sky as if awaiting a word, perhaps a command, until finally, overcome by exhaustion, He allows Himself to lie down. "Thy will be done." The whisper escapes His parched lips, as to that vague oblivion between wakefulness and sleep He succumbs.

Forty days and forty nights, with only hope for sustenance, lies just behind Him. Through the deserts of terrain and of comprehension, wild creatures and angels have remained in attendance, but none have been allowed to interfere with the one who came to tempt and test the Son of Man as He prepares to embark on the mission He was born of Mary to fulfill.

In the end, through the power of His faith and unwavering obedience to His Father, the Son has emerged victorious. In the cocoon of humanity, He has walked the earth for three decades. He has known life as a mortal, navigating the uncertainties and frustrations common to man.

Now, in this transitory place between the human and the Divine, the One known as Jesus of Nazareth must face a future at once magnificent and terrible. For a few measureless moments, on a gentle knoll overlooking His future, He rests. His debilitated human form seeks rejuvenation in the stillness of near death. In silent meditation, His spirit pursues and seizes the courage He must have to go on.

When at last He passes through the purgatory of partial wakefulness, sleep falls upon Him like a heavy mantle, profound and impenetrable. Gentle grasses embrace Him, and angels lead Him on a farewell journey through the life He has known. From His boyhood, through the perilous forty days just passed, Jesus rides the waves of remembrance. Holding on, then letting go. Hungering back, then longing forward, His spirit ebbs and it flows. His heart full of all that has been and will not be again, Jesus becomes the observer, as all of His yesterdays dissolve to make way for His tomorrows.

In the mists of slumber, memories and dreams mingle, revealing truths that lie hidden in the catacombs of His mind. Elation and anguish vie for position as scenes of a lifetime are painted on the canvas of His mind. A sense of freedom in its purest earthly form washes over Him as He dreams of a Boy galloping across a meadow aboard the most extraordinary horse that has ever lived. And for just an instant, He becomes that laughing Boy again, His arms outstretched, His head thrown back, He yearns toward His Father. He feels anew the grace of the glorious creature that was once His partner in a dance with the wind. Then, too soon, assaulted by a less gentle breeze, He is cast into the depths of an old and relentless sorrow.

"Michael . . ." He calls out, reliving the awful day when He and His chosen brother were forced to face separate futures. "Michael . . ." A ragged whisper, tears across dusty cheeks.

Around Him, the earth waits, pregnant with anticipation. The creatures that inhabit the grassy hills begin to stir, but the pain of the Master hushes them. The birds of morning cease their angelic singing, and the rhythm of the world is suspended.

In the stillness, peace at last embraces His heart. Emerging from the abyss of retrospection, Jesus moves toward all that looms on His horizon. And at last, as the dreamer awakens, His hope gives birth to the dawn.

MARY

The morning breeze lifts a lock of the woman's hair. First light burnishes the eastern horizon and draws her eyes across the shelters of Nazareth. In the calm before the town awakens, the gentle soul kneels at work. Dipping water from the urn that sits beside her, she quenches the thirst of the herbs that grow in sweet profusion throughout the rooftop garden above her Son's carpenter shop.

"Oh Father," she prays, bowing her head and closing her eyes against the encroaching sunrise, "grant me, please, the grace to stand beside my Son in the trials my dreams have told me lie just ahead."

Morning birds chirp and tiny nocturnal creatures bustle in preparation for the day. The woman shudders in the chill that descends as the sun pushes aside the night. Today, in rare sorrow, she feels no comfort in the familiar, takes no joy in the song of the birds or the light of morning.

"I know His time is near . . ." She raises her face to the heavens. "I know I must not cling to Him." A muffled sob overflows from within her. "Oh, but how can I face this future of which I have dreamed?" Bowing her head once more, she allows herself to weep.

Then a soft footfall on the stairs beckons and there, in the aurora of daybreak, stands her Son. Her eyes hold fast to His glowing silhouette, and all that she is reaches out to Him in love. As if in answer to His mother's unspoken plea, Jesus takes her hand, helps her up, then pulls her tenderly into the circle of His arms. No words pass between them. Mary rests her cheek on her Son's chest and gives herself over to the beating of His heart. Jesus moves aside the mantle of blue cloth that covers His mother's head and lets His own tears fall into the silken mass of hair that lies unbound across her back.

The world is stilled as the spirits of the Son and His mother intertwine to reach with hope toward their God.

In time, Jesus steps back. Holding His mother at arms' length, He seems to study her face.

Mary wonders what troubles her Son, if there is a battle going on within Him.

He gazes at her, the light in His eyes shadowed by sorrow. "There is a battle, My mother." Jesus answers her wordless question as though she has spoken aloud. "But the flesh will not triumph. I will obey My Father."

"I understand," she says, reaching up to tenderly caress her Son's tear-stained cheek. "I understand."

"We must soon part," Jesus says, holding Mary's eyes with His. "You cannot follow where I am called to go."

"I know, my Son," she says, her hand still on His face. "When I cannot touch You with my hands, I'll reach for You with my heart, and our spirits will travel always together." With a gentle finger, she traces the track of a tear along the curve of His cheek. "I have known from the beginning that You were loaned to me, not given."

Again, Jesus sighs and leans forward to rest His head on that of His mother. Once more their silence draws out.

"Come with Me today," He says at last. "Come with me to the Sea of Galilee." The tone of His voice denies His sorrow. "We can walk along the shore and take a boat out onto the water." Now He smiles and caresses her cheek. "Just us, just you and Me. We can sup together once more and make a memory that will travel with us for as long as we need it."

"Yes, I'd like that." Mary matches her Son's smile. Then, taking His hand in the old way, she leads Him forward.

Together they take the stairs down from the rooftop and go into the house where Mary gathers a few provisions for their journey. Into a basket, she packs sweet bread and wine, goat cheese, and vegetables from her garden. Then they venture out into the awakening village. As they pass through the quiet streets, Jesus holds His mother's hand and gently guides her to a small stable on the outskirts of Nazareth. There He procures a cart and a donkey, and they journey toward the inland Sea. They talk of God's grace and of the loveliness of His creation. Neither the Son nor the mother mentions the future.

MICHAEL

On a bluff above a broad and winding river, a man kneels in prayer. Beside him stands a white stallion, a sentinel overseeing the night. In the valley below rests an immense herd of horses. Mares stand beside foals that rest, innocent in the sheltering grass. An ambient breeze carries the sounds of the awakening herd across the valley and up the hill. Soft snorts, the stomping of feet, the shifting of big bodies ready for motion unite with the abiding calm as this small kingdom awaits the dawn.

The kneeling man raises his eyes to the heavens where shadows of starlight have begun to replace the morning-brittle stars. His mouth moves in prayer, but no sound escapes his lips. A lock of heavy black hair falls across his forehead, and an unwanted tear runs down one cheek as a ribbon of gray morning light tentatively breaches the horizon.

"I heard Him calling . . ." The words escape on a muffled sob. The white stallion lowers his head and nuzzles the man's shoulder.

"Just a few more minutes, old friend . . ." The man reaches up to touch his patient companion and, as though he understands, the stallion raises his head and resumes his vigil.

Returning to his silent reflections, the horseman known as Michael allows his heart to carry him back, far back, to the night of a mysterious Star and a miraculous Birth. Then, to a perilous trail toward an uncertain future with a young mother, her husband and their Child. To danger and escape, to dread and tranquility.

Finally he relaxes into memories of halcyon days and gentle evenings beside the River Nile. Seeing beyond the fetters of time, he watches as the Boy born beneath the Star grows and becomes strong. The horseman's spirit rides once more beside that Boy across the meadows of paradise. And peace envelops him as the scenes of a lifetime continue to unfold before him.

Following the road of his life's journey to the days before the Boy, Michael recalls his mother's illness and her death. He revisits the peril that swept away his youth almost before he had time to grieve for the woman who gave him birth and loved him beyond herself. He rides once more beside the Wise Man who was his father. He recalls their arrival at the camp of his mother's people, and relives their last good bye.

"Oh my father . . ." His words are little more than a soft breath. "Will we ever meet again?"

The stallion nickers low and Michael looks up.

Before the fan of dawn's first light his wife rides toward him.

"I'm sorry," he says softly, rising as she approaches.

"Why?" she asks, stepping down from a golden horse whose coat matches its rider's wind-blown hair.

When he doesn't answer, she speaks again. "Do you fear my displeasure because you're lost to us again?" she asks, her tone kind, a smile warming her eyes.

Still Michael says nothing as touches his wife's face, then gently draws her into his arms.

"Perhaps it is I who should be sorry," she whispers. "Maybe I've failed you somehow."

"No, my love." Michael touches his wife's chin and tips her face up so that he can look into her eyes. "You and our children are my consolation." He shakes his head. "I'm so sorry to make you think otherwise. Since the day we met, you have been the great joy of my life."

"But still, you long for the others."

"Sometimes . . ." Michael lifts a lock of Adrianna's heavy, golden hair. "Jesus and His parents are always in my heart and in my thoughts . . . but because my life is so full and good, my yearning for them is rare."

"And your own father?" the beautiful Adrianna wonders. "Are you thinking of going again in search of him?"

"I don't know." Michael pauses and looks off across the plain where his family's vast herd of horses still rests. When he speaks again, his voice is husky. "He is a very old man . . . if he is still alive . . .

"No older than your mother's brother, John, or our friend, Zadoc, who are both robust and healthy."

"That's true. But if he is alive, if he is well, why has he never returned?"

"Perhaps other responsibilities have kept him away." Adrianna caresses her husband's face, calming him with her eyes. "Perhaps he has looked for you in vain as you have so often sought him." She says nothing else for a moment. Then she goes on. "It's not like you to give up, my husband. You cannot lose faith. You will one day be reunited with all those you love. It is you who have taught this to me."

"I must go to Jesus first." Michael seizes the opportunity to turn his thoughts away from his father.

"Why do you say this?" Adrianna asks.

"This morning I heard Him calling out to me . . . and I cannot get Him out of my mind."

"Then surely you must go to Him," she whispers.

The husband and wife fall silent. Michael holds Adrianna close to him, inhales the sweet fragrance of her hair, and wills his heart to beat in time with hers. After a while, she pulls back and lifts her face to his. "I sense that everything is connected," she says, then hesitates as though she doesn't want to disturb him.

"What do you mean?" Michael asks.

"Jesus and His parents, your father, our future . . . I think that they are all like a seamless garment, more than related, more than dependent on one another . . ."

"As always, you read my own thoughts," Michael says, once more brushing aside the shining hair that keeps falling across his wife's face.

"For me this is all such a mystery." Adrianna's brow is knit in a small frown of confusion. It is at once real and an illusion and always beyond my comprehension."

"Yes . . ." The horseman strokes his wife's cheek, then releases her gaze and looks away, beyond the herd, across the far horizon. "There *is* a mystery," he says. "One voice in my heart tells me that I cannot uncover the secrets I do not understand while another voice demands that I find a solution. Either way, I think that soon I must go in search of answers."

Adrianna doesn't question her husband. She doesn't beg him to stay. And for this element of her abiding courage, Michael is grateful.

"Let us be thankful for the time we have together, for this day, for this hour," Adrianna says, her eyes following those of her husband toward the place where the sun emerges. "We needn't dread tomorrow, my husband. It will come on its own, and we will face it."

ARCHANUS

Shards of moonlight cut the surface of the talking waters and glance from rock to shining rock. The shallow stream moves with purpose while the world through which it travels rests in anticipation of the dawn. Beside the stream, a man kneels in prayer.

"Oh my father . . ." In the stillness, an impression of words reaches the praying man. "Oh my father . . . will we ever meet again?" The question trembles in the listener's heart, and he raises his head to look for the source of the entreaty.

"Too long," he whispers to the freshening sky. "I fear it has been too long."

Time passes with the gentle surety of the stream, and the man's lips move in silent conversation with his God. Just emerging from a long and terrible illness, his gratitude to the One God overflows, pushing forth a low sob from the depths of him. Then he feels a hand on his shoulder.

"Simon, I'm sorry," the kneeling man says, looking up into the face of the friend whose amber eyes match the color of his skin. "I should not have tarried so long in the moonlight." He attempts to stand, wondering as he does so, why he is so stiff and how long he's knelt beside the flowing waters.

"I have come to relieve you, Archanus," the big man says softly, helping the supplicant to his feet. "I am not here to rebuke you."

"I know. I know that." Archanus looks down, moving his head from side to side. "It is only that I feel I have been no help to you and Luke for so long."

"This was not your choice. You did not ask to succumb to the sickness we still battle." Simon's hand remains a steadying force on Archanus' arm. "Luke has gone to rest. He asked that I come and tell you to do the same."

"But the night is the worst time for those who suffer . . ."

"Perhaps. But this night is nearly over. And what of your own torment?" Simon asks. "Will the dawn give you respite from the heartache that takes you from us?"

"I cannot say. That pain is so present just now."

"It is your son who calls to you, is it not?"

"Yes," Archanus says in apology. "It is my son . . . and it is the Savior. I cannot seem to think of one without the other."

"Have you spoken of this to Luke?"

"No. His mind has been too occupied with those who need him. I could not intrude."

"On the contrary." A smile warms Simon's dark and handsome face. "Luke told me only yesterday that he dreamed of your son . . . and another—a mysterious young man of gentle countenance around whom shown what Luke called *the Light of God.*"

Falling silent once more, Archanus ponders this revelation. Time stretches away, and soon the first sounds of morning break into the friends' meditations. Birds chirp in the dawn breeze. Horses, resting on the far side of the stream, stir and move toward the water to slake their morning thirst. Bees hum, beginning their industrious ministrations to the grasses and the flowers.

Archanus watches and listens, yearning to hear the words he now fears were only a morning dream.

"You will have the reunion you so desire," Simon says, breaking the silence.

"How will my son ever forgive me for staying so long away?" Archanus asks. "How could he pardon this offense of which I cannot absolve myself?"

"How can you not be forgiven?" Simon asks. "You have lived a life of service, obedient to your God. And don't forget the times you've gone in search of your son. You could have chosen a more selfish path at any moment. But you did not."

"What if it's too late? What if I've waited too long?"

"We are never too late when we heed God's call." Simon's tone is gentle, yet certain. "Had God ordained that you and Michael should find one another before now, this would have happened. We are not given to understand all that He has in store for us. But now, I believe, the time for reunion is drawing near. Be not afraid, Archanus. You know that God goes before you always."

PART
One

Ten Years Earlier
Around The Year of Our Lord
20 A.D. (Anno Domini)

Through the dark night of the soul,
bright flows the river of God.

Taylor Caldwell

CHAPTER One

D ust motes danced in the noonday sun. The soft footfalls of an easy loping horse were underscored by a rolling churf . . . churf . . . churf, as the animal snorted in time with its rhythmic breathing. At the center of the fifty-foot circle stood a tall man, wiping sweat from his forehead as he turned, keeping his eyes on the horse that moved steadily around him.

The activity took place in a small hippodrome with a sheer earthen wall as a natural barrier on two-thirds of its perimeter. To complete the circular boundary, stones were stacked one upon another to a height of nearly eight feet. A gate constructed of sturdy willow branches secured the opening to the corral where the horseman known as Michael, trained his animals and instructed the young men who wished to learn his art.

The tall man raised one arm perpendicular to his body, and the horse stopped abruptly, dropping its head low, shifting its weight heavily onto its front feet. "Now what have I done wrong?" the man shouted.

Outside the walled arena, Michael stood on a raised stone platform from which he could observe the efforts of the humans and horses within. "What were you trying to do?" he asked, attempting to sound more patient than he felt.

"I wanted him to move faster!"

"You told him to stop," Michael said.

"No I didn't. I raised my arm to urge him forward."

"You raised your arm in front of him, which told him to stop." Michael fought to remain calm. It had always been so easy for him to be patient and sympathetic with the horses, and so difficult to give similar consideration to most humans.

"I'm tired of this." The man turned and stomped toward the gate. "I'm never going to learn your pampering ways. You're too easy on these stupid animals!" He flung open the gate, and didn't bother to close it behind him. "I prefer the old ways of the lash and chain." The student looked over his shoulder at Michael and uttered one last verbal assault.

As the angry soldier strode away, a subtle portent of something fearful shuddered down Michael's spine. Turning away, the horseman moved into the enclosure toward the bay horse that stood warily observing his approach.

"Marvelius is an impatient brute," said a younger student who had been waiting for his turn.

"Marvelius?"

"The one who just stalked away," said the student.

"Oh . . . yes . . ." A fleeting notion touched the edges of Michael's mind, making him wonder why people's names didn't always stick with him as did the names of the horses.

"May I come in?" the student asked from his place near the open arena gate.

Michael nodded his assent then turned back to the horse. He stroked the bay's sweating neck and its back until finally, beneath his hand, the horse's skin quivered and the animal began to relax.

"Marvelius was grumbling last night about how hard it is for him to learn your ways," the young man said as he drew near.

"I knew he was having trouble," Michael said. "I hoped it might help him to work with a well-trained horse. But his angry commands only made that a worse experience."

"I think I know what Marvelius did wrong. But will you show me? I want to learn."

Michael studied the young man beside him. His bare arms were corded and brawny. He was somewhat taller than Michael. But he wasn't gangly as was the angry soldier who had just departed. This boy's conformation was like that of the finest horse, balanced, well proportioned. There was no softness beneath the sun-bronzed skin, only muscle and symmetry. But it was not this physical excellence that most arrested Michael. It was the young man's eyes—deep chestnut pools wherein character overpowered physique and gentleness outweighed strength. At once familiar and mysterious, the eyes were ancient reflections in the youthful face.

"I want the horses to know me as they know you," said the student. "I want to feel the understanding ripple of their skin beneath my hands . . ."

"You're different from the others." Michael still studied the boy's face. "What is your name?"

"I am Phillip." There was a pause then a hint of expectation. "My father is Zadoc."

"The great soldier?"

"Yes. Your friend, and the friend of your father."

"Why have you not spoken of this before? And how could I not have recognized you?" Michael gave Phillip no chance to answer. "Your likeness to your father and older brothers is remarkable." Michael shook his head self-consciously. "What a fool I've been!"

"No . . . you've had other things on your mind . . ."

"That's no excuse," Michael said. "If you had been a horse, I would have recognized in you the family I know so well."

"Perhaps," Phillip said. "And maybe if you didn't have to deal with would-be horse soldiers like Marvelius, you would have had time to notice me."

"But you've been here for days," Michael said. "We would have treated you with the respect due all members of your family."

"That's why I didn't tell you who I was," Phillip said, looking down, pushing at a small mound of dirt with the toe of his boot. "I wish to earn my own way, not to be shown favor because of my father."

"Admirable." Michael paused. "So why do you tell me now?"

"While you were checking the herd this morning, I got word from a soldier who passed through that my father is on his way to see us." Phillip looked up and met Michael's eyes. "I have a habit of hiding my identity . . . and I didn't want to hurt him as I have too often done before."

"You are as different from your older brothers as you are from the other soldiers." Michael smiled and clapped a hand on Phillip's shoulder. "Your father brought both Marcus and Joel to us so that there could be no doubt about who they were or what responsibility I had in their regard."

"They're good men." Again, Phillip looked embarrassed. "They just don't like to waste time, as they say I do. But you haven't answered my question. Will you teach me your ways? Help me to be a fine horseman?"

"It will be an honor. But first I need to understand why Zadoc allowed you to come to us on your own."

The boy looked away and Michael waited. The sun had passed its zenith and the air inside the hippodrome was stifling. Finally, Phillip spoke, his face still turned away.

"My mother fell ill with a terrible sickness that took many in the town where we lived. My father was away in the service of Rome when she died. I could not stay."

"But your father must be beside himself with worry in addition to his grief."

"I wouldn't have let that happen." Now the boy turned and looked at Michael. "I got word to my brothers that I meant to come to you. It was Joel who sent the soldiers that accompanied me."

"Why did they not tell us who you were?" Michael wanted to know.

"I asked them not to. I'm sorry."

"Never mind. There's no need for apology." Michael hadn't removed his hand from Phillip's shoulder. Now in his best gesture of affection, he patted the young man as he might a horse. "If your timing and your determination are half as good as your intentions, you'll become what you wish to be. Your brothers are both good horsemen. Because it obviously matters to you, I expect you'll be even better."

"I have many questions. Will that annoy you?"

"Only if you don't pay attention to the answers."

"I will listen and I will learn. When can we start?"

"Right here and right now, with this patient horse, in this safe enclosure."

"Is that why you work with the horses in this small space, because it's safest?"

"A good question." Once more Michael looked into the boy's eyes. "Yes, it is safer—for the horses and for us. But there's more to the answer than that." Michael turned to the horse, patted its withers and absently straightened a tangled lock of its mane.

Michael talked then about the difference between the predators of the earth and the prey, explaining that horses are the latter—animals that spend their lives being wary of other creatures that might steal their freedom or kill them for food.

"And man is a predator?" Phillip asked.

"I'm coming to that . . ."

"Sorry," Phillip said. "Getting ahead of myself is another one of my bad habits."

Without responding, Michael went on, explaining that horses are herd animals, bound to others of their kind. The bay turned its head and Michael scratched the animal's dusty forehead. "Horses rely on each other for safety, and each one is alert to the signals of the others. Their instincts and their herd dependence are powerful."

"Are they not, then, frightened when you separate them?" Phillip wanted to know.

"Yes . . . another good question. That particular fear helps us teach them to depend on us. In this small, high-walled place, where the horse can't see its usual companions, the horseman becomes the herd mate.

"In an enclosure like this," Michael went on, "there are fewer distractions than there are in open spaces, so the animal pays closer attention to its handler. These barriers give the horse a sense of both safety and confinement." Looking up, he gestured to the surrounding walls. "My own teacher, Jephthah, was the first of our clan to build a miniature hippodrome like this one."

As he told the story, Michael recalled the box canyon where the idea had come to Jephthah so long ago. He saw in memory the huge black horse that had been a unique challenge—a stallion with small, mean eyes and a terrible temper, a horse too strong and obstinate to be handled in the usual way.

He remembered a hot afternoon when the black horse got away from Jephthah and led the horseman and his helper on a wild chase that ended in a canyon. Cut by the arm of an ancient river, sheer cliffs rose a hundred feet and more on three sides. "By the pure grace of God, when we caught up with that wily beast, he was too exhausted to run us over and go back the way he came," Michael said, rubbing the back of his neck as if reliving the struggle.

Michael had watched Jephthah that day as the heavy black horse, his sides heaving and sweat pouring from every inch of his big body, began to come around and pay attention. Lowering its massive head and snorting through flared nostrils, the stallion had looked to Michael as though he was about to charge the riders that had chased him into this place of impasse. But after a while, the animal gave a great sigh and took one tentative step forward. Michael held his breath and waited for Jephthah to make some move. But the horseman stayed still and quiet.

"I learned a great deal that day," Michael said. "About patience, and focus and not giving up. Jephthah was as weary as the horse, but he understood the temporary advantage, so he didn't quit. He just knelt in the dust and the heat and let the horse come to him."

"Did your teacher build the arena there and then?" Phillip asked.

"No. But that was where the idea was born. We were getting ready to break camp and move on, so Jephthah didn't put his plan into effect until we'd settled down on the steppes where we would live for some months. Then, he and I scouted the area until we found just the right place to test his theory."

"And you've been doing this ever since?"

"We have," Michael said. "Over all these years, in little walled places just like this one where the animal doesn't think about running away and we don't worry about it getting loose, we've been learning how the horse thinks and how we can communicate with it. Without distraction, we can concentrate on one another, and we both get more in the bargain."

"Can I ask now? Do the horses see us as predators?"

"Some horses are more frightened of humans than others," Michael said. Then he explained how his family had carefully selected their breeding horses not only for good conformation, but also for tractability. "And," he said, "we've always started handling our foals as soon as they're born to minimize their fear of humans. Other horse breeders aren't always as concerned with disposition. And they don't always treat their animals with as much patience and gentleness as we do ours.

So, quite often, horses from outside of our herd are more fearful of us, less trusting and, therefore, harder to train."

While he talked, Michael had continued stroking the neck of the bay horse that stood at rest beside him, its head low, its body and ears relaxed, its eyes half-closed.

"Why do you take in horses from other tribes if that's the case?"

"We believe it's important to infuse fresh blood into the herd, rather than to continually mate animals that are too closely related," the horseman said. "Once we determine that a well-conformed horse also has a good mind, we'll give that horse a chance as a breeding animal. But we can talk about that around our night fires while you are with us. I'll tell you then the stories of Zabbai, the stallion that has changed our world. Right now, I want you to watch me go through the exercises I was trying to teach Marvelius. Afterwards, you can have your turn."

"So soon? Thank you!"

"I'm sure my confidence is warranted," Michael said with a wry smile. "Now, let's get started. First, I'll practice a few training maneuvers with Bashan." He paused. "By the way, I want you always to know your horse's name. We can only pay proper respect to another if we know and use his name. While Bashan and I work together, I'll explain a little about what we're doing. You can watch from the observation bench outside."

When Phillip had taken his position along the outer wall, Michael, facing Bashan, stepped to his own right, toward the animal's hindquarters. Raising his right arm slightly, creating pressure on the invisible, but very real, bubble of space between them, he urged the horse forward. Walking with the handsome bay, retaining the imperceptible pressure, Michael moved Bashan toward the outside wall. Once that track was taken, the horseman raised his arm higher, and using a single word command, urged the horse into a canter.

"Can I ask another question?"

"Go ahead." Michael kept his attention on the horse as he spoke.

"Why don't you control the horse with a long line when you work with him?"

"That kind of control isn't necessary in a small space like this," Michael answered. "The horse learns to read us, as it does its herd mates, by the way we move our bodies and position ourselves. Using this familiar form of communication, we make the learning easier and more comfortable for the horse."

For the better half of an hour, Michael demonstrated basic training methods, instructing as he went along. When he was finished, he invited Phillip into the arena where he left the boy alone with the horse. Taking his place on the observation platform, the horseman watched without coaching. The longer he observed, the more impressed Michael was with Phillip's singular ability to grasp the subject and to emulate the techniques he could only have seen once or twice.

At the end of the lesson, Michael walked back into the center of the enclosure. "At the risk of encouraging too much pride," he said, stroking the horse's neck, but looking at the handler, "I have to tell you that's the best first try at these maneuvers I've ever seen."

Phillip looked down and moved the dirt about with his foot as he had earlier. The young man's smile was shy, and his humility further endeared him to his teacher.

Michael looked from the horse to his new student. Finally he said, "If you don't mind my asking, how old are you? You look much younger than your brothers."

"I am." Again, self-conscious, Phillip looked at the ground. "I'm only fifteen years. I was maybe a little unexpected."

"Joel must have been about twelve when you came along?"

"He was." Concern knit Phillip's brow. "Does this matter. Am I too young?"

"Some of us are never young." Michael looked away and rubbed Bashan's back. "Besides," he said after a long pause. "I'd rather work with younger students who tend to be less involved with their manhood and more interested in the horses."

"Thank you," Phillip said.

"Now you need to walk Bashan until he's cool, and then make sure he drinks from the stream before you turn him out with the herd," Michael said. "Afterwards come and share the evening meal with my family."

The heavy blanket of night fell, putting the day to rest. After the evening meal, stories were told around the night fire. Children played until their mothers insisted it was time for sleep. Infected with a niggling apprehension, Michael looked on from the periphery as he had when he was a boy.

At length, Adrianna called him to their tent, bidding him to seek relief in sleep. "How do you know that I worry?" he asked as they lay side by side on their mats.

"My heart always reaches for yours." Adrianna turned to look at her husband. "I don't need your words to feel your suffering."

He touched her face, whispered her name, and finally, allowing his eyes to close, he fell into a fitful sleep.

In the still of the night a sound and a strange sensation brought Michael fully awake. Carefully, he moved out from beneath the slender arm that rested across him. His family's tent was set apart from the tents of the other families on a small knoll overlooking the herd. He could hear the soft breathing of his children, who slept behind a curtain within the large enclosure. Adrianna's peaceful expression told him that she too slept soundly.

The full moon was high, and its reflection on the river cut a swath through the dark valley. Michael could see the watchmen in their places around the resting horses. There was no disturbance, and yet within he felt alarm mounting. A small noise like the falling of a chain turned his head toward the ravine beyond the bluff on which he stood just outside his tent. Now a thud and a scrape, subtle sounds, foreign to the time, heightened his alarm.

With stealth he neither planned nor considered, Michael made his way down toward the place where his training corral was set into the hillside. He had chosen the site because it was well separated from the herd and from the camp, minimizing distraction for equine and human students alike. As he approached the enclosure, the sound of a chain striking something solid grew louder and more pronounced. Soon he was running toward the source.

Flinging open the gate to the small arena, Michael was met with a vision more horrible than he could have imagined. The bay, Bashan, stood trembling in the cold moonlight, his sides heaving, blood running from his flaring nostrils and from welts all over his neck and body. His big, soft eyes were dilated in frenzy, his ears flicked frantically back and forth. A powerful kick was delivered to Bashan's side just as a length of heavy chain struck across his bloodied back. All of the wind from the horse's great lungs seemed to expel at once and the animal fell first to its knees, then to its side.

Michael took two long strides from the gate to the center of the arena where he leapt upon the man who tried to continue beating the fallen horse. Ripping the chain from the man's hands and tossing away the brutal weapon, Michael began to pummel the face and the neck and the arms of the now fallen Marvelius. Then, yanking the monster up by his hair, Michael struck him, bare fisted, again and again and again.

Each time Marvelius fell, Michael pulled him to his feet. Blood spurted from cuts around the soldier's eyes and ran from his nose and out of his mouth from empty places where teeth had been. Sweat and blood streaked Michael's face and arms. His knuckles too were raw and bleeding.

Marvelius tried to fight back, but exhausted from his savage assault on the horse, he was no match for the enraged horseman. At length the coward's screams roused soldiers whose tents were nearest to the hippodrome. Michael's night watchmen heard the commotion too, and soon a crowd had gathered. Watching in horror and fascination, no one attempted to interfere until Adrianna ran up and saw what was happening. "Stop! Michael, stop!" she shouted. "You'll kill him! Stop!"

Only then did the night watchmen leap down from their horses and rush into the fracas. Three of them tried to subdue Michael to no avail. Marvelius was on the ground, apparently unconscious, and Michael still pounded the man's face and his chest and his body. One of the horsemen shouted for the soldiers to come and help. At last, two men dragged Marvelius away while four others held Michael back. All the while Adrianna spoke softly to her husband as if to a raging horse. And then it was over.

As if waking from a nightmare, Michael looked around, shaking his head, a bewildered crease in his bloody, sweating brow. With his trembling legs set wide apart so that he could stand, he turned first to his wife and then to Bashan.

"Go to him," Adrianna said, touching her husband's cheek.

Bashan lay flat out near the canyon wall. Phillip knelt beside the horse, murmuring softly, stroking its face and neck. Among the first to arrive, he had gone immediately to the fallen horse. At Michael's approach, Bashan's swollen eye opened and the horse made a small effort to raise its head. Dropping to his knees beside the animal, Michael found the large artery beside the curve of its jaw and felt a reedy pulse. He shook his head and tears mingled with the sweat and the blood and the dirt that caked his face.

Another horseman arrived with a pail of water and cloths and joined Phillip in his efforts to sooth Bashan. Adrianna had left moments earlier. Now she reappeared with Eleazar, the healer. Still kneeling, stroking the horse's heaving sides, Michael watched as the healer drew herbs and ointments from the large bag he carried and then began to minister to the brutalized horse.

Adrianna put a hand on her husband's shoulder. At her touch, he let his chin fall forward onto his chest and forced himself to face the horror of all that had just transpired. Never before had he felt such rage. Never had he lost all control in such a way. As though he were watching another, not himself, the scene played out again in his mind. He had a terrible sense of not knowing who or where he was, an utter disassociation from himself and his surroundings.

Adrianna bent low and reached for her husband's hand. Now he looked up into her beautiful face and his comprehension began to return. Without a word, Adrianna bid Michael to follow her. He stood, and though his legs were weak, he walked beside her through the gate and out into the open meadow beyond the arena walls.

"You've done nothing wrong," Adrianna whispered when they were well away from the others. "You couldn't have done anything else."

"I was lost . . ." His own whisper sounded ragged inside his head. He clutched Adrianna's hand, then feared that he was hurting her and let go.

"What you saw was too awful," she said, turning to face him, taking both of his hands in hers. "You were protecting a helpless creature. You've done nothing wrong."

Just then one of the soldiers walked up. "I'm sorry to interrupt you," he said. "But I thought you would want to know that Marvelius is alive."

"Thank you," Adrianna said. "What does your healer say of his injuries?"

"He will survive." The soldier's tone was grim.

"That's good," Adrianna whispered. "That's good."

"Perhaps . . ."

The soldier was cut short. "Michael, Adrianna . . ." Phillip called from the hippodrome. "He's up!"

The three turned as one and sprinted to the small arena. In hope, Michael forgot his own weakness. Bashan stood, his head low, his legs splayed, his whole body heaving with the effort to breathe. In front of him, Phillip held an earthen pail filled with water. Eleazar stood beside the swaying animal as if he could support it. Sweat glistened on the healer's brow and his expression was grave. "I don't know how he'll be, if he'll ever trust us again. But I think he'll make it . . ."

Michael, Adrianna and Phillip stayed with Eleazar and Bashan until it was nearly morning and the horror of the night began to fade.

"It's over," Adrianna said, breaking a long silence as the moon slipped beneath the western horizon. "It's time to move on."

"I don't know . . ." Michael shook his head sadly. "I fear, my love, that this long night has just begun. I have a terrible sense that I've started something I will not soon be able to bring to an end."

CHAPTER *Two*

Bright ribbons of flame twirled in a low, rhythmic dance. Dry willow kindling crackled in conversation with the snap, click and rustle of the small burning logs, and the saffron glow of the night fire touched the faces of the horsemen and their families gathered around it. In the shadows nearby, a young man softly strummed the lyre and hummed a melancholy tune.

It was the night after the terrible altercation between Michael and the soldier, Marvelius. Adrianna had convinced her husband that he must spend the evening with his people to help calm the still present tension and to give them confidence and a sense of normalcy. Supper was finished, and the adults sat around the night fire, while the children expended the last energies of the day.

"Will you tell me now of Zabbai?" Phillip asked Michael. "When you didn't join us last evening, some of the herdsmen told me a little about him. Now I hunger for more."

"Yes, I'll tell you about the great horse." Michael smiled ruefully. "Perhaps the telling of old tales will help us all to continue pretending that nothing awful has happened."

"I'm sorry," Phillip said. "You must want to go away alone again."

"It's all right. But aren't you exhausted? Did the long night and the hard day have no effect on you?"

"No. I am more eager than ever," Phillip said.

"You'll want my apologies before this is over." Zadoc, who had arrived that afternoon as his son expected, made a wry face. "This boy's energy is only surpassed by his curiosity. It's likely that you'll tire of him before he's satisfied his insatiable desire for learning."

"I warned him too," Phillip said, looking at his feet and then, turning his eyes to his father. "But he says all will be well as long as I listen."

"Is this the path you wish to follow, then?" Zadoc asked. "Will you join Michael?"

"I want to be a fine horseman, but I don't think I'll join these good people. I think, instead, I'll one day have charge of the cavalry so that I can change the way the horses of war are treated. I'll be their protector."

"That's another of my son's small faults." Zadoc spoke with good-natured sarcasm. "He has so little confidence!"

"It's an admirable goal," Michael said. "And I'll do all I can to help him attain it."

"No one could ask for more." Affection lit Zadoc's still handsome old face as he looked from the youngest son of his blood, to the eldest son of his heart.

"So, how about the story of Zabbai?" Phillip persisted.

"As soon as Michael has bidden his children good night." Adrianna, trailed by three small children, answered Phillip's question as she joined the circle of friends.

Michael held out his arms, beckoning his children. When he was finished hugging them, individually, then together, he turned the two handsome boys and the enchanting little girl toward Zadoc. "Do you remember who this is?" he asked them.

"He is the great soldier," the largest boy spoke solemnly. "He is the friend of our grandfather."

"Come here, boy," Zadoc commanded. "Let me look at you."

The child walked bravely up to the big soldier and stood before him as though at attention. "Junias, you are the reflection of your beautiful grandmother." Zadoc captured the boy's gaze and held it.

"But I am a boy," the child said, obviously insulted.

"Indeed you are, and a strapping boy at that." Zadoc appeared to suppress a laugh. "But in your eyes and the shape of your face, I see Junia. Your hair too is like hers—the color of spun gold. And in your heart, I know you carry her courage."

"I can ride like the wind!" Now the boy smiled.

"How old are you?" Zadoc asked.

"I am nearly six years."

"Big for your age! Come. Introduce me again to your brother and sister. I doubt they remember me as you do."

Junias turned and reached his hand out toward his younger siblings. "Come here, Matthias. You must meet the great Zadoc . . . Matthias will soon be five. He too will be a fine horseman."

A dark haired boy stepped forward. Intense blue eyes fringed by thick lashes looked gravely into the face of the old soldier.

Zadoc took a great, deep breath. As he spoke, he shook his head in wonder. "You are your father all over again."

The child said nothing. Nor did his gaze waver.

"A stoic like him too, I see . . ."

"I am Veronica." A clear, small voice chimed like the high, melodious notes of the lyre, as an exquisite girl child stepped in front of her older brothers and introduced herself. "I am three, and I am my Abba's princess."

Luxurious waves of black hair fell to the child's waist and framed a face of breathtaking beauty. Huge eyes of translucent turquoise sparkled with vitality above dimpled cheeks and an impish, curving mouth.

Watching as his daughter spun her web of enchantment, Michael's heart ached with love and gratitude. For the first four years of their marriage, he and Adrianna had remained childless. Two miscarriages and one stillborn boy had, early on, dashed their hopes for a big family. But just when Michael had finally resigned himself to the fact that he would never be a father, Adrianna announced that she was again with child, and that this time she was sure she would give her husband a healthy son.

She had been correct. Junias was born vigorous and strong. Then, in quick succession, came Matthias and Veronica, whose difficult birth had nearly killed her mother and had made it impossible for Adrianna to bear any more children.

Now Zadoc reached for Veronica, who moved fearlessly into his outstretched arms. "You have stolen my heart, dear princess." The soldier laughed. "I will be your slave forever!"

"Where has this brazenness come from?" Adrianna asked, shaking her head in mock disapproval.

"From the women of her heritage!" Zadoc and Michael said in the same breath.

"Her name suits her perfectly," Zadoc said. "She *is* an icon—the true image of those from whom she comes." Like Matthias, Veronica had her father's features and his coloring, but in her attitude and her carriage, she reflected her mother and her grandmothers. "From now on, I'm going to call you Neeka," Zadoc said, "just as I did your mother's mother."

"I like that!" The child giggled, ran to her father and wrapped her arms around his neck. "Abba, from now on, I will be Neeka."

Michael laughed and buried his face in his daughter's fragrant hair. "Just like the horses," he said, looking up and across the child to his wife, "the female line is always the strongest and surely the most important."

"But what about stallions like Zabbai?" Phillip asked, evidently determined to return to the subject of his interest.

"All right, time for bed," Adrianna said to her children. "Your father has stories to tell."

"I want to hear," Veronica protested.

"Me too," the boys said as one.

"They can stay up." Michael was still smiling. And before their mother could disagree, the boys sat down beside their father and their sister.

"The horses are a great mystery," Michael began, his eyes meeting those of the eager Phillip. "And yet, they offer some predictability. They're like life itself—a combination of so many elements that a student can never become too sure, never assume that all of the necessary lessons have been learned."

"If it mattered to you," Zadoc interjected with a patient smile, "you might notice that everything you know about horses can be applied equally to the study of people. The way the horses learn, the ways they protect themselves, the way they teach their young—all have parallels in the human theater."

"I leave this philosophy as it regards people to you and Adrianna," Michael said. "I'll stick to the horses, who are more reliable and far less devious."

Earlier, when the other children of the clan had been sent off to their tents for the night's rest, Michael had expected their fathers to follow, exhausted as everyone obviously was from the events of the past twenty-four hours and the fears that had nagged them all day. But apparently, as word got around that he was going to tell a story, all those old enough to avoid a forced curfew had drifted back to the night fire.

Michael watched now as a number of soldiers approached tentatively. Understanding their reticence, in view of their association with Marvelius, Michael was cordial and welcomed the men.

⟨≈⟩

Zadoc sat silent near Michael, surveying the growing assembly and observing the way both horsemen and soldiers were drawn to this leader. The fierce devotion paid to Michael by his people was legendary. Reserved, often unapproachable, Michael was an enigma whose very reticence seemed to inspire admiration. The respect he received was less difficult to understand. He was a horseman without equal who naturally garnered the honor of those who recognized his gift. And even before his decisive, potentially disastrous, action of the preceding night, he was known among the cavalrymen for his courage.

"What is the condition of your comrade?" Zadoc asked one of the soldiers.

"He's no comrade of mine," the man said. "He is a barbarian . . . as cruel to humans as he is to horses. But in answer to your question, he is, unfortunately, going to survive."

"May we stay and listen?" one of the horsemen asked, turning the focus away from the evil Marvelius.

"Of course," Michael said. "But I'm not likely to say anything you haven't heard before."

"No matter," the man said. "There is always more to be learned."

"So where do I begin?" Michael looked at Phillip, the instigator of the night's storytelling. "Is it a tale of adventure you want? Or shall I continue telling you about our philosophy and our understanding of these great creatures?"

"Abba, you must start with Zabbai." Neeka, cuddled up next to her father, tipped back her head, looked into his eyes and spoke with authority. "You must start with his name."

"A good place," Michael said, returning his daughter's gaze. Squeezing her to him, he turned again to Phillip. "Do you know what the word Zabbai means?"

"No," Phillip said. "I don't."

"A gift from God," Matthias said, his tone soft but sure.

"Oh . . ." There was wonder and excitement in Phillip's response.

"And there is a great deal in a name," Adrianna said into the silence that followed. "For instance your name, Phillip."

"What does it mean?" Neeka wanted to know.

"Horse lover." It was Zadoc's turn to answer. "His name means horse lover."

"How did you know to name him thus?" Adrianna asked, a puzzled little wrinkle crossing her pretty forehead. "When he was just a babe, how did you see that he would love the horses?"

"I knew nothing." Zadoc shook his head. "Phillip's mother named him, as she did all of our sons. My wife was the keeper of our wisdom . . ." He looked away, unable to say more.

"I'm sorry," Adrianna said, reaching over to touch the Tribune's arm. "How thoughtless of me."

Zadoc looked down at his hands. Then he turned back toward Adrianna. He knew she would see the emotion in his eyes, but that didn't matter, somehow. Adrianna was like a daughter to him, and with her it didn't seem necessary to hide the grief that had lived within him since the loss of his beloved wife some months earlier.

Neeka looked up at her father, then stood and went to Zadoc. Placing her tiny hands on each of his weathered cheeks she gazed into his glistening eyes. "Don't be sad," she whispered. "My Abba has told me that we will meet the ones we love in heaven."

Zadoc wrapped his arms around the child and looked at Michael. "You have taught her well," he said softly.

"Sir, I'm sorry . . ." The commander of the Roman cavalry unit presently in residence with the horsemen stepped into the circle of light that emanated from the night fire to address the Tribune.

"Yes," Zadoc said.

"I'm sorry, sir," the officer said again.

"What is it?"

"The . . . uh . . . the injured soldier is demanding to see you."

"On what pretense?" Zadoc asked.

"He insists that he has recourse to you regarding the . . . uh . . . the incident. He says you are familiar with his father . . ." The officer's voice trailed off and he looked away.

"And?" Zadoc said.

"I know this is irregular, Tribune, sir—but I think you should come."

"All right," Zadoc said, still holding Neeka in his arms as he stood. "You wait with your Abba. Help him tell his story. I'll return soon." Then he placed the little girl in her father's lap and turned to follow the officer to the soldiers' tents.

❧

Michael watched his friend walk away. An uneasy hush had fallen on the little gathering, and the air was pregnant with tension.

"Please, Michael, tell us the story." Adrianna broke the heavy silence.

"Another invitation to think of something other than the calamity I have brought upon our people?"

"There is no calamity," Adrianna said, shaking her head. "It's good that Zadoc is here. He'll avert any trouble that might have come from your doing the only thing you could have done."

Grateful to his wife, though unconvinced, Michael forced himself to begin the narrative that would take him away for a time from the anxiety of the present.

"Zabbai, like all the best, was the son of a great mare," the horseman began. "Indeed. Lalaynia was the greatest mare I've ever known." His voice drifted off as the sorrow of a long ago parting took captive his heart and his thoughts.

ARCHANUS

In the warm light of the fading day, Archanus sat greeting the sick at the door to the hospital and assessing their needs. A young mother with her son came to him and spoke of a lingering illness that had plagued her—an illness from which she seemed unable to recover.

As the old Wise Man listened, his heart began to ache with a ferocity beyond what was natural to such an encounter. The sun lowered toward the western horizon behind the woman, making her down-turned face indistinct within the shadows. The soft glow of evening shimmered through her golden hair. For just a moment she became Junia, the wife too long gone from the path Archanus had walked, and the dark haired boy beside her became his long lost son.

The moment passed. He tended to the needs of the woman and her child. Then, alone again, he could not escape the sorrow that journeyed always with him. It was an agony of spirit that sometimes receded into the dark corners of his heart, but never left him. It was an old grief that could neither be fully observed, nor entirely put to rest. Somewhere in the wide world was his son—the one he must see again before he could glimpse the peace he sought.

"Have I not tried hard enough?" he whispered into the encroaching darkness. "Has the One God kept my son from me because I have not been good enough?" He listened and he waited. But no answer came. Only the sounds of day's end in the town square met his ear and accompanied him as he left another day behind.

CHAPTER *Three*

When the sorrow at last faded back into the recesses of his heart and his mind, Michael began his story right where he had left off.

"Lalaynia carried me to the most monumental events of my life," he said softly. "She will always be the horse that holds my heart."

"Tell about the journey, Abba," Neeka begged.

"You've heard that story a hundred times." Michael and Adrianna spoke together.

"But I haven't," said Phillip.

So Michael told once more how he and Lalaynia and her brother, the old warhorse, Ghadar, had traveled for many days and many miles. He talked of the desert pirates who accosted them and of the angels he believed had been their guides and protectors. He recalled for his listeners the great Star that had guided the travelers on the last leg of their journey. "I've always been certain of one thing," he said at the end of his story. "That night will be remembered as the moment when the whole world was changed forever."

"So the colt—Zabbai—came after that?" Phillip asked. "After Lalaynia touched the hand of the Babe in the manger?"

"Yes. Zabbai was born some months later in Egypt," Michael said. "But that's another story, too long just now for the telling."

"Just one last thing," Phillip said. "You told me earlier that Zabbai has changed your world. Please, tell me how."

"You are insatiable," Michael said with a good-natured shake of his head. "All right. But for now, you only need the short version of the story. You'll learn more as you work with the horses."

"Good . . . good. That's what I want."

"Zabbai passes on to every one of his offspring his very best characteristics," Michael began. "Even the oldest of our horsemen cannot recall having ever heard of such a potent stallion."

"What are those characteristics?" Phillip wanted to know.

"The most obvious have to do with physical beauty and athleticism," Michael answered somewhat vaguely.

"But there is much more," said Adrianna. "And my husband doesn't usually talk about the rest."

"Why not?" Phillip frowned.

"Because it's hard to explain," Michael answered. "And for most people, harder to believe."

"Please try," Adrianna and Phillip spoke at once.

"I'll believe whatever you tell me," Phillip said.

"Well . . ." Michael paused, bent his head forward, and rubbed the back of his neck and then looked again toward the herd before he spoke. "Before Zabbai, no amount of careful training could produce the kind of trust his offspring have in us. Even though horsemen like my mentor, Jephthah, had started perfecting kinder, more intelligent methods of handling the horses than those most commonly employed before, we never got the kind of results that we get consistently from horses of Zabbai's line."

"Like what?" Phillip asked.

"I don't know how to define it except to say that Zabbai as well as his sons and daughters and all those that hail from them have become our willing servants. They're still creatures of the herd. They're still wary, as are all animals of prey. But the horses related to Zabbai seem to have a true desire to please us."

"Is that why your training methods are so different?"

"Yes, at least that's a good part of it. I've learned so much from these Zabbai-related horses that nothing, for me, will ever be the same."

"But can you use the new methods on horses that aren't related to Zabbai?" Phillip asked.

"We can." Michael paused, considering the rest of his answer. "The results aren't as good, generally. But even with the most difficult of horses, we have much better long-term success than we ever did before."

"Some of the soldiers my brothers ride with don't approve of your new methods," Phillip interjected.

"They miss the days when they could prove their manhood by taming the wildest of horses at our annual procurement gatherings," one of the horsemen said, laughing.

"That's the truth," said a soldier. "And most men, even after they've spent time with you, are still caught up in trying to master these big, powerful animals."

"That's why I won't sell to the cavalry any horses that are related to Zabbai," Michael said, turning to look at the soldier. "I hope that you, like Phillip, will be different."

"Perhaps you'll join me, Maximus," Phillip said to the soldier, then turned his attention back to Michael. "When you have taught me your new ways, I'll teach them to the other cavalrymen. Anyone who refuses to learn can travel on foot instead of being a part of the cavalry."

Two of the other soldiers seated nearby looked at one another and shook their heads. Noticing this Michael spoke directly to them. "Never underestimate the power of faith and determination." Then, turning to Phillip, he added, "You're a brave one. I'll teach you everything I can. And I hope Maximus will join you. Now, this has been enough for tonight. You can't learn everything in a single session."

With that dismissal, Michael hugged his children, then looked up at Adrianna who waited patiently. "I'll be along in a little while," he said. "I want to wait here for Zadoc."

"I understand. We'll say a special prayer tonight, won't we?" Adrianna looked at her children who all agreed. When they had moved away only a few yards, Neeka let go of her mother's hand and ran back to her father.

Wrapping her arms around his neck she whispered, "The One God will take care of us, Abba. Do not be afraid."

Michael held his daughter close, once more breathing in the sweet smell of her, wishing his own faith could be so innocent and so strong.

"Come, Neeka," Adrianna called. "We'll ride with your Abba tomorrow. How will that be?"

The beautiful child let go of her father's neck, kissed his cheek, then followed her mother without argument. Right behind them, the others got up and left. The last to go was Phillip.

"No more stories tonight," Michael said. "You need to get some rest if you're going to be of any use to me tomorrow."

"But what about you?" Phillip wondered. "Aren't you tired?"

"I am. But I need to hear from your father before I'll be able to sleep."

"And you don't want me to stay."

"Not tonight," Michael said with a sad shake of his head. "Not tonight."

Once Phillip had disappeared into the darkness, Michael stirred the still crackling fire and then added a few more pieces of wood. He allowed his gaze to be held by the ardent glow at the center of the small conflagration. Something inside him ebbed and flowed with the changing colors of the living fire. The fever in his heart matched the swelling heat, and he lost himself for a time in regret and reverie.

"Are you all right?" Zadoc's voice was deep and gentle.

Michael turned from the fire to face his friend. "Yes . . . I suppose . . ."

"Come, sit with me for a while," Zadoc said. "I'll tell you of my plans."

They moved a few feet away from the fire ring and sat down, resting their backs against a rock.

"I'm not going to lie to you," Zadoc began. "This situation could be dangerous—for you and for your people. But there are ways we can forestall this."

Zadoc told Michael about the father of Marvelius, a man whose military career had been destroyed when he failed a mission of particular importance to King Herod.

"Darkon was given the responsibility of finding and killing a child born in Bethlehem some twenty years ago," Zadoc explained. "He was a centurion who had earned high regard— a hard, cruel man expected to advance through the ranks. Many male children died at his hand when the One he sought could not immediately be found."

When Zadoc paused, Michael did not fill the silence. Finally, the Tribune went on.

"After that horror, Herod sent Darkon as second in command to a brute named Carvelius on an expedition to Egypt in search of the same Child. The evil pair returned in disgrace, having failed their mission. Although Darkon was not demoted, he was forever after held in the lowest regard and he did not again advance in rank. Carvelius suffered a similar fate."

Another pause begged comment from Michael. But again, he remained silent.

"Darkon's wife died soon after his return, when their three sons were still very young. Some say the woman perished of a broken heart. Others insist her demise came at the hand of her husband. It is said that from then on, Marvelius and his brothers suffered beatings beyond the endurance of most. Though it is not an excuse for repeating that behavior, I believe this to be the source of the savageness that drives Marvelius today."

"What have I brought upon my people?" Michael looked down at the back of his bruised hands, then turned them, palms up, and continued to stare as though they held some answer.

"I will see to it that Marvelius is deployed with an infantry unit under a leader who is loyal to me," Zadoc answered indirectly. "He will be sent as far away as possible from the areas you and your people commonly travel."

"Will that not only anger him more?" Michael asked.

"It may. But at least it will keep him away from you and give me time to figure out what else to do. I'll keep track of his whereabouts and of his attitude."

"How can I thank you?" Michael asked, his voice echoing the heaviness of his heart. "You have been saving my life since I was a boy. How can I ask you for more?"

"You are as my own son," Zadoc said, placing a hand on Michael's bent shoulder. "I would give my life for you."

"I pray, with all my heart, that will never be required." Michael looked into the eyes of the old soldier then fell silent once more. Throughout the long night, they sat together, waiting for the dawn, speaking no more of that which lay ahead.

CHAPTER *Four*

The sun shone above the eastern horizon. Not a cloud breached the hard blue sky, and already heat rose in subtle, translucent waves above the morning-warm ground. The horsemen and soldiers, who had shared the day's first meal, chatted amiably. The women visited with one another, while their children played nearby.

Suddenly the sound of hooves pounding across hard packed ground broke the calm. A dozen horsemen jumped up as one and ran to the line where their mounts stood tethered for easy access in case of an emergency. With equal haste, the women rushed their children toward shelter and safety. Adrianna got her hands on her daughter and youngest son before they could follow their father. But Junias escaped his mother's protection. Among the first mounted, the boy, who had been taught well that the horses were always to be considered first, rushed toward the resting herd without waiting to see where the other horseman were headed.

While some of the horsemen rode to the edges of the herd, others went to the trails that led into the camp. Additional riders made their way to the high lookout points from which the whole valley could be observed. On the trail that led to the north, two of the horsemen were met by a cadre of mounted soldiers. Pulling his horse to a rearing stop, the leader signaled his men to follow suit. "Has the Tribune Zadoc arrived in your camp?" he shouted. "We must find him at once!"

"He is here," the younger of the two horsemen said. "Please calm your horses before you proceed. The herd is unsettled by your arrival and could be in danger."

"That is not our concern!" The soldier, who simultaneously yanked at his reins and spurred the sides of his confused mount, forced the massive animal between the horsemen and galloped again toward the camp with his men following at the same breakneck speed. Shaking their heads, the riders joined their kinsmen who were doing their best to quiet the frightened herd.

"Tribune Zadoc!" the lead soldier shouted as he and his men thundered into the camp. "Where is the Tribune?"

"I'm here you fool!" shouted Zadoc, grabbing the reins from the man's hand and jerking him down off of his horse. "What is the matter with you, charging into a peaceful camp, endangering people and animals?"

"There is trouble in Gaul. You are being called to quell an uprising. There is no time to waste." The soldier's anxious harangue was not accompanied by an apology.

The rest of the soldiers had dismounted and were quieting their horses. Hearing the interchange between Zadoc and the agitated soldier, Adrianna had left her children with one of the other wives and stood now at Zadoc's side. "Calm down and make sense," she said with an authority that at once startled and subdued the soldier.

"My apologies," the soldier said, nodding in Adrianna's direction. "But this is a matter of gravest importance."

Adrianna took the reins of the soldier's horse from Zadoc and the snorting, stomping animal calmed visibly. Sweat foamed around the edges of the saddle pad and girth and along the horse's neck. His sides heaved and his nostrils flared with labored breathing. But he dropped his head low, submitting to Adrianna's gentle touch.

"We will care for your horse. Your riders can see to theirs. There is food for the animals and the men." Adrianna looked at the soldier, speaking to him as she might a recalcitrant child. "You, explain yourself and your errand to the Tribune."

The man gave no argument.

"Your name," Zadoc demanded.

"I am Clovis, a Centurion in your command."

"Your message."

"You are to come at once. Your son, Marcus, has been sent ahead with his troops to deal with the insurgents. But your presence is required . . ."

"My men and I will prepare for the journey," Zadoc said. "When your horses and men have rested, we will depart. Before that departure, you will apologize properly to Michael, the leader of this tribe, and to his people for your rashness and the danger you caused."

"Yes sir," said the Centurion, his voice now tinged with fear.

Phillip had returned to the camp when the herd grew quiet. "I'll prepare your horses and ride with you a short way," he said to his father.

"That will be good." Zadoc recognized in his son an unusual sadness. Uncertain of its source, he offered the only consolation he had to give. "I'll return, son, as I always have," he said. "If it's Marvelius who troubles you, don't worry. I'll take him away with us. Gaul might be just the place to keep him distracted." The Tribune paused. "Right now, I need to borrow your horse so that I can ride out to talk with Michael."

Phillip handed his father the reins, then turned and walked toward the small corral where the horses that belonged to Zadoc and his men were kept.

"He'll be at the highest lookout," Adrianna told the Tribune as he rode by her.

"Thank you," said Zadoc. "And, Adrianna, don't worry . . ."

"I'm not worried, dear friend." Adrianna moved close to the horse, rested her hand on its neck and looked up at the rider. "I'm only sad at yet another goodbye."

"I'll be back," he said, and then he rode away.

Zadoc found Michael standing beside Zabbai on a high bluff that overlooked the meadow where the horses again grazed peacefully.

"I must bid you farewell, my friend," Zadoc said as he dismounted.

"I feared something like this when the soldiers arrived in such haste. But what has happened?"

"I must go to Gaul to quell an uprising," Zadoc said. "Marcus has been sent ahead and, though I trust him completely, I don't want to leave him on his own."

They fell silent then, standing side by side, looking across the herd into the unknowable distance.

"Do not worry," Zadoc said after a while. "I'll still deal with Marvelius."

"I hadn't even considered that," Michael said, a deep, sad furrow in his brow.

"What is it then?"

"Each time I must bid you farewell, my heart is drawn to the long ago parting with my father. And when I think of him, I wonder where to search next." Michael turned to look at the old soldier. "Perhaps I should follow you to Gaul. Maybe he's there."

"Your family and your people need you with them right now," Zadoc said, looking into Michael's eyes and placing a hand on the horseman's shoulder. "I'm sorry I have not been able to locate Archanus for some time. But I'll make inquiries along the way, and if I hear anything, I'll get word to you."

"Thank you," Michael said tentatively.

"Is there something else?"

"I'm just hoping that one day you'll be able to get word to my father that he's no longer in danger."

"I have never ceased that effort," Zadoc said, "And I won't stop now."

A pair of colts playing war games in the pasture below caught the friends' attention and made them both smile.

"Will we ever meet again?" Michael asked when the colts loped off together.

"You and I . . . or you and your father?"

"Both."

"As I told Phillip just moments ago, I'll return, probably soon. My heart tells me that your father is still alive and that you will be reunited. When my mission in Gaul is ended, I will find a way to leave the army and spend the rest of my life—if that's what it takes—searching for your father and seeing to it that the two of you are brought together once more. Please trust me, Michael. I have never given up hope, nor must you."

"Hope can be hard to find." Michael met Zadoc's eyes. "Even when such a gift is offered by the most trusted of friends."

ARCHANUS

The sun had reached its zenith. A bright flowing river cut through a meadow. On the western bank Archanus sat aboard a pretty gray horse that slaked its thirst in the easy moving waters. Shadows of anxiety crossed the age-lined face of the rider as he strained to discern the source of a nearby commotion. Across the river, dust rose like steam into the hot midday air and mingled with the voices of soldiers who seemed to be having some sort of disagreement.

"It is the horses that draw you, is it not, Archanus? As though to your son?"

So engrossed was he in his effort to hear what was being said by the soldiers across the river that the old man hadn't noticed the approach of another on horseback.

"Luke, I'm sorry, I didn't hear you ride up. How long have you been beside me?"

"For many years, dear friend."

Archanus looked into the blue eyes of the handsome Greek physician with whom he had, indeed, spent so many years. "How true . . ." Archanus said softly. "How true."

The riders sat for a time beside the river. As they watched, the three soldiers dispersed. Two of the men made their way around the band of horses. The third, whom Archanus had heard the others call Joel, walked between the animals, touching them, appearing to speak softly to them as he headed toward some unknown objective. The young man reminded Archanus of his wife's people—the horsemen he had left behind in a time too long gone.

The old Wise Man looked down and brushed away a bit of dust from his light tunic. Then he reached up and stroked his horse's mane.

"Archanus, look at the river." Luke's tone was gentle.

"Why?"

"Just take a few moments," Luke said. "Watch and listen.

Beneath the harsh midday sun, the river flowed. Birds called; men conversed and sometimes shouted. From a tree or bush near the riverbank an occasional leaf fell into the current. Now and then a mare brought her foal to refresh itself in the cool waters, or to cross from one portion of the pasture to the other. Fish fed on the insects that landed on the water's surface. And the river rolled on, undisturbed.

"Long ago you taught me that life is like this," Luke said at length. "Like a river that knows nothing of time and has neither fear nor guilt. No matter what happens, it goes on. And one day it arrives at the place its heart has always sought."

"I wonder, does the river know as it travels where its journey will end?""

"Yes, my friend," Luke said, reaching over to rest his hand on Archanus' shoulder.

"The river knows, as do you. You will both reach your hearts' desires. It is only the course you must take that remains a mystery."

"This time and the river you speak of, did I tell you if they were friends?" Archanus asked, the hint of a smile visiting his tired eyes.

"Yes, you taught me that time and the river are life's dear companions, accepting one another and heeding God's call."

"I know that you and I are such companions, Luke." Archanus looked again into the eyes of his friend. "No longer am I your teacher. You have become the one with all the wisdom." Archanus paused, raising an aged yet strong hand to wipe beads of sweat from his face. "I know that we must continue to care for the sick throughout the land. I do accept that this is God's will . . ." The words were sure. But the tone was tentative.

"Perhaps," Luke said, finishing his friend's half-spoken thought. "But do you also have faith that it is God's will for you to be reunited with your son?" the physician asked.

"I want to believe this." Hope whispered around the edges of Archanus' heart as he studied Luke. The physician was thirty years his junior, but the younger man's face had begun to age. Exhaustion had etched itself into the lines around the Greek's blue eyes and his once black hair was already threaded with silver. Only his physique remained as perfect as it had been in his youth. He still held his broad shoulders erect above a straight, strong back. Firm muscles were evident beneath the thin cloth of his tunic. And he sat aboard his horse like the young horsemen Archanus recalled from the family of his beloved and long-deceased wife.

"And yet?" Luke ventured, interrupting Archanus' thoughts.

"I am an old man, Luke." He shook his head sadly. "I fear that I'll have neither the faith nor the courage to go again in search of my son." He paused. "Besides, even if I find him, Michael might never be able to forgive my long absence."

"Dear Archanus, it is you who taught me of faith. You are the one who encourages me, who keeps me believing that I can and must go on when I only wish to give up."

"But the teacher cannot always do what he requires of his student."

"You must." Again Luke reached for his friend, gripped the drooping shoulder and forced Archanus to meet his gaze. "You must follow your own teaching and, like the river, you must go on."

Around The Year of Our Lord
25 A.D. *(Anno Domini)*

Blow the trumpet in Zion:
sound the alarm on my holy hill.

Let all who live in the land tremble,
for the day of the LORD is coming.

It is close at hand . . . Yes, it is near . . .
Like dawn spreading across the mountains.

And everyone who calls
on the name of the LORD will be saved.

From Joel 2:1-2, 32 NIV

CHAPTER
Five

O nce in a time, there was a wise man who had to leave his son behind. Before he left, the man told stories to his son and his son grew up and had boys and a girl with his wife, and he told stories to them. And before the girl had babies of her own, she told stories to her horses . . ."

Sunlight danced among the glistening ebony strands of hair that fell in soft waves to a place below the child's waist. Her cheeks dimpled in a smile, but her eyes were serious as she admonished the foals gathered around her to pay attention.

"I'm telling you a good story," she said. "You should listen."

Eight foals, all under the age of six months, surrounded the child, Neeka, who sat cross-legged in the tall grass. A big-eyed bay colt tickled the back of her neck with the inquisitive twitching of his soft muzzle. A filly, the color of bright copper, nipped at one of the other colts, vying for position near the seated child.

Neeka laughed. "Don't be fighting over me. I have plenty of love for all of you, and lots of stories to tell."

On a nearby knoll, Michael sat astride a five-year-old son of Zabbai that had become his favorite mount. As he watched his daughter with the foals, a smile creased his sunburned cheeks and his eyes were bright with love.

All at once, the stallion, Jaanai, tensed. Raising his head high, he snorted and gave a startled little jump, just enough movement to plant his four feet in a wide, braced stance. Jolted out of his tender thoughts, Michael strained to see what had caught his horse's attention. In the distance, a cloud of dust swelled and moved toward the herd. Soon the ground began to rumble with the heavy footfalls of at least two hard-galloping horses. Mares, frightened by the disturbance, raised their heads and whinnied to their foals. The babies nickered with fear in response to their mothers' warnings.

Confusion plain in their erratic movements, the mares and foals prepared to flee the predator they sensed. Michael urged Jaanai forward and the big animal began a plunging descent down off the knoll. But before they could reach Neeka, her mother appeared, seemingly from nowhere. Dashing across the meadow on a golden mare whose flaxen mane blew wild in the breeze, Adrianna bent low, reached for Neeka's outstretched hand and flung the child easily up behind her, onto the palomino's back. Riding toward his wife and daughter, Michael was amazed as he often was at Adrianna and Neeka's grace and their miraculous timing. No sooner had Adrianna pulled their daughter out of harm's way than the mares bolted into a terrified stampede, followed by the foals that had moments earlier surrounded the young storyteller.

The drumbeats of thundering hooves became a cacophony, and the discord further incited the herd. The source of the ruckus drew nearer to the place where Michael, with his wife and daughter, tried to calm their horses while a cadre of herdsmen did their best to circle the mass of stampeding horses and bring them under control.

From the narrow strip of dusty plain where their race had started, Michael's sons and their horses bounded into the grass, heading straight for their parents and sister.

"Not again!" Adrianna gasped, realizing as the boys drew near, that her sons were the cause of the disturbance.

When the laughing Matthias pulled his black gelding to a stop in front of his father, the horse reared up and teetered precariously on its hind legs. Recognizing the expressions on his parents' faces, Junias tried to bring his sleek bay to a more controlled halt. Understanding appeared to dawn on the boys at roughly the same moment, as they saw the small disaster their lively competition had caused.

"Go and help the others contain the herd," Michael commanded. "Then come back here and we'll talk."

His sons looked at one another, their expressive faces showing mingled worry and excitement. Then they kicked their still fresh horses into another gallop and took off toward the milling herd.

"A part of me wants to beg you not to be too hard on them," Adrianna said. "But the rest of me wants to thrash them myself. Neeka could have been trampled!"

"The foals wouldn't have hurt me," Neeka said with the assurance of the confident child that she was. "They love me and they would have protected me."

"Fear is a dangerous thing," Michael said, his voice and his countenance stern. "The horses never want to run over us, but when they're frightened, anything can happen."

"My brothers were just testing each other," Neeka said, sounding now like a wise old woman. "They didn't mean to hurt anything."

"No, they didn't," Adrianna said with a rare hint of impatience in her tone. "But when they're playing they don't think any more clearly than frightened horses do. The harm they did today could have been a lot more serious than it was."

"But I'm not hurt," eight-year-old Neeka insisted.

"Don't argue with your mother." Michael's grave look did as it was meant to do and his daughter fell silent. "And remember," he added, "you aren't the only one who was in danger. There's a whole herd of horses that can be badly hurt in a stampede. We don't know yet how much damage has been done."

⧼⧽

Around the night fire, at the end of that long and near disastrous day, the men laughed among themselves and recounted their own youthful antics while the women wondered aloud if their sons or their husbands would ever grow up.

As it happened, none of the horses or herdsmen had been injured. Still, ten-year-old Junias and nine-year-old Matthias were in disgrace. They would not be allowed to ride or to play with the other boys until the coming of the next full moon nearly thirty days away. They would, instead, spend their time in camp helping the women prepare meals and wash clothes in the stream that flowed out of the mountains toward Lake Hula and the Sea of Galilee beyond. Michael and Adrianna had agreed that this would be the most humiliating punishment they could impose on their rambunctious sons.

Now the chagrined parents sat apart from the other horsemen and their families. "I'm afraid I haven't been a good father," Michael said. "Our sons are the last children who should cause the kind of trouble they made today."

"You're a fine father," Adrianna assured her husband. "Your sons are just being boys. They're not malicious, only playful."

"I was a boy and I wasn't wild like they are."

"You were never a child, at least not by the time you came to live with our people." Adrianna smiled. "It is said that you were born a man grown."

Michael thought back to that time so long ago, after his mother's death, when his father had been forced to leave him with his mother's people. Even now, all these years later, it was hard not to relive the terrible sadness he had felt at the loss of his parents. Now, watching the children at play, he remembered how unfriendly the other children his age had seemed when he came to live among them. As though the rejection occurred just that morning, he again saw boys and girls running and riding and playing together, excluding him.

Until his mother's passing and his father's departure, Michael had never thought about playing with other children. He had only wanted to be a great horseman and a scholar in the traditions of both sides of his heritage. And he had only needed the company of his parents.

Picturing his daughter sitting in the grass earlier that day surrounded by curious foals, he recalled the sunlit afternoon, three decades earlier, when the great horseman, Jephthah, had found him similarly engaged. This man who trained the horses of the tribe had befriended him that day and ultimately become his mentor. And with that, his life had changed forever.

Learning from Jephthah filled his days as he worked beside the great horseman. The horses filled his heart and carried him over the abyss of his sorrow. He wondered, this night, if he would ever learn to trust people in the way he had always trusted the horses. It wasn't something he thought about often, and as quickly as the thought crossed his mind, it was replaced by another old sorrow.

"Jephthah, how I miss you . . ." The words escaped in a whisper, unbidden.

"I miss him too," Adrianna said, tears pooling in her eyes. "What made you think of him just now?"

"Neeka sitting with the colts," Michael said. "And the trouble today—my own sons misbehaving, acting just like the boys who hated me when I came to live among you."

"They didn't hate you," Adrianna touched her husband's cheek. "You seemed so self-possessed, so aloof. The others your age were just trying to show their power . . . silly, stupid boys." She paused. "Many of those same boys now revere you as their leader."

"Perhaps. But today, our sons have disgraced us . . ."

"That's your pride talking," Adrianna said. "Please, my husband, instead of being ashamed, or feeling guilty, take pleasure in your sons and thank the One God for the good life He has given them—the life that allows them to laugh and play."

"You're right, as always." Michael put one arm around his wife. Just then Neeka and her brothers ran by. They were playing a game of tag, separate from the other children, obedient to at least a part of their punishment. When they noticed their parents, they stopped abruptly. The boys looked sheepish, but the ever-cheerful Neeka ran to her father, flung her arms around his neck and turned to her mother.

"Tell us a story, Mama," the laughing child begged.

"Are you trying to help your brothers out of trouble again?" Adrianna smiled at her daughter.

"No," Neeka lied. "I just want to hear a story. Tell us about that beautiful place you went that you can't find anymore."

"I've told you that story too many times to count. But come and sit with us. I'll tell it once more," Adrianna said, taking her place at the center of the family circle.

As his wife spoke, Michael allowed himself to be immersed in her story. As always, he enjoyed her reminiscences and her view of the idyllic world that he sometimes thought could not have been real but perhaps merely a product of his own wishful imaginings. It was a validation and a relief to hear Adrianna tell of that place and that time. Through her clear memory, the treasure became real and present once more.

"A part of my heart will always reach toward those mountains, and that time and that amazing Boy," Adrianna began. "You will meet Him one day," she said, looking from one of her children to the next, engaging the eyes of each individually.

When the storyteller paused too long, her daughter broke in.

"Tell about the Boy and Zabbai," Neeka said.

"Who's telling this story?" Adrianna tousled her daughter's hair. "But you're right to ask. He is, after all, the heart of the story." She fell silent for a few moments, appearing to gather her thoughts. "I've never encountered anyone like Him, never seen anything as true and full as the love between that Boy called Jesus and His horse, our beloved Zabbai."

She paused again and this time no one tried to fill the silence. "No matter how hard I try," she went on finally, "I can never explain how watching that Boy and that horse affected me."

Listening, Michael was drawn into a clear memory of those halcyon days, and once again he saw the Boy and the stallion in a mystical pairing of spirits that he had never seen before, nor since . . .

It was as though the Child and the stallion were one. No matter the gait, the action or the speed, the little body of the Boy melded with the great back of the horse, and on the wings of a miracle they soared across forever. With only a subtle shift of His balance, a small pressure from His short legs, the Boy communicated and the horse did His will. Gliding across the land, Jesus and Zabbai made the most beautiful picture Michael had ever seen of freedom ~ made sweeter by love and pure devotion.

"Michael?" Adrianna said.

"I'm sorry. Your story took me back to Him." The horseman turned away, not wanting his children to see the emotion in his eyes and not ready to come back from that far away time he believed was lost to him forever.

Again the children waited, unusually silent. Adrianna laid her head on Michael's shoulder, and the family listened, as one, to the sounds of the evening.

Now memories of too many heartbreaking goodbyes nudged aside all else in Michael's mind. For the first time ever, he admitted to himself that it was Jesus he most yearned to see again. In the acknowledgement of this longing, deeper even than the heartache he still knew over the loss of his father, he felt something shift within him. But full understanding of that transformation eluded him, and he shook his head in confusion.

Adrianna drew her husband's hand to her lips.

"You are the heart of my heart," Michael said, responding to his wife's tenderness, wondering, as he often did, at the gift she was to him and fighting the fear that she too would one day be taken from him.

"I know this, my husband." She looked up at him through a veil of thick lashes. "And you must know that I am not fearful of your other love, of that yearning that draws you away from us."

"Jesus," Michael whispered.

"Yes . . . only Him . . ."

Adrianna caressed her husband's cheek. Though their children sat with them, they were alone for a time with the One they both loved—the One who had lived for so long in their hearts and in their memories.

When Adrianna spoke again, there were tears in her eyes and her voice was husky. "One day He'll come and fill that empty place He left inside of us. I know He will. Until then, we must not grieve, but only wait and hope and thank the One God for the time we had with Him."

ARCHANUS

From a sun baked hill that overlooked the town and the surrounding countryside, Archanus watched as people went about the business of their lives.

Turning away from the simplicity of this ordinary day, he looked up into the hot blue sky. "My dearest Junia," he whispered, "can you ever forgive me?" He dropped his chin to his chest and listened to his own labored breathing. "I thought it was best to leave him. I thought he would be safe. I thought . . ."

The ache in the old Wise Man's heart was fierce and relentless. He forced himself to breathe in and breathe out as though the nature of this action had deserted him. He thought that he had lived too long, seen too much. And yet, he knew that for one reason alone, he must go on. He could not let go of his life on earth until he told Michael that he had loved him always and begged his son's forgiveness. Only then . . .

CHAPTER
Six

Months passed in the usual way. Foals were born and young horses were started for riding as the horsemen and their families lived out their days as had their clan for a thousand years and more. But the yearning in Michael's heart did not cease. And although Adrianna could feel his discontent, she could find no way to broach the subject or to help the one she loved beyond herself.

For Michael's part, he existed with a strange anticipation, hoping for something he could not quite name and wishing he could open up to his beloved wife. But he was unable to do so in the formless perplexity that riddled his heart and his mind. Mystified by the air of disquiet that emanated from their parents, Junias and Matthias and Neeka fell somehow quieter and drew closer to one another. The horses that Michael worked with were less cooperative than normal, spooky and generally unable to settle into their training.

On a still, cool evening after Michael and his family had retired to their tents some distance from the others, the subject of Michael's malaise was brought up by one of the women.

"This is not a topic for discussion," said her husband. "Whatever is troubling our leader . . ."

Before the man could finish his admonition, the herd began to stir. Mares nickered low to their foals and the stallions stomped and snorted. Alert to the smallest disturbance, the herdsmen who had been reclining around the night fire rose as one and headed for the animals they kept ready for any emergency.

While the others mounted their horses and began to circle the herd, Michael dashed on foot from the place outside his tent where he had been sitting alone, to the hilltop overlook where he could see Zabbai standing watch, his head high, his whole body alert.

At twenty-five, Zabbai was as fit and youthful as he'd been at five. Only his pure white coat suggested he was no longer a young horse. A light wind ruffled the stallion's mane and lifted his forelock. His huge black eyes focused on something in the distance. His nostrils flared as he inhaled the incense of the breeze.

"What is it, old friend?" Michael said softly as he moved to stand beside the stallion. The herd milled about, restless, uneasy. Riders circled, containing the animals, avoiding a full-scale stampede. In time, the mares settled and soon the other's followed suit, but even then, the air remained rife with a strange tension.

After a while, Adrianna joined her husband. "Have you seen anything?" she asked. "Any reason for alarm?"

"No," Michael said, "nothing at all. But Zabbai is still uneasy so I'm going to stay here with him." He turned at last to Adrianna. "Would you go and tell the herdsmen that I want extra sentries tonight?"

"Yes, of course." Adrianna took from her shoulders the blanket she had thrown around herself and gave it to Michael.

"You'll need this," she said, then brushed her husband's cheek with her lips and walked down the hill to do as he had asked.

There was a chill in the night air. Brittle bits of starlight decorated the moonless cerulean sky. Surrounded by the night watchmen and their dogs, most of the herd rested, calm and still. But a few mares with young foals were edgy, and Zabbai remained tense. His ears tight forward, his nostrils still flaring, he drank deeply of the wind, as though in anticipation of a certain sound, a particular scent.

Finally, exhausted from his response to the day's events, Michael sat down, wrapped Adrianna's blanket around himself, leaned against a rock at the stallion's feet, and allowed himself to drift into a light sleep. Fitfully, he dreamt of long ago journeys. First, beside his father, fleeing from sure death toward the fearful unknown, then riding to the top of a mountain and saying goodbye. Later, filled with hope, racing toward a miraculous Star, finding an unexpected Treasure—but no reunion. Through the long watches of the night, the horseman's dreams tumbled over one another, holding him captive, shifting and repeating themselves, altering course, at once expectant and mysterious.

Near first light, a sensation of warmth on the back of his neck drew Michael up out of his uneasy dreams. Zabbai bent low at the withers and reached toward Michael, and the stallion's grass-sweet breath brought the man gently into the pacific calm of pre-dawn. The still dark earth and most of its creatures were cloaked in the pregnant hush that comes before morning. In the cool air, stars appeared to retreat as the subtle pink of awakening insinuated itself into the rich, nocturnal black.

Michael stood and stretched and found his body strangely devoid of the aches that should have followed a long night spent sitting against a rock. Not wishing to invade the uncontaminated hush of the morning with words, the horseman stood close to the stallion, communicating in silence and receiving sweet warmth from the great horse.

Together they resumed their watch. Michael was still gripped by the same curious unease that had accompanied him into a restless sleep the night before. And once again, time escaped him until finally, just when he was about to give up his anxious sentinel and walk down into the comforting sameness of his temporal world, the answer came.

On the eastern horizon, dawn spread across the mountains. Nudging aside the subtle effulgence that had implied the end of night, brilliant rays of light soared toward the heavens in a golden fan above the emergent sun. And in the arched portal of that glory, appeared the glowing figure of a Man.

A hush fell over all the earth, and within the quiet an angelic symphony throbbed like a beating heart. There was no sense of time for Michael, only a sureness of hope—a knowing that All-that-was-and-is-and-ever-shall-be-Love was moving toward him, reaching out to embrace his heart.

Then at last, the Love stood before him, with a countenance at once gentle and all-powerful. Although the sun had found its way into the morning sky, rays of pulsing gold emanated from the Man as though He was yet standing before the aura of dawn's first light. And in the grip of pure silence, the whole world seemed to hold its breath.

"It can't be You," Michael whispered.

"It is I." The voice was deep and resonant and strangely familiar.

"You are a man I have not seen," Michael said, slowly moving his head from side to side in disbelief. "But Your eyes . . . I could never forget those eyes." The horseman bowed his head, drew a hand roughly across his face, then looked up once more. "No, no," he shook his head again. "It cannot be." Michael heard the huskiness in his own voice, but he could not stop the flow of his words. "I must be deceiving myself. It can't be You. I have waited, but I have never believed I would see You again."

"You are not deceived. Be still and know that I am here, that I am with you always."

"Say Your Name," Michael begged.

"I am Jesus, the brother of your heart."

At that, all restraint deserted the horseman and he flung his arms around the Boy he had loved beyond understanding—now a Man he wondered if he could ever know.

And then he surrendered, accepting his own weakness, knowing that he was safe. And Jesus held him. Zabbai reached his long neck around the brothers, pressing the underside of his jaw against Jesus' back, holding his men in the embrace that belongs alone to the horse.

In the solace of the only complete refuge he had ever known, Michael wept with neither reserve, nor shame. In time, Zabbai relaxed his hold and the brothers stepped apart so that they looked into each other's eyes and searched one another's faces. Soon they were smiling. Then Michael heard his own laughter mingling with that of his Brother as Zabbai begged for attention, nuzzling Jesus, nickering softly. Jesus wrapped His arms around the stallion's neck and rested His face on the white mane that shimmered in the morning sun.

As Michael watched this reunion, a thousand questions pressed against the door of his heart. But he could not speak. He could only wait.

In a little while, with one hand still resting on Zabbai's withers, Jesus turned to Michael and began to answer the horseman's unspoken questions. The brothers' conversation took off then as if in mid sentence, as though there had been no parting, no fifteen-year-lapse in their time together.

"I don't know how to be with You," Michael said. "You are a man grown . . ." He paused. "Your voice is no longer like a chime in the wind, no more a boy's sweet song."

"The Boy is still within Me," Jesus said, His deep voice soothing. "I am the same inside. Only the façade is changed. Be at peace with Me, My brother. I still love you as I always have, as I always will."

Once more Michael shook his head in awe. "I don't know how to be with You," he said again.

"Be patient with yourself as you once were with Me. You'll know Me again."

Jesus had dropped His hand from Zabbai's withers. Now the stallion rubbed his forehead up and down Jesus' arm. It was plain that there was no barrier between Zabbai and his beloved Master, no difficulty of recognition, no sense of change. Michael could see that, for Zabbai, Jesus remained the same today as He had been at their last parting, as He surely would be forever.

From the camp below, the sounds of morning wafted up on a light breeze. In the meadow foals romped while their mothers grazed. There was comfort for Michael in the routine of the horses and their people, in the song of the birds, in the familiarity of the world he had chosen.

"Please tell me of Your life," the horseman said, turning back to Jesus. "Where have You been, how have You lived? Tell me of Your Mother, and Joseph . . . and Shadow."

"Of course I'll tell you everything. And will you do the same for Me?"

"Have I ever said no to You?"

"Never," Jesus said.

While the day proceeded around them, Michael and Jesus began to share the stories of their lives since their sad parting on the shore of the Great Sea. Miraculously, no one interrupted the brothers' reunion. At length their storytelling brought them to the present moment and Jesus said it was time for Him to see Adrianna and to meet Michael's children.

"There's so much more I want to hear, so many things I want to ask You," Michael said.

"It is the same for Me. And we will have time for that. But let Me first come to know your children."

When they walked into the horsemen's camp, it was as though Jesus had always been a part of this extended family. No one acted surprised to see Him, just joyful and welcoming.

Michael's children gathered round and Jesus caressed each one, laughing with them, filling their hearts with His love.

During the long greeting process, Adrianna stood apart, watching, her hands resting one on the other in front of her, silent tears finding their way to the creases beside lips that quivered with her efforts to smile. When Jesus met Adrianna's eyes, the love that passed between them was almost tangible, and a peace beyond all understanding settled into Adrianna's no longer aching heart.

❦

During the short period that Jesus spent with the horsemen, He worked beside men and women and played like a boy with the children, sharing Himself and His love with no limits. One morning when Michael and Phillip took two colts out into the desert for training, Jesus rode along on Zabbai. As they traveled, Jesus filled the other men's hearts and their minds with the story of Creation. He spoke about the fall of humankind and the part played by the devil known as Satan who He told them still prowled the earth seeking the ruin of souls.

When He had fully unfolded this tale in words and pictures that filled the sky, Jesus revealed to His friends the truth of the One God's great gift of Zabbai. He talked of the Zabbai effect that would completely change not only the millions of horses that would descend from him, but ultimately—and of even greater significance—the very course of civilization.

"You must speak of this to no one," Jesus admonished, directing His words primarily to Phillip. "Most people would not believe you and would brand you a lunatic. But a worse fate could befall you at the hands of those who believe just enough of your strange claim that they would try to take from you the treasure you describe."

"Could not my father and his great army protect us?" Phillip asked.

"No man, no army, can provide adequate protection when envy gives birth to hatred," Jesus said.

"But why should there be envy?"

"Greed and envy are among the most common bequests of the devil," Jesus said. "When one receives a gift that others desire, there is often envy from some quarter. But that, Phillip, is something you will learn in this life. For now, you must promise to keep to yourself all that you have heard and will yet hear today. These horsemen for whom you care so deeply would be further endangered if you were to talk to anyone about what you have learned. If you will not protect yourself, I know you will act to protect your friends."

"If You ask this of me, I will promise," Phillip said solemnly. "I would die rather than cause harm to these good people." He paused. "But what do You mean about Michael's people being *further* endangered."

"I have come with a warning," Jesus said, turning to Michael. "I did not wish to tell you of these things until I had shared some measure of peace with all of you. I wanted first to prepare you for what lies ahead. Now it is time."

"To what do You refer?" Michael asked.

"You and your people are in grave danger, My brother. There is a soldier of some rank who incurred your wrath a few years ago—before he achieved the military status he now holds."

"Marvelius," Phillip said.

"Yes, that is his name."

"Do You know what happened between us?" Michael asked.

"Perhaps you'd like to tell Me."

"He was beating a horse with a terrible fury," Michael said. "The animal was down and bleeding from its head and its neck, its back and its legs . . ."

"And you fell upon the man to protect the horse," Jesus said.

"I did. And, to my great shame, I lost all control. I might have killed him had not some of my kinsmen and soldiers pulled me away."

"That monster deserved far worse than Michael gave him," Phillip said.

"I have heard this from others," Jesus said. "The ones who told Me of Marvelius say that he is a fiercely proud and angry man. They say his rage has been fueled by the humiliation you caused him and that this single emotion has driven him ever since your altercation. Now he is in a position to do you and your people great harm."

"So that is why You came?" Michael said, his brow furrowed. "Only to warn us?"

"That is only a small part of My reason for coming," Jesus said. "The rest is that I could no longer stay away. When the longing to come to you became too great to ignore, I prayed for guidance. I spoke with My mother of My decision and she agreed that I must listen to the voice of My Spirit and make the journey."

"Have You known before of our whereabouts?" Michael asked.

"I have."

"Why, then, have You not come before?" Michael's hurt was plain.

Jesus didn't answer at once. Stroking Zabbai's neck, He looked forward, with the stallion, along the path that lay ahead.

"I can't go back to being the Boy I was," Jesus said finally. "I have a mission in this life, a purpose that I won't disobey. With you and the horses, I might be tempted to forget."

"And there is danger for You," Michael said. "I can feel this."

"You must not fear, My brother."

"Is it the devil—the fallen one of which you have taught us today?" Michael asked. "Am I right in thinking that he must hate You even more than he hates us?"

"You are right. But My Father will prevail. You must not fear," Jesus said again.

"So what happens now?" Michael asked.

"When this visit that I will always treasure is over, I'll return to My mother and My work. And you must flee again to Egypt, as you helped my family to do long ago. You'll be safe there, at least for a time. The Nile River valley is too far out of Marvelius' domain for him to venture."

"What of Joseph?" Michael changed the subject. "You have spoken little of him. Is he well?"

"I wish that I could say yes, but this is not so. His dear eyes are shadowed now, he moves with caution, and he tires at the least exertion."

"Can You do nothing for him?" Michael asked. "Can You not heal him as you once healed the birds and the creatures of the forest?"

"In this case, it cannot be," Jesus said. "When it is time for Joseph to leave this earth, I am bound to let him go to be with the Heavenly Father. For My mother's sake, I can only pray that his departure does not come before I return."

"I'll prepare my kinsmen for the journey we must make. Then I'd like to ride with You to visit Mary and Joseph," Michael said. "One last time."

"Yes," Jesus nodded. "We'll have to take great care that you're not recognized. But I agree. You must see them again."

From that moment until they arrived back at the horseman's camp, the companions rode in silence. Michael wondered how he would announce to his people that they must undertake a perilous journey without him. Phillip wondered what part he would play in the drama that must soon unfold. And Jesus prayed.

❧

Jesus stayed among the horsemen for only seven days. But in those gently passing moments every member of the clan saw eternity through His eyes. There was no change in routine, yet when He left, every man, woman and child felt as though they had done nothing but spend time with Jesus. Everyone was drawn to Him. Everyone wanted to be near Him, to ask Him questions, to tell Him of their own lives, to touch Him, to be touched by Him. And somehow, there was time for this. Afterward, throughout all the years of their earthly journeys, each man, woman and child would recall how Jesus had singled her or him out to receive a special measure of His love and His Truth.

Zabbai never left his Master's side. Where Jesus led, Zabbai followed. Only when Jesus took him to the river or sat beside him in the grass did Zabbai drink or eat. And when Jesus rode out, no matter His companions, it was always aboard Zabbai. Michael's children were almost as ever present as was Zabbai, yet they took nothing away from the others who hungered for Jesus. With Him, they learned to be quiet and unobtrusive, small conduits of His fathomless love.

And so, for the tribe known as The Horsemen, the world began anew. Every spirit was liberated and granted peace. Divine Mercy gave birth to a new and deeper hope, in a bequest from God that would last far beyond the generation directly blessed by this legacy.

A part of Jesus would live forever in every heart He touched. And for these people who knew the merciful love of Jesus, nothing would ever be the same again.

CHAPTER Seven

S even grace filled days had passed. Now it was the day of parting. In the chill before first light, mares stood at rest, their foals curled or sprawled in the grass at their feet. Jesus, followed by Zabbai, made His way toward the stallion's hilltop lookout, skirting the herd so as not to disturb, stopping now and then to take in the beauty of these creatures He would not soon see again.

Jesus paused beside a small chestnut mare that turned to Him and nickered softly. He spoke to her, stroked her neck and ran a finger along her pronounced tear bone and down across her nose, to her muzzle. There, He opened His palm and bade her to rest in Him, and the breathing of the mare synchronized with that of the One who touched her in the silence of the star bright pre-dawn.

"She is Lalaynia all over again, is she not?" Michael's words, like his approach, were so soft as to be almost soundless.

"She is. A daughter of Zabbai, no doubt, given to you in the image of his mother," Jesus said, a smile lighting his eyes. "You have always been able to move among the Father's creatures like a gentle breeze. Neither they nor I were disturbed by your approach."

"That is the One God's gift to me. The animals know that I love them before myself, even as You love this world He has given You to save."

"How do you know this?" Jesus asked.

"When I was a boy, my father told me of Your birth and Your mission. When You were a Boy, Your mother confirmed to me that it was You of whom my father had spoken." Michael paused. "And more than this, I have known You and You have shown me the truth of who You are." Michael looked away, across the backs of the still sleeping horses.

"You will see Archanus again," Jesus said. "This I promise."

"As always, You see into my heart. And if this is Your promise, I can only believe."

"It is My assurance to you. But for now, we must think of other things. I have been considering our travels," Jesus said, "yours and Mine, and those of your people."

"As have I, and I am lost. Please, tell me what we are to do."

"Your people cannot travel any of your customary routes," Jesus began. "Marvelius has made himself familiar with your habits, and there will be those in debt to him or in fear of him watching every by-way customarily traveled by your people."

"There aren't many pathways to Egypt that offer enough sustenance for the horses," Michael said with a worried frown.

"This is true. And yet, such a trail does exist. Instead of following the shore of the Great Sea, the horses and their caretakers will make their way along the steppes east of the inland seas outside the territory claimed by the Romans. They will travel with the grasses to a place below the southern tip of Lake Asphalititus. From there, they will pass through the desert to the Red Sea. They will cross both arms of this body of water entering Egypt near the great fork. They will then move south along the Red Sea's western shore until they come to a path that will lead them to the Nile."

The brothers didn't move away from the horses as they talked about the journey, but remained beside the chestnut mare and her sleeping foal. A faint light was beginning to warm the sky, diminishing the brilliance of all but the bright morning star. And the rumor of dawn whispered into the silence of the night.

"But surely many will perish if we try to take them across these barren wastes," Michael said, shaking his head and running a hand through his thick, dark hair. "In the steppes there is grass, but precious little water. The deserts are barren and the Red Sea is deep. I cannot imagine how my people and our horses will survive this journey."

"Do you trust Me, My brother?" Jesus asked.

"With my life, and with the lives of those I love."

"Then know that God will provide. Every man and woman, child and animal will have plenty of all that they need along the way. And they will all arrive safely beside the banks of the River Nile. On this route, they will only be within Roman jurisdiction for a short time near the Red Sea in an area rarely visited by anyone, least of all the Roman Army. They will settle in a place some distance south of Thebes in a broad river valley outside the circle of Roman influence."

"And when will I meet them again?"

"Are you having second thoughts about going to Nazareth with Me?"

"No, none at all. I must see Joseph, and, of course, Your mother. I only wish to know when I will rejoin those whom I've been chosen to lead."

"I can't tell you the day or the time. I can only say that there will be trials and there will be danger as there often is when one obeys the call of God."

"I don't fear for my safety," Michael said. "But I cannot abandon so easily my sense of responsibility for God's people and His horses."

"The youngest son of Zadoc will be your surrogate. He can be trusted."

"But he's scarcely more than a boy."

"Phillip is half a decade older than you were when you guided My family to Egypt on your first visit to that safe harbor. He has been with you for five years. He knows your ways and loves your family and the horses. And his loyalty is beyond reproach."

"All of this is true," Michael said, turning to look into the herd.

"Be at peace, My brother," Jesus said, placing a gentle hand on Michael's shoulder. "The Father demands nothing of you. If this is too great a sacrifice for you to make, He will love you nonetheless."

"No, my choice is made. But what about Phillip and Adrianna? What if they don't see things in this way?"

"Then we'll make other plans. And again, the Father will understand. Come now, it is time we meet Phillip and Adrianna on Zabbai's hill."

❦

"I had a strange dream," Phillip said when Jesus and Michael arrived at the vantage point from which Zabbai stood watch over his herd. "It was as though someone was calling me to come here."

"I too had such a dream," Adrianna said. "Is something wrong?"

The sun was making its presence known, it's subtle effulgence illuminating the curve of the land in the east. Zabbai stood with his head high and his ears forward. In the wide meadow below, foals were beginning to stir. Many of the young stallions were making their way to the stream that separated them from the mares. Night watchmen were riding around the edges of the herd, checking on their charges in the emerging light. In the camp, morning fires were being stoked and from them, ribbons of smoke undulated toward the wakening sky.

"You have both been called," Jesus said. "Ahead of you is a perilous mission and a great responsibility. You may choose to accept the call, or to deny it."

"Who has chosen us for this task?" Phillip asked.

"My Brother," Michael said, nodding toward Jesus.

"Then of course I will accept." Standing just a little taller, raising his chin, shrugging back his shoulders, Phillip assumed the stance of his father.

"I can do no less," Adrianna said, looking into her husband's sad eyes.

"You *are* your father's son," Michael said to Phillip then, reaching for Adrianna's hand and looking into her eyes, "And from you, my dear wife, I would expect no less."

"My father taught me to obey," Phillip said. "Now, may I ask what Adrianna and I are to do?"

"Together, you will lead Michael's people and the horses into Egypt," Jesus said.

"But what of Michael?"

"As you heard yesterday, Phillip, and as I told you last night my dear wife," Michael said, "I will be traveling to Nazareth for a short visit. When my time there is over, I will come to you."

"But why can we not all travel together?" Phillip wanted to know. "Surely there are places near Nazareth where we can find grass and water for the horses."

Adrianna moved nearer to her husband. In her eyes were fear and unshed tears. But she did not speak.

"Marvelius and his minions will be less likely to recognize Michael if this well-known horseman travels alone and on foot," Jesus said. "You, Phillip and Adrianna, will lead the herd on a different route to Egypt than any of you have traveled before, and you will all be safe."

"I am Your servant," Phillip said, looking first at Jesus and then at Michael and Adrianna. "I will do whatever You ask."

In agreement, they left the hilltop and went down into the camp where, for the next hour, they met with the horsemen, explaining the situation and outlining their plans. Adrianna remained at Michael's side—a faithful, if silent, presence.

Michael made it clear to everyone that, in his absence, Adrianna would share leadership with Phillip. There was a little grumbling and some jealousy in regard to Phillip's elevated position. And there was righteous concern over the route of travel and its lack of food and water. But in short order Jesus allayed all fears and made clear the reasons behind both Phillip's assignment and the path the horsemen were to follow.

"Phillip is the son of one of the greatest military leaders of our time," Jesus explained. "From his father he has learned the ways of the army. This son of Zadoc will be better able to anticipate the plans of those who would cause you harm than might one of you who has not witnessed the sort of treachery common to Marvelius and his kind."

"But we've never gone this way before," said one of the horsemen.

"I know this is true," Jesus said. "And I know you fear. But I ask you to trust Me and to believe that God will provide for you and see to your protection."

"Will someone travel with Michael?" another horseman asked.

"No," Michael answered. Then he reiterated what Phillip and Adrianna had learned earlier. "I'll go with Jesus on foot to Nazareth. The Romans will be looking for me on horseback. They'll be less likely to recognize me without a horse."

"And from Nazareth?" the first horseman wanted to know.

"When my visit is over, I'll go on alone. I'll make my way toward Egypt and will hope to meet you somewhere along the way. It's safest for all of you if I'm not in your company too soon. And I would not endanger any one of you by asking you to accompany me, or even to suspect my route of travel."

"What about my brothers?" Phillip asked. "Couldn't one of them escort you?"

"We cannot take that chance either." Michael shook his head and there was a sadness in his voice. "Marvelius knows of our association. Marcus and Joel may already be in danger because of this."

"Michael will not be alone—nor will you," Jesus said, looking around the assembly, engaging the eyes and the hearts of each one present. "Armies of angels will accompany you."

"How will we know when they're with us," the second questioning horseman asked.

"They are always with you," Jesus said. "Know this and travel in peace, with faith."

❧

"Adrianna, you have asked nothing," Michael said, when the meeting was over and everyone but Jesus had left them. "Are you disappointed with me?"

"No, my husband. Only sad to be away from you."

"He will return," Jesus said.

"I believe You." Adrianna's lips smiled, but her eyes were sad. "I have experienced the intervention of Your angels. I know You do not tell us of their presence just to placate." She moved closer to her husband. "It is only that Michael is the heart of my heart and has been for most of my life. It is difficult for me to journey without him."

Jesus took Adrianna's hand in His. "Know, dear one, that you and Michael will always be connected to one another by God. Your separation will only be of a physical nature. In spirit you will always be as one."

"And what of You, dear Jesus?" Reaching up to touch His cheek, Adrianna beseeched Him with her eyes. "Will we meet again, You and I?"

"In a time and a place beyond the troubles of this world we will walk and ride together once more. There will be no danger then, no sorrow, no more parting."

"These words are a mystery to me," Adrianna said. "But I will hold them in my heart until we meet again."

Just then, Junias, Matthias and Neeka appeared, as though they had been summoned.

"It is good that you have come," Michael said, reaching out to his children. "I want to tell you what lies ahead." The children said nothing, only exchanged anxious glances, then turned their attention to Michael. "Jesus and I must make ready for a journey," he said.

"I want to go with you, Abba," Neeka begged, interrupting her father before he could go on. Tears filled and overflowed the child's eyes and made small streams through the dust on her cheeks. "You always take the boys when you ride off . . ." She choked on a small, mournful sob. "But you never take me. I want to go . . ."

Michael picked up his weeping daughter and held her to him. "No one is going with me this time," he whispered into her hair. "And I am not riding off. I am walking with Jesus."

"But why, Abba, why?" the child cried.

"It is what I must do. I will be back. In the meantime, you and your brothers must help your mother and the herdsmen— and Phillip. You must be obedient. No trouble from you two," Michael said, engaging each of his sons in turn with a stern look. "Everyone must work together."

"Come to Me." Jesus sat down on a big rock and beckoned the children. Michael put Neeka down and with her brothers, she moved into the circle of Jesus' arms. In that shelter, the children fell silent.

"You will take a road you have never before traveled," Jesus told them. "There will be adventure, and there will be danger. As your father said, you must obey your mother, and you must help her to keep the spirits of all the others high. No one should fear. Along with your mother and Phillip, you will be the leaders. Can you do this?"

"Yes, yes, we can," the three children said in unison. "We can be brave."

"And can you obey?" Jesus asked.

"Yes. We will do this," Matthias said looking first at his brother, then at his sister. "Won't we." It was not a question.

"But where are we going?" Neeka asked.

"To a place where the grass grows belly deep to the tallest horse," Michael said.

"To a place near the river valley where your father and I began our life's journey together," Adrianna added.

"But how will we get there?" Matthias wanted to know.

"By faith and faith alone," Jesus told him.

"I do not understand." The boy frowned.

"Perhaps not now, but one day you will." Jesus stood up, drawing the children with Him. "Now," He said, "I need some time with Zabbai, and then, your Abba and I must go."

The boys stepped back. Junias kept his eyes on Jesus, while Matthias looked from the Son of God to his own father.

Neeka clung to Jesus. Burying her face in the folds of His robe, she wept again as though her world was ending. For a long while He held the child to Him. Finally, He leaned slightly away, tipped her chin up so that she could look into His eyes, and gently wiped her face with the blue cloth that encircled and hung from His waist.

"We will meet again, Veronica," He said as He took off the blue sash and wound it gently around and around the thin waist of the little girl.

"This I promise."

"When, Jesus?" she sobbed. "When?"

"In My Father's time. Perhaps sooner than we can know."

"I don't understand," Neeka said.

"There are many things that we are not given to understand," Jesus told her, then paused, caressing her tear-streaked face. "But some things are certain," He finally went on. "And, as I promised your mother, we will surely meet again when our time on earth is finished." Gently, He brushed back a lock of her hair. "Be still, dear one, and know that I am with you always, until the ends of the earth. Wherever you go, there I am also. Just call on Me and I'll touch your heart. You'll never, ever be alone."

At those tender words, Adrianna's tears overflowed at last. She held her arms out summoning her children as Jesus urged them forward with a touch of His hand.

"I must go and bid farewell to another," Jesus said, rising.

Michael put his arm around Adrianna. The children huddled close to their parents. Together, they watched as Jesus walked away. And then they waited.

❧

Jesus and Zabbai made their quiet way through the herd to the stallion's hilltop. For a time, they stood there together, surveying all that they loved. Then Jesus swung up onto the great horse's back and urged him into an easy, ground-covering lope. At that gait, they glided across the grassy plain until they reached the foot of a steep hill with a switchback trail that led to its summit. There, Zabbai dropped down to a walk, lowered his head and carried his Master upward, to a high place from which Jesus could see past the valley and the foothills and this present moment.

A light wind sighed into the stillness. Jesus slipped to the ground, knelt beside Zabbai and bowed His head. In remembrance, He passed through the years behind Him. In prayer, He begged strengthening and peace for Michael and his family—and for Himself—throughout the trials that lay ahead. Hours went by. Time and Zabbai stood still. Thunderheads gathered and became a blanket of dark, ominous clouds.

In the fullness of that suspended place in time, Jesus stood and walked around to stand in front of Zabbai. The stallion lowered his head to rest on his Master's chest, and Jesus spoke to the animal's great heart. He did not weep as He had all those years ago when He first bid Zabbai farewell. This time, He spoke comfort to His beloved horse. "We'll ride together again, dear friend," He whispered, "across the hills of Heaven, back here for the last battle, then forever, and beyond.

They stood together until the sun broke through the clouds as it had on the day of their last parting. Broad rays of light fanned out and spread across the land. Then all at once, like the breath of God, one single brilliant shaft of light escaped the others and came to rest on the Son of Man and His horse.

In the horsemen's camp, every eye turned toward the faraway hill where Jesus and Zabbai stood, bathed in the light of glory. No sound broke the lengthening silence. No motion indicated the passage of time. When the moment was over, none of the horsemen had any idea how long they had been still. When conscious thought returned, they only knew a mysterious peace and an understanding that they had been called, that they would obey, and that they could go on.

MARY & JOSEPH

In a room too warm and still, Joseph lay tossing and turning, soaked in the sweat of fever. Beside him Mary knelt, praying and caressing his face with cloths soaked in cool water.

"Be at peace, my husband. I am here."

"Jesus . . ." A hoarse whisper escaped the dry lips of the sufferer.

"Soon, my dearest. Soon He will return." Mary's soothing voice belied the sadness she could not share with her life's beloved companion—the man she knew would too soon be gone.

In her sorrow, Mary recalled a long ago day and the visit of an angel. In her heart she pondered once more the lonely road she had chosen to travel.

Resting one hand on Joseph's laboring chest, she looked up and saw beyond the confines of the room. "Thy will be done, Father," she whispered. "Thy will be done."

CHAPTER *Eight*

O n a sheltered knoll at the end of their first day's journey Jesus and Michael reclined. Walking the paths made wide and smooth by thousands of hooves over the course of hundreds of migratory years, the brothers had begun sharing the stories of the lives they had lived since their long ago parting.

Tomorrow, they would travel on and soon they would walk down the hill to Galilee and then on to Nazareth.

Now they broke bread and, enjoying the simple feast that Adrianna had packed for them, they continued their conversation.

"Before we left camp, I heard the words You spoke to Adrianna," Michael said. When Jesus didn't respond, he went on. "You told her You came to this earth so that the faithful might meet one day in heaven."

"Yes," Jesus said.

"What does this mean? And why do I fear there is danger for You in this mission?"

"It means that My Father has sent Me to atone for the sins of mankind, so that He can forgive them and welcome them one day into His Kingdom."

"And the danger?"

"You sound like My big brother scolding me." Jesus smiled.

"I am Your big brother. Don't change the subject. What about the danger?"

"That which lies ahead is not for either of us to fear."

"Should I not be concerned for Your safety, as You are for mine?"

"That's different."

"How so?" Michael asked.

"What good would come from your being murdered by a thug?"

"What good can come from You suffering some mysterious fate about which You're not willing to tell me?"

"All right," Jesus said. "I can see that you won't give up."

"No, I won't."

"Your father studied more than just the stars, did he not?"

"Yes, he did." Michael nodded. "I don't remember a lot, but I know he wanted to understand what he called man's inhumanity to man."

"Did he find any answers?"

"I don't think so. He used to talk about patterns, about how civilizations repeated the errors and the sins of their predecessors. Sometimes he weighed the order of the universe against the disorder of humankind." A smile came into Michael's eyes.

"What are you recalling?" Jesus asked.

"I was thinking how my mother used to compare the horses to what she called 'foolish' humans."

"In what ways did she make these comparisons?"

"She always said that horses could be understood, if one paid enough attention. She thought that humans were much more difficult to know. I think she spent her life trying to treat people with the same kindness and love she had for the horses," Michael's voice trailed off.

The sun hung low in the amber sky. Long shadows were reaching toward dusk. A night bird called somewhere in the distance, and the creatures of the evening were beginning to scurry about. Seeking peace in the predictable cycles of nature, Michael looked to the horizon and breathed deeply of the cooling air.

"And what happened when your mother made this effort?" Jesus asked.

Michael thought about the question. When he finally spoke, his words held no sense of assurance. "I think people kept disappointing her," he said with a confused frown. "They kept being inconsistent, often cruel."

"Was that your mother's view?" Jesus asked. "Or is it your own?"

Considering this, Michael didn't answer at once. "Perhaps more mine," he said at last. "Why is it that You have always known me better than I know myself?"

"It is My gift," Jesus said. "I know why you don't trust people as you do the horses. I only hope you will one day learn to forgive these flawed humans and to love them without so much expectation."

"I don't understand what You're asking of me."

"When a man cares for other people with the hope of receiving some earthly reward, he is destined for disappointment, even heartbreak."

"So I shouldn't care so much?"

"On the contrary," Jesus said. "You should care beyond what you think is your greatest capacity. Learn to be even more patient and loving with people than you naturally are with the horses."

"But people aren't drawn to me as are the horses."

"What of Adrianna?"

"She's different. She and our children love me in spite of myself."

"So you don't think you're lovable?"

"Not particularly."

"Why not?"

"I don't know . . ."

Jesus said nothing, only looked into Michael's eyes until the horseman became uncomfortable and went on.

"Maybe it's because I was so angry when my mother died and my father had to run away and leave me behind. Maybe these feelings I harbor have made me difficult to love."

"And even though these sorrows are long behind you, they still ride along."

"Yes, I guess they do."

"Do you love Me, My brother?" Jesus asked.

"Of course I do. You know that."

"Then do this for Me. Give love and it will be given back to you. Choose those to whom the giving is most difficult and show them the kind of love and respect you show to the horses."

"But why? Why do You want me to do that?"

"Because this is how we are called to show our love for God, by loving our fellow man."

"And loving God is a commandment of Your people, is it not?" Michael said.

"You still recall what My mother taught us long ago." Jesus smiled.

"I have forgotten almost nothing of that time we spent together in Egypt. What she taught You was always important to me."

"That is because her teaching was for you as well as for Me."

"Yes, I guess I knew that."

"Still, you've let those truths lie fallow in some lonely corner of your heart."

"I guess I have." Michael shook his head. "How have we gotten so far away from what we were talking about? I thought You were going to tell me about the danger You face."

"In a way, I am telling you," Jesus said. "I want you to understand from within yourself what I have come to do. Knowledge is as nothing without depth. You must know the important things with your being, not merely with your mind."

"Again, I am confused."

"We've been talking about human nature, have we not?"

"Yes, we have. And what am I to learn from this?"

"You see people as unpredictable and often untrustworthy, correct?"

"I do, and worse."

"But not better?"

"Well, sometimes. Some are good. My mother was good, as is Yours, and Adrianna."

"These alone?"

"No, well, maybe."

"What about your father and Joseph?" Jesus asked. "Your aunt and uncle, your teachers?"

Michael hesitated and looked away, then turned back to Jesus.

"Are you still angry with your father for leaving you?" Jesus asked.

"Perhaps I am."

"Did he go away because he loved you and wanted you to be safe?"

"Yes. But why did he never return? Zadoc has told me that the danger passed for my father many years ago."

"You cannot know the story of Archanus' life until he tells it to you. Only then can you assess the reasons for his long absence."

"But You know, don't You."

Jesus didn't give Michael a direct answer. He said only, "I promise that you will see him again."

"Will You still not tell me when this might happen?"

"When your heart is ready for that reunion," Jesus said. "Then you will have it."

"Again, we've departed from the answers to my questions." Michael was afraid to ask what Jesus meant about his heart being ready, afraid to look within himself where he suspected he would have to face unpleasant truths.

"Do you imagine that My Father created man to be unkind?" Jesus asked.

"Not if You are His perfect image, as Your mother once told me." A confused frown creased Michael's brow.

Jesus looked up into the darkening sky. Michael watched the rise and fall of his Brother's chest and listened to His rhythmic breathing as he waited for his Brother to respond. But Jesus' gaze did not waiver and He did not speak.

Though the air had no chill, Michael began to shiver. "I am afraid," he said, breaking the silence. "I have never felt this kind of fear before. Please tell me that You'll be all right. That You won't suffer in whatever it is that lies ahead of You."

"My brother, you must understand that I come as a gift of My Father's merciful love. So that all of humankind might be forgiven, I will suffer joyfully," Jesus said, placing a hand on Michael's shoulder in the gesture of love that He so often used.

"I feel like the child now." Michael shook his head sadly. "Like You are the big brother and I the one who needs to be led. I feel a terrible weakness."

"This weakness is a gift," said Jesus. "Through it, you are drawn to ask the Father for His strength. Even fear can be a grace when it leads you to seek greater faith in God."

"The fool again, I ask You to explain," Michael begged.

"Fear is the opposite of faith and the two cannot live as one," Jesus said gently. "As your faith and trust in God increase, your fears will die and you will know the peace and freedom that only this faith can give."

Utter quiet enveloped the brothers as all around them the echoes of night were hushed. Not even his own breathing breached the silence that held Michael in its grasp.

"Tell me, please," he begged when he could wait no longer for a word from Jesus. "What is going to happen to You? I don't think I can bear not knowing and imagining the worst."

"Soon I'll be called to teach of My Father. I have been sent to set the captives free, to heal the sick, and give sight to the blind."

"But there is grave danger in this effort . . ."

"Yes, there is," Jesus said.

"Is there no other way?"

"With My Father all things are possible. But this is the way He has chosen to save the world."

"What does this mean?" Michael was angry with himself for not understanding, and even though he was ashamed of this shortcoming, he could not stop the asking.

"Remember what I explained to you on our ride a few days ago," Jesus said. "My Father created humankind in His image and gave all of you complete freedom of choice. This is the reason I've been leading you to answers that lie within you, instead of simply feeding you My thoughts. As I've said, only when the knowing settles into your very being—like the seed taking root in the good earth—can it begin to mature."

"I have felt this," Michael said. "And, I have seen it in the horses. It makes me think about the teachings of my father and the other Magi. And still, I cannot bear the thought of losing You."

"Look at the dark sky, My brother," Jesus said, raising one hand and sweeping it like a great paintbrush across the horizon. "Listen to the silence of the night. And remember that the sun will return . . ." Again Jesus paused. "As your father told you, there is order in the universe. To reap a harvest, seed must be sown, must die to itself and give up its original form so that it can be born again."

"Yes, " Michael said. "I can understand when You speak of things I know. I can see the grain fall from the wheat and the grass. I know how the shell opens and allows the root to reach into the ground from whence it will come again." Then the words Jesus had spoken found their way into Michael's heart, and the horseman was gripped by a deep and desperate sorrow.

"Please, my Brother, tell me that You are not this seed."

For some moments, Jesus had been lifting handfuls of sand, watching as He let the shining particles fall gently back to the ground. Now He turned His face to Michael and, with His eyes, embraced this brother of His heart.

"I want you to make Me a promise," Jesus said.

"Anything. Whatever You want, I will promise."

"No matter what happens to Me in the years ahead, no matter how badly you want to save Me, you must not."

"How can You ask this of me?" Tears pooled in Michael's eyes. "What You expect must be more awful than even I can imagine. How am I to stand by and allow You to sacrifice Your very life as I know You are telling me You must do?"

"My brother, you must embrace the truth that I sacrifice willingly and that My suffering will be for your salvation, and that of all mankind. You must not try to stop it," Jesus said. Still holding Michael with His eyes, He added, "Promise Me."

Michael couldn't speak. His breathing was a violent mistral in his ears. His heart pounded as if to escape his heaving chest.

"You will be given the courage, My brother, to accept what lies ahead for us both. And when it is over, you and your children, and everyone who believes in Me–in every generation–will share eternal life with Me. As I promised Adrianna, you and I and your family will meet again in the lush meadows of heaven." Jesus gave Michael time to accept all that he had just heard.

When He spoke again, His own eyes were bright. "Always know, My brother, that love is stronger than death. With this truth in your heart, you will be able to face anything."

A mysterious peace enveloped Michael then. The winds within him settled and his heart resumed its calm, steady rhythm. Once more he could hear the soft rustling of the field mouse and the rabbit that shared the hillside where he and Jesus sat side by side. And, as though this were an eventide like any other, Michael relaxed into the dark of the moon and found a measure of joy in the dancing of the stars.

The brothers spoke no more that night, but reclined in silence to await the dawn. When he awoke the next morning, Michael understood that in the time left to him on the earth, when the dark nights of his soul threatened to consume him, he would be able to return to this place and this time. And in this moment of blessed clarity, he knew that this oasis would reside forever in his spirit, where he could revisit it and find the peace that can come only from resting in Jesus.

ARCHANUS

The Roman sun scowled its disapproval over the teeming city. In a sultry square, perspiring men complained and sought shade beneath the statues of minor gods and other undeserving semi-current celebrities. Women, watching their children at play in the fountains of this park, laughed and gossiped amongst themselves.

Down a long side street that shot away from the eastern border of the square, a low building rested in the afternoon shadow of a taller edifice that stood before it. The curtains had been drawn away from the doors and windows in front of which old men and women stood waving fans in a vain effort to cool the furnace within. In spite of a continuous effort at cleanliness, the air was rife with the stench of illness and death. The moans of the sufferers were punctuated by their cries for help or surcease, and soothed by the whispers of those who tended to them.

Suddenly the somnolent drone of the day in this makeshift hospital was split by the sound of galloping, heavily shod hooves and the shouts of more than one soldier.

"Lucanus! Lucanus! Where is the physician?" The shouts rang out, amplified as their sound ricocheted off of the stone walls that lined the alley. "We need the physician!"

Simon, the dark skinned one who lived to protect the two men he served, stepped to the main doorway, barring entrance. Behind him, Archanus created a second barrier to the infirmary, and to Luke.

"The physician!" Another shout from the rider who pulled his horse to a stop just in front of the door. Metal horse shoes slid across the cobbled stones of the street sending out sparks like fireworks in every direction. The lather of heavy sweat fell in globules from the animal's neck and its flank and its haunches. In the creature's eyes, as in those of its rider, there was determination without fear. The set of the horse's head, and that of the man, bespoke both power and confidence.

Dismounting with the elegance of a powerful athlete, the man pulled off his helmet and bowed low. "Forgive the noise and the violence of my arrival," he begged. "It is my father on whose behalf I come. It is the Tribune, Zadoc!"

"What is your name," Archanus asked, standing to meet the young man.

"I am Joel," the soldier said, looking squarely into the old Wise Man's eyes. "Do you not see my father in me?"

Archanus drew in a deep breath. It was as though a quarter of a century had slipped away and he was standing once more face to face with his old and dear friend. "You are indeed his image," Archanus said, shaking his head in wonder. "Speak, now. What is your purpose?"

"My father lies gravely ill. He was in Gaul where they could not help him, so we tried to bring him home, but the journey proved too tedious and his condition has worsened."

"How far away is he?" Hearing the exchange, Luke had come up behind Simon and bade his protector to step aside.

"I have ridden hard for two days from the place where I left him with two centurions and their forces, as well as those who do their best to aid him in the extremity of his illness."

"Have you fresh horses?" Archanus asked.

"Yes. At the outskirts of the city," Joel said. "Will you come?"

"We will," Luke gave the answer. "There is a cart and horses just behind this building. We will follow you." He turned to Simon. "Archanus and I must go. I ask that you remain here in charge of the hospital. The caregivers can do as much as we would for a short time. Will you accept this mission?"

"But who will protect you?" Simon asked.

"This fine soldier," Archanus said. "He will see to our safety. You have heard me often speak of his father. Zadoc is the one who long ago saved my son and me from certain death."

"Then you must go and I must obey."

"We will return." Luke placed a gentle hand on Simon's arm. "This I promise."

CHAPTER *Nine*

ADRIANNA

Through the long hours of this first night she had spent in many years without her husband beside her, Adrianna could find no rest. Every little sound awakened her from a too light sleep. Be it the scratch of a field mouse scurrying about or the snort of a horse in the distant meadow, no noise was too small. Even the breathing of her children, sleeping peacefully in the tent they shared, could startle her into wakefulness. Finally, when the guard changed at the third watch, she abandoned all effort to sleep. Rising quietly, she went to the hill where Zabbai stood, waiting.

Adrianna talked to the stallion as she approached. He nickered in response to her words, but he did not turn toward her. Even when she moved up beside him and placed her hand on his withers, Zabbai's gaze stayed fixed on the path that Jesus and Michael had taken the day before. She wondered how he could be coaxed away from this lookout point when it was time to embark on the journey that lay ahead.

After a little while this usually calm woman, whose now ever-present anxiety threatened to overwhelm her, dropped to her knees and began to pray. She asked for guidance and strength. She begged for hope. She didn't know how long she had knelt there in the stillness when she felt Zabbai's soft muzzle on the back of her neck. As though the One God had whispered to her on the breath of the great stallion, she understood in that moment that Zabbai at least had heard some answer to her prayers and that—guided by the hand of God— the stallion would lead the horsemen through whatever they must face in the days and weeks ahead.

Heartened by this revelation, Adrianna stood and swung up onto Zabbai's back. Without being asked, he carried her down the hill to the field where the mares still rested with their foals. They circled each separate part of the herd, and as they passed, every horse turned toward them in soundless recognition.

When they had seen that all of the horses were safe, Zabbai took Adrianna to a nearby hill where Phillip stood—alone. In the morning calm, this son of Zadoc seemed to be studying the encampment below and the lay of the land around it. Adrianna wondered what the young man was thinking. Might he too be feeling the sadness that everyone else seemed to share at leaving their well-loved winter home to traverse an unknown land?

"What do you see out there?" Adrianna asked Phillip as she slid down off of Zabbai's back.

"Nothing that seems familiar to me beyond these hills."

"How can I comfort him?" she asked herself in silence. "What do I have to offer him when my own fears are so overwhelming?"

Over the five years he had spent with her family, Adrianna had observed Phillip as a student, and then as a dear friend to her husband. In that milieu, she had seen him to be both intrepid and faithful. Watching him grow from a handsome boy to a physically powerful young man, she had seen him become more and more like his father. As he drew closer to her children, taking on the role of an uncle, she had, in her heart, adopted him as the younger brother she once longed for. But because his interaction with her was so reserved, she had no idea how to give him her support, no clue what he might accept from her, and what he might consider intrusion.

The minutes drew out as the two whom Jesus had charged with a truly fearsome responsibility stood side by side in silence. Finally, Zabbai became impatient and pawed at the ground and nickered. Then he nudged Adrianna and Phillip in turn, rubbing his forehead on each of their backs.

"What do you suppose he's trying to tell us?" Phillip asked.

"I think he wants us to talk to each other," Adrianna said. "I think he knows we won't be able to find our way if we don't communicate, somehow."

"Ah, the great stallion, so wise." Phillip shook his head and ran one hand through his mass of thick hair. "Until today, I thought I was a man grown." He gave a short, self-deprecating laugh.

"And now?" Adrianna looked at him, but he did not turn to face her.

"Now, I am younger than your sons, and surely far more frightened. They see what lies ahead of us as a grand adventure, while I see it as a burden I may not be strong enough to shoulder."

"Do you recall who entrusted you with this mission?" Adrianna said softly.

"I do." Phillip turned at last toward Adrianna. She had looked away in discomfort, but she felt his eyes on her and turned back to face him.

"Do you not trust your friend and his Brother?" she asked.

"Well, yes. But . . ."

"Then you must trust that they have made the right choice for all of us."

There was another long pause before Phillip spoke again. "Adrianna, will you help me?"

Now it was her turn to consider her answer. Of course she would help, but she did not want to demean him. Finally she turned and their eyes met. "I will aid you in any way that I can. But you must ask. You must let me know where my assistance is welcome, and where it is not."

"Why are you so cautious?"

"We can only succeed in this mission if we work together as partners," she said. Her tone was soft, but her words were firm. "If we become adversaries or compete in any way, we will fail. The very nature of men and women makes some disagreement probable—unless we learn to talk things through and to identify the boundaries over which we should not cross."

"And you are a woman of such strong character that you fear I might not receive your counsel well?"

"Yes." Adrianna smiled. "Something like that."

"Then I must make my position clear," Phillip said, turning his whole body toward Adrianna and taking her arm gently so that she would turn toward him. "Even as I respect your husband, I respect you. I have observed the partnership that is your marriage for one quarter of my life thus far. I pray that one day I'll meet a woman with whom I can have such a bond." He paused. "Meanwhile, I will honor Michael, my friend and my mentor, by honoring his wife as does he."

"Thank you, Phillip. I ask that you make me just one promise."

"And that is?"

"If I begin to overpower you with my bossy ways," she said with a small laugh, "you must speak to me. You must not fall silent and brood over my unjust behavior."

"I agree to this." He matched her smile. "And I'll ask the same of you."

"Then it's settled," Adrianna said. "We are partners. Now, we must prepare for tomorrow's departure."

Again, Zabbai nickered low and nudged Adrianna. "Oh my." She laughed. "Already I've failed to mention something that's very important."

"What's that?"

"Zabbai will be charting our course. I prayed for guidance this morning." She paused. "And, well . . ."

"As did I," Phillip said. "And I received the same answer."

With their covenant sealed by shared faith, the partners made their way down into the wakening camp; and the day began.

Hours passed in a flurry of activity with the whole tribe pulling together as families sometimes do. At the end of a long, arduous day, Adrianna led her people in the prayer they had said for all of her lifetime on the eve of every momentous departure. In this prayer the horsemen asked the One God to lead and protect them and to provide for His horses and His people all along the way.

Later, Adrianna lay in her tent and, wakeful once more, she wondered if anyone slept as they waited for the dawn.

⬷⬳

The next morning, with Adrianna riding Zabbai in the lead, the horsemen left one of the places most dear to them and headed for a land they neither knew, nor wanted to know. The procession was as orderly as a massive herd of horses followed by wagons filled with families and their goods could be.

For three days they traveled in relative peace, camping each night beside a stream or some small body of water. With their bellies full and their thirst quenched, the horses were content to move over the hills and into the valleys. The guardians of the enormous herd were wary, but calm. The women soon became tired, as they always did, of trying to confine their children to the wagons. But even they began the journey without protest.

Each day, Zabbai chose the course and set the pace. But on the morning of the fourth day, he seemed to hesitate. And once they got underway, Phillip admitted to Adrianna that for some reason he was feeling uneasy.

"I feel this as well," Adrianna said. "And I'm sure Zabbai wavered this morning because he shares our foreboding."

They traveled for some hours until, early that afternoon, Mathias came galloping up beside Neeka and their mother and Phillip.

"We have some trouble," the boy announced, speaking with the composure that belonged to his father.

"What is it?" Phillip and Adrianna asked in almost the same breath.

"Two of the colts were playing war games and one got hurt. He's badly lame and I can't find Eleazar." He paused. "The healer seems to have disappeared."

Phillip looked to Adrianna as if for guidance. "You've done well, Mathias," she said. "Now, I think I should stay here, allowing Zabbai to remain in the lead, while you take Phillip to the source of the trouble. We must not send up an alarm, so say nothing about Eleazar—just yet."

"We understand," Phillip and Mathias said together, and then they rode off.

As the herd descended into a long valley that was rimmed on three sides by hills of varying elevation, Adrianna looked back over the sea of horses that followed her and Zabbai. From her vantage point, she could see the wagons that drew up the rear as they crested the last hill and started down. The horsemen traveled with ten wagons in all, each filled with families and provisions. Counting only nine, Adrianna watched in growing alarm as the tenth failed to appear. She counted again, hoping against hope that this was only a trick of tired eyes too long on the trail. But soon she had to admit to herself that there was no illusion involved and her heart began to race.

In unison with his rider's mounting fear, Zabbai seemed to grow taller, to collect himself, to prepare for flight. Adrianna stroked his neck and tried to calm him. "It's all right," she whispered, not believing her own words. But Zabbai knew better. No sooner had she spoken than a horde of wild men, shouting and brandishing all manner of weaponry came flying down from the hills to the east.

"Neeka!" Adrianna shouted to the child who had been riding along singing, a short distance behind her mother. "Neeka! Ride into the herd with the mares!" The child obeyed without question.

"Please God, send Your angels," Adrianna said, looking to the heavens, feeling a strange calm embrace her heart even as she spoke.

On his own, Zabbai turned to the side so that his body was like a barrier, signaling the horses behind him not to pass. The horsemen had already begun to circle the herd in hopes of averting a stampede. These were a people who met crisis head on, who did not wait for disaster, but took charge in an attempt to prevent it.

The desert pirates knew nothing of the victims they had chosen—nor could they have imagined what unseen forces had been called to protect these apparent innocents. In their ignorance, the pirates rushed the herd, whooping and shouting, trying to scatter the animals and terrify the people. It was the pirates' way to chase as many horses as possible down box canyons where they could be easily captured, to maim or kill as many of their caretakers as necessary, and to take the women and children hostage for their own purposes, or to be sold at a slave market.

A long held knowledge of this went through Adrianna's mind as she sat aboard Zabbai who continued his efforts to calm his herd. All her life, she had heard tales of men such as these. On two occasions when she was a child her people had been attacked in similar ways. Each time the horsemen had fought valiantly. Each time a few horses and a few people had been lost. But their losses were nothing compared to those she had heard about from other tribes, nor had the pirates she'd seen before numbered anywhere near the mob her people faced on this terrifying day.

The horsemen were poorly armed and they were outnumbered. Adrianna watched in fear and awe, as three sword-wielding pirates attacked a single outrider. Rearing, the horseman's young stallion struck one of the pirates on the knee with a flashing forefoot. When the assailant bent to examine his wound, the stallion's other foot connected with the man's head and he fell to the ground.

At the same time, the other two assailants began to duck and to cover their heads as though they were being attacked by a swarm of bees. While altercations such as this were going on all around the herd, keeping the horsemen from attending to their charges, the sea of animals began to swell outward as those on the edges surged ahead, frightened by the shouting and the noise of battle.

While Zabbai jogged back and forth in front of the moving herd, Adrianna sang a low and soothing song, the words an ancient prayer, the tune lilting, but clear. Within the herd, Neeka took up the melody and the two rode together—yet apart—in harmony.

But the horses would not be stilled. Behind and all around them, some of the pirates chased the animals, lashing at those on the outer edges with long whips, while their cohorts kept up their brutal assaults on the horsemen who tried in vain to quiet the herd.

Nonetheless, by some miracle that Adrianna would only understand much later, none of the herd even attempted to pass Zabbai. From a jog to a lope to a gallop, he increased the speed with which he moved back and forth in front of them whirling with such force and speed as he reversed direction that any lesser rider than Adrianna could not possibly have stayed with him. As though the great stallion's movement created a kind of wall, the animals remained behind the line he established. Zabbai moved with lightning speed and power beyond anything a horse of his age should have possessed. For Adrianna, the ride was at once exhilarating and terrible.

As the action escalated, Adrianna's song was silenced. Now and then she could capture a glimpse of her daughter deep within the core of the mare and foal herd, and though she could hear the child's voice no longer, she could see that Neeka was laughing as though this were a great game as she sat aboard a galloping horse, surrounded by a surging sea of animals.

Dust billowed up from the dry ground, blinding the combatants and the horses. The heat and the dirt in the air were suffocating and fearsome. Then all at once the sky went dark as mammoth yellow-green clouds rolled across the surrounding hills and settled over the melee in a leaden, silencing blanket. Thunder bellowed all around, but the lightning that gave birth to the awful sound could not be seen beyond the heavy cloud cover.

Adrianna's heart nearly burst in terror. But Zabbai carried on, moving with the same purpose, holding the line, undisturbed by the cataclysmic storm and the battle that raged on. In the darkness that had descended, Adrianna knew a helplessness she had never felt before. She could see nothing around her. In the extremis of her fear, she surrendered to the God of whom Jesus had taught her. She began to pray for His help and soon, by His grace, the storm and the battle were over.

The clouds rose, forming a deep blue-gray mantle above the hills and the valley. The dust settled beneath the soft rain that fell, slaking the thirst of the dry land. The horses ceased their fearful rushing, slowing to a jog and then to an exhausted walk. The horsemen who had moments earlier been engaged in fierce warfare all around the outskirts of the herd looked around in wonder, checking their own bodies for wounds and finding none, surveying the herd for injured animals, and finding none.

Finally, at the head of this weary band of horses and humans, Zabbai stopped. Turning to face his followers, he signaled them to go no further, and they did not. Mares dropped their heads to taste the sweet grass that had appeared beneath their feet and foals began to nurse. Shaking their heads in wonder, the herdsmen that Adrianna could see allowed their mounts to relax. Some went to the stream that wound through the deep canyon into which they had surged on the great stampede that was now over.

Completely baffled, Adrianna watched as her oldest son, Junias, rode quietly into the herd and took his sister's hand. Side-by-side, their horses carried them toward their mother. A few minutes later, Phillip and Mathias, followed by Eleazar, the healer, rode up.

"Has anyone checked the wagons?" Adrianna asked. The men and boys looked at each other and shook their heads.

"I'll go," Junias said, and rode off before anyone could suggest otherwise.

"I don't know what happened," Eleazar said. "I have never seen anything so strange. And I've never been so frightened."

"Where were you?" Adrianna asked.

"I was riding along beside the last wagon. The left-hand wheel horse was showing some lameness and I wanted to watch him for a few minutes to try to determine what was wrong." He paused and shook his head. "Then all at once a swarm of riders descended on us. Two of them rode up beside the lead team and grabbed the reins. One leapt onto the wagon seat and shoved Joanna, the driver, into the back of the wagon. Another threw a noose around me, while his partner did the same to my horse. Before we even knew what was happening, we were drug off to a camp hidden deep within one of the small canyons that fork off from this thoroughfare."

Again he paused and looked around.

"They pulled me off of my horse and Joanna from her wagon and bound us to a post beside a fire pit. Thank God Joanna's boys were old enough to be riding with their father, and not in that wagon!"

"Did they hurt you? Either of you?" Adrianna wanted to know.

"Only my great pride was wounded." Eleazar managed a small laugh. "I was most terrified for the beautiful Joanna. I do not have to tell you why. Just one man was left to guard us when all the others rode away. Our only torture was the vile words he used to frighten us, promising the worst when his evil compatriots returned."

"How did you escape? And what of Joanna?" Adrianna asked.

"That is the strange part," said Eleazar. "A great cloud fell upon us, blocking not only the sun, but all else as well. We could not even see our feet, so dense was the damp blanket that surrounded us. Then came the sound of the fiercest thunder I have ever heard. Joanna remained stoic and brave through it all. But our pirate guard shrieked like the coward he was when the storm overtook us. I do not know how long that tempest raged. It seemed at once like an hour and only a moment. When the cloud lifted, we were miraculously free of our bonds. There was not a pirate anywhere in sight. My horse and Joanna's team all stood quietly, as if they were waiting to bring us back to the herd, which is just what they did."

"It was the same for us," Phillip said. "The clouds and the storm and the disappearance of the pirates—everything was the same. I don't know how this could be."

"It was the angels," said Neeka. "I saw them."

"You have such an imagination." Matthias smiled at his sister.

"No," Neeka shook her head. "I saw them."

"Perhaps you'll tell us about this around the night fire," Adrianna said, hoping to reason with her daughter before the child could begin telling some unbelievable tale. "Right now we must check the herd. This is a good place to camp for the night."

"But what if the pirates come back?" asked Mathias.

"They will not return," Adrianna said, wondering at the source of her words.

"How can we be sure?" Phillip wanted to know.

A small frown creased Adrianna's brow. "I cannot answer this question in any way that will give you peace. I can only ask that you accept what has come into my heart on faith, as I must do. We will not be attacked again."

"My mother is right," said Neeka in a solemn tone. "You should believe her."

And so they did believe. Everything that had transpired that day was beyond their comprehension. Why should this call to faith be any different?

Junias rode up then. "The wagons are safe," he said. "The women are all gathered around Joanna and she's telling them the strangest story." He paused. "But I guess what she's saying isn't any harder to believe than what happened to us."

"It was the angels," Neeka said again.

"I believe you," said Junias. "You have always been able to see them when the rest of us could not."

Adrianna wanted to hear more. But she knew that this was not the time. She must turn her attention to settling the herd and the people. She would talk to her children when the day's work was over. And then she would decide if what she learned should be shared with the others.

It was a time of great consequence in Adrianna's life. She had always considered herself a strong and capable woman. She had never been greatly concerned with the opinions of other people as they related to herself. But on this dark night, both her strength and her confidence were drained. And, even worse, she felt she could not, at this juncture, ignore the opinions of those whom she had been given the responsibility to lead.

CHAPTER *Ten*

MARY

Mary knelt beside the mat where Joseph lay, still and quiet. The dark night of her husband's suffering was nearly over. Long ago she had surrendered herself to God. Now she knew she must find the will to give back to Him this dear man whom He had sent to be her companion and the earthly father of their Son.

For days while Joseph tossed and turned in the extremity of his pain, Mary had left his side rarely, and then for only moments. She accompanied him on this journey toward his death, and the life she knew beckoned him, as he had accompanied her these many years across the earthly plain from which he must soon depart.

Joseph's breathing was labored. His eyes no longer opened but his eyelids fluttered now and then as though he wished to see once more. And so, Mary painted for him pictures with words that flowed from her heart, telling him stories of the life they had lived, together with Jesus. Beside her dear husband, she rode again on the back of a donkey into the teeming city of Bethlehem. She talked of the warm place he had found for her to give birth to her Child. She described the night and the Star, the angels and the shepherds. She spoke to him of the mare and her boy, Michael, and the Blessing.

Joseph stirred, and Mary went on, reliving with him their escape to Egypt and the idyllic life they had lived beside the River Nile, and in the mystical mountain paradise to which God had led them. She brought to life the travels that had returned them to their homeland. At the heart of every memory was Jesus, a smiling Babe, a laughing Boy, a beautiful Man. His was the life they had lived together. His was the path they had trod.

Each time she mentioned Jesus' name, Joseph's breathing became less strained, less ragged. Sometimes he became so still that Mary feared he had left her. In her mind, she knew that he must go–that Heaven awaited him. In her mind she knew that it would be a great blessing for God to take Joseph home before Jesus embarked upon His perilous mission. This was all very clear in her mind, but in her heart the pain was almost beyond enduring.

"Never . . . alone . . ." The first words Joseph had uttered in many days came forth on a frail breath.

"No, my husband, you are not alone."

"You . . ." Joseph whispered. "Never . . . alone."

And Mary wept.

A ray of sunshine filtered through the eastern window, and warmed the small room. Birds chirped outside, and one tiny bluebird perched on the windowsill, singing its sweet song to Mary and the morning. The sounds of the day's beginning entered the house as though nothing had changed, as though all things remained as they had been for a thousand years. But for Mary, the Mother of Jesus, this was not so.

JESUS & MICHAEL

The brothers arose before the dawn and walked the short distance down the hill to the Sea of Galilee where they caught fish and ate their day's first meal. Today they would arrive in Nazareth. In Michael's heart, there was a mingling of joy at the prospect of reunion, and sorrow at the sureness of yet another parting.

"It is the way of life, My brother," Jesus said. "Look to the joy and embrace it. When the sorrow comes, you will be given the grace to pass through it."

"And the cycle of life goes on," Michael said. "It seems to me that we are born only to die."

They sat beside the water, watching the movement of tiny whitecaps born of the wind only to disappear when they reached the shore.

"Mankind's death was not a part of the Father's plan," Jesus said, touching gently the sad music of Michael's heart.

"You have said this before." Michael turned his face to Jesus and looked into his brother's eyes. "But is it here, now, to stay? Must the world created in love by the One God exist for all time cursed by the hatred of the devil?"

A sea bird landed nearby and hopped along the shore, stopping now and then, tilting its head curiously toward the intruders. Jesus watched the bird, and Michael waited.

"It will not always be so," Jesus said after a while. In His voice there was a hint of something that Michael did not understand.

"In His Love, and in His time, the Father will redeem His world," Jesus said. "Until then, you must take heart. And you must have faith."

Jesus stood up and extended His hand to Michael. "Let us go now to My Mother and Joseph. It is time."

❧

The noonday sun heated the streets and the walls of the small town known as Nazareth. Sweating men talked and argued and sold their wares in the town square. Women watched from whatever patches of shade they could find while their children ran and played, laughing as though nothing mattered but the joy of the moment.

Assaulted by the sights and sounds of the settlement, Michael saw only the discord. His heart beat like that of a trapped creature and he found it difficult to breathe.

"Come, My brother," Jesus beckoned. "You will not be here long."

"I am sorry," Michael said.

"There is no need for apology. The Father created you to be a man of the wilderness. And to it, you will soon return."

As they made their way through Nazareth, people greeted Jesus and looked with curiosity at His companion. In a short time, they arrived at the community's western edge. "Journey's end," Jesus said.

Michael drew in a deep breath, trying to steel himself against the grief that had begun already to pierce his heart. And, unbidden, came a memory of a time long ago . . .

A pliant breeze undulated through the open windows of the carpenter's shop. Gathering shadows encroached upon the amber twilight that illuminated the hands of Jesus. In a dim, cool corner, the dog Shadow lay dreaming, his paws twitching, little whimpers escaping his slack jaw.

Dust motes danced on a late ray of sunlight that broke through the open window. The chuf-chuf rhythm of a saw moving smoothly through a piece of wood was punctuated by the tap-tap of a small hammer. The hardy odor of cedar mingled with the aromas of less pungent woods, bringing life to the air in the carpenter's shop.

Kneeling in a pool of light where the sunray struck the floor, eight-year-old Jesus concentrated on his efforts to make a little wooden box. His lower lip clamped between His teeth, His eyes focused on His target, a chokehold on His child sized hammer, Jesus carefully aimed every stroke toward the nails that relentlessly eluded Him.

And then they were there, at another carpenter shop, so much the same that time long gone and time present collided in the mind and heart of the horseman.

An unfinished chair sat on a workbench at the center of the room. On the wall, the tools of Joseph's woodworking and masonry trades were hung with the same care and precision the man had always given to his work. In one corner of the room a small pile of sawdust sat beside a broom. In the shade of the opposite corner, an old dog that was the very image of Shadow, lay dreaming, until he sensed the presence of his Master.

Tears sprung to Michael's eyes as the dog jumped up and ran to Jesus. The days of their childhood and youth were gone. But the memories were alive and poignant and painful. In the stillness of the little shop, Michael tried to hold fast to the time he would never know again, even as the present moment clutched at his heart and bade him to face what lay ahead.

There was a fine film of dust on Joseph's usually shining tools and on his workbench. About the room there was an air of abandonment and disuse. No more was the life of the craftsman evident. No more did the hope of a new day linger in the silence.

"I am sorry, My brother," Jesus whispered, resting a hand on Michael's shoulder. "We entered this way so that you might be prepared. Perhaps I should have spared you this visit—and this farewell—all together."

"No," Michael said, the word sounding too forceful inside his own ears. "No," he whispered more softly. "I must say this goodbye, knowing that it is forever, not hoping for a never-to-come reunion. And You were right to bring me this way, through the memories. I'm ready now. We can go to this one who has given us both so much."

"First you must understand and believe something that will carry you beyond today and all the days that will follow," Jesus said. "No matter what happens on this earth, there *will* be reunion. When this journey through a land that is not our true home is over, we *will* meet again all those dear ones we have known and loved. Put your hope in this, My brother, and do not despair."

❧

They passed through the door, then, and it seemed to Michael as though the river of time stopped flowing through his heart.

The room was cool and dim. On a mat beside the inner wall lay the man Michael knew to be Joseph, though in the near absence of his life force, this sufferer appeared so old and so small as to be all but unrecognizable.

Beside the mat knelt Mary who appeared nearly unchanged. Beneath its blue mantle, her hair was still dark and shining. And when she looked up at her Son, her eyes were still like crystalline pools of unfathomable depth.

"Joseph has waited for You," she said to Jesus. "Please come to him." She rose to her feet steadily, as though she had not been kneeling for hours and days on end. She reached her hand out to Jesus and He took her place beside the mat.

Mary turned to Michael and reached for his hand, drew him forward and with a glance bid him to look into his old friend's weary face. The men's eyes met and their hearts reached out to one another as they had once upon a long ago. Michael did not know how long Joseph's gaze held him before the old eyes closed. It was at once a moment and a lifetime, a reunion and a farewell.

Jesus placed His hand on Joseph's cheek. Then He bowed His head and began to pray. "Our Father, who art in heaven, hallowed be Thy Name, Thy Kingdom come, Thy will be done."

Once more Joseph opened his eyes to gaze at Jesus. The carpenter's parched lips moved, but no sound reached Michael's ear.

"Yes, I have come," Jesus whispered. "Go in peace, now. I am with you and our Father in Heaven is calling you home. You need tarry no longer."

Gently, Jesus reached beneath Joseph's shoulders and, supporting the old man's head as though he were a baby, Jesus drew to His chest the man who would be for all eternity the beloved father of His earthly sojourn.

And so it was that Joseph drew his final breath in the arms of Jesus, with the Son's tears falling softly onto his face. "Go in peace," Jesus said again. Then He held Joseph for a long while, praying and rocking him gently, His cheeks awash with silent tears. When He lay the fragile body back down onto the mat, He stood and turned to His mother. And as though He were still a boy, she took Him into her arms. He dropped His face to her shoulder, and she stroked His head and His back as she whispered, words of comfort and of love to Him.

Time had no power as the Mother and the Son held one another in an embrace that transcended all that was, all that had ever been, all that ever would be.

Some part of Michael felt that he was intruding. But his heart knew better. The glimpses of truth he had been given in the company of Jesus and Mary since the day he had first come to them so many years before were graces beyond the explainable, graces he could neither deny nor describe. Now, between the Mother and Son, there was an almost palpable exchange of strength that Michael would recall and draw upon in all the days and years that remained to him on earth.

At length, the two moved slightly apart, still holding one another with their eyes and their hands. And finally, Jesus broke the long silence. "Without your life's companion, can you face what lies ahead, My mother?"

And Mary said yes. As she had so long ago, when the Angel Gabriel asked if she would bear the Son of God, Mary said yes.

❦

Michael stayed in Nazareth for many days, helping with all that needed to be done, praying with Jesus and Mary, loving them and being loved by them. A few days before Michael was to leave, he and Jesus went to a quiet place that overlooked the Sea of Galilee.

They sat together, watching vagrant clouds glide across the sky, listening to the wind as it danced upon the waters, and waiting—for what, Michael did not know.

Finally Jesus spoke. "You must not travel by land any longer than necessary. Tomorrow, when you depart from us, you will follow a southwesterly path through the hills and the valleys to the little town of Dora on the Great Sea. There, you will meet a group of fishermen who will lead you to the port of Caesarea where you will board a ship. You will earn your passage on that ship which will carry you to Alexandria in Egypt."

"But I know nothing of fishing or any other part of life on the sea," Michael said.

"The fishermen you meet at Dora will teach you all that you need to know and they will procure a position for you on the right ship."

Trusting his Brother, Michael didn't ask how he would know the fishermen of whom Jesus spoke. Nor did he ask how these men would know him.

The night before he was to depart, Michael lay on his mat in the carpenter shop wondering what he would face on the journey ahead. When he finally fell into a fitful sleep, it was nearly dawn.

⌘

When it was time for Michael to depart, Jesus and Mary accompanied him to the outskirts of town and walked with him up a low hill where they could look together toward the Great Sea.

"Remember what has been, My brother," Jesus said. "Face the future strengthened by the past."

"I will live in the strength that is You," Michael said.

"I know that you will, My brother. Just remember that you must not try to change anything that happens to Me. You have not promised Me this, but you must do so now."

"I cannot."

"I ask you again, as I have asked before, do you love Me?"

"You know that I do," Michael said.

"Then give Me this last gift. Make Me this promise. Tell Me that you will obey God. Say yes, as has My mother."

Michael looked to Mary then bowed his head, unable to answer at once. "God's will be done," he said finally. "May He grant me the graces to know this will—and to obey."

Then, Jesus spoke the same words with which He had released Joseph from the bonds of this earth. "Go in peace," He said. And grief gripped Michael's heart as he heard the words that he felt sure must herald their last goodbye. They all embraced and Michael, with tears overflowing his sad eyes, turned to walk down the hill into the fearful unknown.

ARCHANUS

While Archanus and Luke gathered their supplies, Simon hitched the horse to the cart that rested in the shade behind the hospital. When they were ready to leave, Simon accompanied his friends to the outskirts of town, where they were given fine horses to ride. They left in haste and Simon drove the cart back to the hospital where he would wait in hope for his friends' return.

At the end of two days and two nights of wild and perilous riding and precious little rest, Joel brought the travelers to a house beside a running stream. The spreading branches of an ancient olive tree shaded the entry. Outside and within the dwelling, servants waved huge fans in an effort to move and cool the stifling air. In a dim corner the great Zadoc lay sweating, diminished almost beyond recognition by the illness that ravaged him.

Exhausted as they were, Luke and Archanus set to work. For many days and nights, they ministered to their old friend. As the hours passed, the physician and his assistant took shifts, one resting while the other tended to the man for whom there seemed precious little hope.

Throughout the long siege, the woman who had opened her doors to the soldiers, cooked and cleaned and prayed. The murmur of her patient petitions became a song and the only glimmer of relief in the darkness of despair that surrounded the apparently dying Tribune.

CHAPTER *Eleven*

ADRIANNA

From the crackling night fire, bright sparks soared into the air. Alone, the tiny bits of fire burst upon themselves then returned as ashes into the small conflagration from which they had been born. The ground and the vegetation were still damp from the rain, and the air was cool and moist. The horsemen and their families huddled near the warmth, feeding the fire with wood they had carried along from what they would always refer to as their home camp. Unusually quiet, they sat mesmerized by the flames, some reliving the events of the day just passed, some worrying about what might happen in the days ahead.

On a small rise overlooking the camp, Adrianna stood beside Zabbai, watching the herd. Feeling utterly alone and overmatched by the responsibility she had accepted, she listened for the words her people did not speak and wondered what she could say to calm their fears and give them hope. In the valley below she saw Phillip and her children riding quietly around the edges of the herd. They had assumed this task so that the other horsemen could sup with their families and rest from the hard day. This was the way of Michael and his family and it would continue even in his absence.

One rider broke away from the herd and came toward her. In the darkness she could not tell which of her sons this was, but she guessed it would be Matthias, who had been so caring, so solicitous since Michael's departure. She thought about this beautiful boy who seemed always to consider himself the least loved by his father and because of this, always tried harder than either of the others to please Michael. She thought about how difficult it seemed for Michael to see his second son in the same way he saw his other two children. Matthias was the image of his father in all things, from appearance to attitude, hence Michael expected more of him and feared more for him. It was a terrible conundrum that tugged at Adrianna's heart.

"Are you all right?" Matthias said when the bay gelding he rode crested the small hill. "Should you not eat and rest with the others?"

Adrianna smiled. And, in that moment, she realized that sometimes it was only this child who could cause her to smile. She loved all of her children equally, but there was something different about Matthias—something she could not name.

"My mother?" he said when she did not speak. "Is something wrong?"

"No, son. I'm sorry. I was just thinking."

"About today and what happened?"

"Yes, and other things." To escape her thoughts, she turned her attention to the camp and saw that four men were preparing to mount their horses to take over the night watch.

"Go fetch your brother and sister and Phillip," she said, looking back at Matthias. "We'll eat and rest together."

Without question, Matthias rode down the hill to do as he had been told.

❧

When Adrianna and her children sat down with Phillip beside the night fire, people began at last to speak.

"Though I do not know what you did today," one woman said, looking directly at Adrianna, "I know that we should thank you."

"And Phillip as well," said the woman's husband.

"It is not us you must thank," said Adrianna.

"Who then?" This question from Eleazar, the healer.

"It was the angels," Neeka said before her mother could begin to answer.

Adrianna drew in a long breath, unsure of what to say in the face of this revelation. But Neeka went on.

"I saw them. They were huge, and they had shining wings and great swords. Every time one of our men was attacked, angels came to his rescue, beating the pirates with great blows, knocking away their weapons and dashing the bad men to the ground. And when the horses tried to stampede, the angels wouldn't let them. They circled and sang softly the same song my mother sang. The greatest angel stayed with Zabbai as he ran and spun back and forth in front of the herd. And another beautiful angel rode right beside me with the mares and the foals."

Amazingly, no one interrupted. They all sat in rapt attention as Neeka went on describing details of all that had transpired that day. Adrianna shook her head in wonder, thinking about how worried she had been all afternoon and evening. She and her sons had witnessed before this phenomenon of her daughter's visions. On other occasions when some unexplainable assistance had come, Neeka had seen the angels and described their actions perfectly. And, although only her eyes had beheld the miracles, her descriptions could never be disputed. The difference this night was that Neeka shared the revelation with the entire tribe— something she had never done before. Perhaps, Adrianna thought, this is how our people are to be given courage and hope, not through me, but through Neeka.

"The child is right," said one horseman. "I knew there must have been some miraculous intervention. We had meager weapons and we were grossly outnumbered, yet the pirates fell as though they had been slashed by mighty swords."

"Yes, it's true," said the man's wife. "When the pirates tried to take control of the teams that pulled our wagons, they were struck down and fell beneath the wheels. Only their horses escaped."

"Right after we were captured, I felt a strange presence," said Joanna, the woman who had been taken by the pirates along with Eleazar.

"I too felt this," said the healer. "And when they took us to their camp, we were never alone."

"How did you escape?" asked another of the horsemen.

Eleazar repeated the story he had told earlier to Adrianna.

"Just as it happened to us," said a horseman. "I've asked others and no one seems to know how long we fought the pirates or how long we were engulfed in the cloud. But when that cloud lifted, the horses were calm and so were we."

"Little Neeka, what is it like to see the angels?" asked Joanna.

"It is nearly as beautiful as seeing Jesus who sent them," Neeka said.

"How do you know Jesus sent them?" asked Eleazar.

"Because the angel who rode beside me told me this," said Neeka. "But I would have known by my heart, even if that angel hadn't spoken. Jesus promised me that He would be with us always—and sometimes He has to send angels when He is busy with something else."

"Who is this Jesus?" Phillip asked. "I mean beyond the man who walked and rode with us. Who can He be?"

"Jesus is a man of great mystery," said Adrianna. "We may not know in this lifetime all that He is. But just as Neeka said, He is with us always and one day, beyond this life, we will know Him in all His fullness and glory."

No one questioned the truth of Adrianna's and Neeka's words.

MICHAEL

On the evening of the second day of his journey, Michael arrived at the shore of the Great Sea where the sweet song of the wind played across the Sea and lulled the horseman into a gentle sleep. He awoke the next morning to the sounds of fishermen talking and laughing as they began their day. He watched as a handsome black and white dog walked with patience and dignity beside his master as the man approached.

Michael stood up to meet the man. "I am Simon, son of John," said the fisherman. "You look a bit lost."

"Perhaps, a little," Michael said. Not offering his own name, he bent low and reached out to the dog that licked his hand and moved to stand beside him.

"Are you a fisherman?" asked Simon.

"No, I'm afraid not," said Michael feeling at once shy and foolish. "I'm a traveler and I need to find passage aboard a ship headed for Egypt."

"Come," offered Simon, "my friends and I will teach you to fish. Then we'll help you find work aboard a ship that will take you where you need to go."

"Why would you do this?" Michael asked. "You do not know me . . ."

"But the dog has recognized you," the fisherman said with a small laugh. "I trust this animal's judgment well beyond my own. Now, come along. You look hungry and we've had a great catch this morning."

Michael stayed with Simon and his companions for many days, learning the fisherman's art and regaining the strength he had lost during the travels that brought him to the shore. At the seaport of Caesarea, Simon introduced Michael to the captain of a ship bound for Egypt. The captain and the fisherman were obviously acquainted, and on Simon's recommendation, Michael was given passage in exchange for his labors. The new friends bid one another farewell as Michael departed that afternoon on a journey that would be for him both tedious and uneventful, a moment in time that would soon recede from his conscious memory.

The rolling sea lulled the horseman into a strange sort of lethargy. But he did the work he was given, keeping to himself and praying constantly for the safety of his family. He would not dwell on the danger they faced. Instead, he continually willed himself to call on Jesus and to trust in His protection.

Adrianna

For some time after the pirate attack, all was quiet. There was so much grass and water for the horses that many of the horsemen questioned why they had not traveled this route before. A few wondered if this abundance was another angelic gift. Some still complained about the forced exile, fretting about what Egypt would be like and how long they might have to remain there. But for the most part, they were at peace.

From their favored winter pasture near Lake Semechonitis, they had taken the new route set out for them by Jesus, avoiding both their usual path beside the Jordan and the North/South trade route once known as the King's Highway, that wound along near the crest of the eastern mountains. In the foothills and the steppes, grass grew in abundance, springs bubbled, and streams flowed. But this changed when they reached the desert south of the Dead Sea.

For two days after they passed the southern tip of that small and brackish lake, there was plenty of vegetation and water. On the third day, they came to a land so barren that hope began to abandon even the hardiest and most hopeful among them. Forced into a long canyon that ran between red, rocky hills, the horses and their people endured awful heat and deprivation. By the pure grace of God, two days into this desolation, a freak rainstorm poured from the heavens, leaving small pools of water in every surface indentation. After the horses had drunk their fill, the women of the tribe gathered every container they could to fill with water that was slightly dirty, but nonetheless a much needed blessing.

Hungry and thirsty, traveling at half their normal speed, it took another three days for the tribe to reach the northernmost tip of the Red Sea's eastern arm, where the King's Highway met the ancient route of the Exodus. By this time, the sense of mutiny that surrounded her was so palpable that Adrianna felt she could reach out and touch it. And with this realization, she came to realize just how important Phillip's commanding presence actually was.

There had been no night fires since the herd entered the hot and dusty canyon. Still, families gathered in the evenings to share the meager supplies of nuts and dried fruits that they had brought in case of such emergency. Until just days earlier, there had been no problem for the women to find berries and greens and for the men to bring home the meat of wild game. But now, obliged to begin using their stored supplies, Adrianna's people were ready for revolt.

"We are turning back in the morning," Arnon, one of the elders of the tribe announced to Adrianna when the evening meal was finished. "Everyone knows what lies ahead. There is only more of the same kind of wilderness we've just crossed. Knowledge of this has been handed down among us for generations. It is why our people have never traveled this way even on the rare occasions that they chose to go to Egypt." He emphasized the word chose.

"We cannot know what lies ahead of us." Adrianna spoke with feigned calm. "But we can be certain that at least four days of emptiness lie in the way we have just come. Not many of our horses, especially the young ones, will make it back over that wasteland alive."

"Then we'll purchase new horses and start again!" shouted another of the horsemen.

"Do you care more for the horses than your children, and ours." These angry words were hurled at Adrianna by a woman whose voice was both edgy and cold.

"That is a foolish question," said Adrianna. "There can be no distinction between our families and our horses. We are as one, each existing to serve the other."

"Yes, this is true," said Arnon. "That is why we are taking over the herd and our own destiny." He looked around as if seeking approval. Heads nodded and tentative words of assent were exchanged. "You can go wherever you want to," said the troublemaker with pride and self-satisfaction. "We'll be safer without you and your children. It is your husband and their father who placed us in this danger in the first place."

"Enough!" Phillip walked into the center of the circle around which everyone was gathered. "Anyone who wants to turn back alone may do so. But the horses stay with us."

Matthias and Junias moved to Phillip's side. The boys were tall and strapping for their nine and ten years of age, daunting in their own way. But in the image of his father, Phillip was a huge and powerful presence. Towering nearly a head above the tallest of the horsemen, with wide shoulders and muscles that glistened in the heat, he was more than just imposing. With the attitude of a soldier, he commanded respect, and all those around him seemed at once to realize that he would settle for nothing less.

"What of our families?" Arnon whined.

"For hundreds of years, your people have trusted whatever leader was given charge of this herd, and this family. If you lack the courage to continue in this tradition, you must go your own way."

"But our leader is gone," said the foolish woman who had spoken earlier. "And before he left, he betrayed us."

"Shut up, woman," said her husband. "Michael did only what had to be done, and this is not a matter for you."

"Thank you," said Adrianna.

"Let's take a vote, then," offered Arnon. "Let everyone decide what they want to do."

"This is not a democracy. We do not subscribe to rule by the mob. Our journey will continue toward the destination that has been set out for us. And we will go on without you." Phillip's demeanor, even more than his firm statement, dissuaded any argument.

"Who will go with me?" Arnon shouted, trying to regain control.

No one spoke and no one stepped forward.

"Have you all gone mad?" Arnon's voice trembled as he spoke. "The woman was right. We have no leader."

Adrianna stepped into the circle beside her sons and Phillip. "My husband left Phillip and I in charge. We are your leaders. If you choose to follow us, we'll be leaving in the morning, heading southwest along the path it is said the Jewish people traveled long ago to escape their cruel slave masters in Egypt."

"We will find the place of which Jesus has told us," Phillip added.

"What of our maps," Arnon shouted. "Every hill and valley, river and spring has been recorded, and there is nothing in the land of Ethiopia beyond Syene."

"Maps don't tell us everything," said Neeka who had been standing, unusually silent, beside her mother.

"Go away child," said Arnon. "You have no place with the men who are discussing your fate."

"This is not a discussion," said Phillip. "Our plans are firm, Arnon, and you have no more part in this. Tomorrow you will take your family and five horses, in addition to the team that pulls your wagon. At some point you'll doubtless find another tribe you can join or a different life you can build."

"You cannot send me away from my people." Arnon's eyes narrowed in hatred.

"I can, and I have," said Phillip. "Prepare to depart in the morning."

"Who will go with me?" Arnon asked again.

And again, no one spoke or stepped forward.

"Cowards, all of you! Even my own kinsmen! Will none of you stand with me against this usurper?"

Still no one responded and after a while the people began to disburse and to move toward their separate tents. The air of defiance seemed to have mostly dissipated. But Adrianna was uneasy. What if Arnon managed to re-incite some of the others? What if they tried to use physical force to take control?

That night, Adrianna took her usual post beside Zabbai. Resting her hand on the stallion's withers, she followed his gaze to the western horizon where there was still a dim glow from the sun that had long since set. "What lies ahead old friend," she whispered as a new terror began to take seed in her heart. What if Arnon betrayed both Michael and his people to Roman authorities? What if all was still to be lost? In the extremis of her fears, she forgot to ask the One God for help and protection, and the empty place in her heart filled with despair.

⤳

Following the rebellion among her people, Adrianna traveled in constant dread, sleeping and eating little, speaking almost not at all. Phillip remained a commanding presence who tolerated no disrespect toward Adrianna or himself.

Consulting the ancient maps of the tribe's cartographers, Adrianna and Phillip followed the path recommended by Jesus. And just as He had promised, they found ample food and water as they headed south toward Mount Sinai. When rain miraculously fell or grass covered the ground where it seemed as though nothing should grow, Adrianna thought of the stories Jesus had told her about the homeward migration of the Jews after their exile in Egypt. He had spoken of the manna that fell from heaven so that those wanderers could eat. And He had told of the grumbling that had gone on despite these blessings. As she recalled the story, it occurred to her how little people differed from one another and how little humans had changed over the centuries.

At Mount Sinai, the horsemen turned to the north, still following in reverse the route of the Exodus. When they arrived at the shore on the westerly arm of the Red Sea, the spirits of one and all seemed to lift. A cool breeze wafted across the waters. Birds unlike any they had seen before graced the land and the water and their songs filled the air. A fresh water stream ambled toward the sea, and beyond the sandy beach, grass grew belly deep to the tallest horse. They camped for three nights in this peaceful place before they resumed their journey.

It took the tribe many days of northwesterly travel to reach the King's Highway at the northern tip of the Red Sea. At that juncture they headed west to the River Nile where they turned south.

Embarking on this leg of their journey, the travelers didn't depart from the Roman Empire until the moon reached its fullness. By then, the people had begun once more to complain. The vegetation that had been lush and plentiful along the riverbanks became more sparse each day, and the crocodiles that called that great river home became more abundant.

Borne on the hot southern winds, dust storms came nearly every afternoon. While traversing the desert east of the settlement of Syene, they saw on the distant hills what looked to be a cadre of foot soldiers. They were at once terrified and heartened by this first sign of human life they had seen along the Nile. Their maps marked four cities along the Nile between Memphis and the Roman border. Anticipating each city, they had crossed over the hills and gone out into the desert to avoid notice. On these forays, the desert had become to them anathema.

Around the night fire at the end of the tribe's first day beyond the Roman border, the grumbling reached fever pitch. The next day, Phillip took Adrianna's sons and three other young horsemen on an expedition in search of a continuing route of travel, or a place to stay. Before midday, they crossed the shallow Nile and rode into the low western hills. The land was barren, but something told Phillip to explore it nonetheless. At the convergence of the narrow gulch down which they had traveled through three other ravines, the riders stopped to consider how they should proceed.

"We have only enough water to search for a short time," said Phillip. "Then we must return to the river. We'll cover the most ground if we separate. Junias and I will take the north draw: Matthias, you and Caleb follow the western canyon. Erech and Anat, go south. We'll meet at this dry spring when the sun is halfway between its zenith and the western horizon."

At the appointed time, Phillip and Junias met Erech and Anat at the dry spring. But Matthias and his companion, the twenty-year-old Caleb, were nowhere to be seen.

"Our water is gone," said Erech.

"As is ours," Phillip and Junias spoke in the same breath.

It was decided that Erech and Anat would ride to the river leading Junias and Phillip's horses. There they would refill the water carriers, then return. While they waited, Phillip and Junias tried to follow on foot the trail left by Matthias and Caleb. The searchers had walked only a short distance when the hoof prints they were following disappeared in the deep sand of what looked to be an ancient riverbed. As the sun lowered, its heat became even more intense, and soon the man and the boy were forced to take shelter in the shade of an east-facing hill.

By the time Erech and Anat returned with the water, the light left behind by the falling sun had begun to fade and the moon had not yet appeared.

"We'll stay the night," Phillip said, looking at the other horsemen. "In the morning Junias and I will continue our search while you return to camp. Adrianna will be beside herself and the complainers will be even more agitated."

As it happened, it was not necessary to put this plan into effect. Matthias and Caleb arrived at the meeting place beside the dry spring just before dawn. Even the firm scolding from Phillip could not dampen the spirits of the intrepid pair.

"We have found paradise!" said Matthias, jumping down from his horse. "We must go for the herd and bring everyone here at once. It's less than half a day's ride from here, but the path between the mountains is narrow and the horses will all have to travel in single file."

"Wait, wait," said Phillip. "You need to tell us more before we rush back and start moving the herd."

"It is like the magical place where our father lived with Jesus and his family," said Matthias.

"There are trees and streams and great valleys," said Caleb. "There is enough food on the grassy plain that spreads forever between the high mountains to feed many more horses than we might dream of for all the time to come."

"And there is rain!" Matthias said with a laugh. "While we were riding along beside a bubbling stream, clouds gathered and sweet rain fell upon us. There is no dust and no sand. Truly, it is a paradise."

"You're certain? You haven't eaten any strange berries, or succumbed to thirst?" Phillip asked.

"This is not a dream," said Matthias, raising his full water carrier. "We have not been thirsty and we have eaten nothing but the rations we brought, even though there are trees laden with fruit and berry bushes in great abundance."

"Matthias knew that everyone would be suspicious," said Caleb, "so we did not even taste the fruits of that fine land."

"Perhaps you should ride back there with us," Matthias said. "Then you can see for yourself."

"No, I trust you. And we must return to your mother. We should not have left her this long to deal alone with that quarrelsome mob."

Returning the way they had come the day before, the riders were able to make far better time than they had traveling into the unknown. When they arrived at the camp before midday, Adrianna, with tears of joy running down her cheeks, ran to her sons. Matthias jumped down from his horse and threw his arms around his mother. "We have found a paradise like the one you knew long ago," he said, his voice full of laughter and excitement. "We must ride back there together at once."

There was some grumbling amongst the people, but Phillip quelled this in short order by reminding them of Arnon's departure and offering the loudest complainers the same choice, which no one accepted.

ARCHANUS

From the moment Joel arrived in Rome, Archanus had felt a sense of deja vu, as though he had seen the young man somewhere before. He tried to reason away this sensation by reminding himself that Joel was the image of his father long ago, when Zadoc was a young and handsome Centurion. But that explanation wasn't good enough.

"I'm an old man with a failing memory," he told Luke one afternoon while they sat outside in the afternoon sunshine. "I keep picturing Joel walking about within a herd of horses. Could I be confusing him with my own son?"

"I don't think so, my friend," Luke said, placing a gentle hand on Archanus' shoulder. "I believe this memory is true and that it will come back to you in its own time."

When he could stand it no longer, Archanus questioned Joel about his life as a soldier, asking where he had been and what he had done. Through this conversation, the old wise man learned that Joel and his brothers had studied horsemanship with Michael and that the youngest of them, Phillip, was still with the horsemen, as far as he knew.

When Zadoc finally recovered enough to recognize and talk with his old friends, he shared with them his desire to go home to his vineyards in the hills outside of Rome. "I no longer have the heart for battle," said the old soldier. "I wish only to live out my years in peace."

When Zadoc seemed strong enough, Joel explained Michael's present situation, telling the tale of the evil Marvelius and asking his father's advice.

"My heart breaks knowing that my inattention has contributed to this trouble. You and Marcus must keep track of this man's movements," Zadoc said. "From now on, no matter where I am, Michael's safety will be the first matter on my mind. You must keep me appraised of all that you learn and we will plan what needs to be done."

"And I must go again in search of my son," said Archanus. "I cannot let him be murdered by this madman," He dropped his face into his hands and, shaking his head in sorrow, fell silent.

"You cannot do this," Joel said. "Michael and his people have escaped for the time-being. Marvelius has spies in every quarter. If he hears that anyone has gone in search of Michael, he will have the seeker followed. Should you find your son, this very thing could bring about his demise."

"I will be near you in Rome," Zadoc said, reaching for the hand of his old friend. "I will keep you abreast of everything that transpires. When it is safe, we will go together in search of Michael. Until then, you must trust my sons."

CHAPTER *Twelve*

ADRIANNA

A strange and foreboding calm settled over horses and humans alike as they departed from the Nile before dawn, heading once more into the dim unknown. Even the irrepressible Neeka was unusually subdued. All three of Adrianna's children rode beside her in front of the herd on this portentous morning.

For a good part of the day they traveled steadily with Matthias guiding them toward the convergence of canyons where he and Caleb had begun their exploration two days earlier. Because of the distance they would have to travel to the next source of water, they tarried longer than usual at the Nile, giving the horses plenty of time to eat their fill of sweet grass and to fully satisfy their thirst. So, by the time they reached the dry spring, the sun had passed the halfway point of its descent.

"How much further?" Adrianna asked Matthias as the herd began to gather behind them in the arid little valley.

"If we don't tarry, we can make it before nightfall. But we must keep the horses moving, which shouldn't be too difficult in the narrow draw ahead."

"All right," Adrianna said. "Lead the way."

As they went on, the canyon walls became higher, creating the sensation that the riders were descending, although the path seemed level. Shadows obscured the sun and the deepening hues of the rocks added to the illusion of darkness. When it seemed they had been within the ever-narrowing confines of the ravine for too long, Matthias began to look around with alarm.

"What is it, my son?" Adrianna asked.

"I don't know." He shook his head. "I feel as though we must have passed the almost hidden passageway to the valley we seek."

Just then, Caleb appeared behind them. "It wasn't easy making our way between all of the horses," he said. "But I'm worried. I fear we've ridden beyond the place where we should leave this part of the trail. It seems so much narrower than it was when we first came here."

"We're not there yet," said Neeka.

"How do you know this?" Junias asked.

"The angels," she said simply.

The boys and Caleb looked at one another, but said nothing.

"Zabbai can find the trail," Neeka said. "Let him take the lead."

Matthias nodded and moved his horse aside. With his head low and his ears forward, Zabbai lengthened his strides and walked forward, moving a good deal faster than the hesitant pace Matthias had set in his rising confusion. The sky directly overhead had gone from a pale, dusty blue to deep azure. Voices echoed off the canyon walls, amplifying the fear in their words and in their tone.

Dread gripped Adrianna's heart in anticipation of awful danger. And just when it appeared to her that all was lost, Zabbai stopped. He planted his forefeet wide apart and gave a great snort as though a snake had crossed his path. Adrianna held her breath and everyone behind her fell silent. Even the sound of moving horses was dulled. Moments later, Zabbai shook himself all over, then raised his head, took two forward steps and made a sharp right turn. At first it seemed to Adrianna as though the stallion had decided to walk right through the rock wall of the canyon. But where he turned, there was an opening just wide enough for one horse to pass through.

"This is it!" Matthias said, laughing. "This is the way!"

"Wait here a moment, Junias," Adrianna said. "Hold the horses in place. Matthias, come with me. I want to be sure before we lead the others any further."

Matthias followed without argument. The corridor was so tight that the riders' legs brushed against the sinister rock barricades that jutted so high on either side of the path that the sky was almost obscured and only a sliver of dim light shone above. But, in the length of only about ten horses, the walls broke away and before the riders a glorious field spread out. The last rays of a setting sun shone over the western horizon, and the mist left behind by a recent rain glistened on the waving grasses and the trees and the wildflowers.

Again, Zabbai stopped. He looked around and this time his snort was one of satisfaction, not alarm. When Matthias and his horse broke from the corridor, the boy was laughing and the horse raised his head to let out a great whinny.

"Isn't it beautiful?" Matthias said. "Can you believe me now?"

"I always believed you, son," Adrianna said, leaning over and hugging Matthias. "Doubt only assailed me at the last when the ravine and the light kept shrinking. We'd better hurry back for the others. I know they're terrified."

But they didn't have to go back. Necka had come rushing down the corridor when she heard the call of Matthias' horse.

Junias and Caleb had followed, and on their heels were the horses at the front of the herd. When all of the riders cleared the portal, they moved aside and let the herd and the horsemen flow into the valley like a river emptying into a great and shining lake.

The horses spread out, jogging and loping, rearing and calling out to one another in that timeless salute to freedom that belongs so purely to the horse. When the herd settled at last, the vast sea of horses was only a speck on the face of the grassy plain that spread out toward the west and the north and the south.

The horsemen talked and laughed and planned how they would dismantle the wagons that could not make it through the final passage into this magical land. Some of the men unloaded the wagons and brought their tents and provisions into the valley. The women found a place for their fire circle and prepared the evening meal while other men set up the tents. By the time darkness had fully descended, everyone was exhausted from the tension of the day and all but the night watchmen drifted off into the most peaceful sleep they had enjoyed since their departure from the far north.

MICHAEL

In the fullness of time, the ship that carried Michael arrived at the Egyptian seaport of Alexandria. But in this teeming city, the horseman felt none of the relief and freedom he had expected. Instead he was assaulted by a terrible sense of crowding and confusion. His anxiety continued to mount until at last he thought to beg the One God for help. No sooner had he whispered his prayer than he recalled a few forgotten words Jesus had spoken to him before they parted.

"Go to the marketplace near the port in Alexandria," He had said. "There you will meet an old friend who will help you to set forth on the rest of your journey."

When the memory of Jesus' words finally came to him, Michael asked a passerby how he might find the marketplace.

"You are at its outer edge," said the man, pointing to the west. "It is a huge market. Do you know who or what you seek within it?"

"The horses," Michael answered without thinking.

"Follow this street," the man nodded toward a narrow byway that forked off of the thoroughfare on which Michael had been traveling. "You will come to the place where they auction slaves and horses."

Soon, just as the man had promised, Michael arrived at an enormous square with a platform in the center around which a noisy crowd was gathered bidding on the slaves that huddled fearfully together behind the auctioneer. On the far side of the square a small herd of horses was corralled and tethered and held by their sellers. Between Michael and his goal a dozen or more Roman soldiers milled about the square.

To avoid the danger of meeting a soldier who might recognize him, Michael headed down a side street and eventually found his way to the rear of the corral. As he surveyed the horses and wondered how he might acquire one, a heavy hand fell upon his shoulder. Startled, he turned to face the fear rising inside him. But lo and behold, it was a friend, just as Jesus had promised.

"I can't believe my eyes," said the old man, grasping Michael in a strong embrace.

"Ben Faroan, is that really you?" Michael shook his head in wonder.

"It is I, my son. It is I." Abu Ben Faroan stepped back and looked Michael over as he might a fine horse. "You are in grave danger," he said. "There are soldiers here who have been looking for you. They say that you are wanted for high treason. What is this about?"

Briefly, Michael told Ben Faroan the story of Marvelius and of how this situation had forced him to part from his family. "But I don't understand why the soldiers are looking for me here." he said. "The last they knew I was camped with my people near Jerusalem."

"Their leader told me that one of your people betrayed you, a man called Arnon, who is also here in the city."

Michael looked away then back at his friend. "I need to buy a horse," he said. "But I have no money. Will you trust me?"

"I owe you and your family far more than a single horse," said Ben Faroan. "Have you forgotten that I am alive today because of your uncle? I will begin to repay him by helping the son of his heart."

"I have not forgotten. Still, I can't put you and your people in danger."

"Nor will you," said Ben Faroan. "I will provide you with a fine horse, a son of your own Zabbai, a colt born to us from one of the mares we purchased from you some years ago. Two of our young men will show you the way you must travel in search of your family. You will ride out tonight under cover of darkness when the soldiers have all succumbed to drunkenness and depravity."

⌘

Two days later, riding alone on the powerful horse he had named Faroan, the horseman covered ground with great speed. Stopping only to rest and water his horse, Michael arrived at the Nile in under five day's ride, even though he had followed Abu Ben Faroan's advice to travel through the hills and desert far to the west of the river, avoiding all settlements.

He camped one night at Lake Moeris, southwest of the Great Pyramids at Memphis. From there, he followed the lush valley that led to the Nile. Then, staying to the hills west of the river, going near only to feed and water Faroan, he rode south for what seemed days upon endless days. Hope remained with him thanks to the signs of the herd that he found all along the way.

Only once on this long southward journey did he catch sight of a Roman battalion. But they were a great distance away and either did not see him, or paid him no mind. The further he traveled, the less Michael thought about anything but reunion, and so he pushed himself and his horse beyond normal endurance, riding each day from before dawn until after dusk. When he arrived at the place where the herd had obviously rested for some days, the dark of the new moon engulfed him and he fell into a deep and healing sleep. When he awoke the next day, far behind the sun, Faroan grazed peacefully nearby, birds sang all around him, and the sound of gently flowing water eased his spirit.

Having deciding that Faroan needed a good day's rest before they embarked on the next leg of their journey, Michael explored the area on foot while the sun rode across the sky. In the back of the horseman's mind was a troublesome feeling that something unknown, perhaps dangerous, lay just ahead. He wondered if his unease had started with a dream he could not quite remember. And though it felt strange not to press on, he listened to the vague warning that pushed against his heart. That night, he camped at the foot of a sandstone cliff near the river. Again, a sense of foreboding had sent him away from the river to a more sheltered place. And once more he fell into a deep sleep.

During the third watch of the night he was startled into wakefulness by a loud and unremitting reverberation. At first he thought the sound was that of a huge number of horses galloping hard along the butte above him. But soon he realized that the rumble came from the heavens. Lightening flashed all around, preceding the rolling and crashing of thunder. Then the deluge began and for hours sheets of rain fell upon the land. In the end the dark clouds and the rain were swept away on a gale.

The sun rose in fierce opposition to the cool and the damp. Soon Michael's clothes were dry and before long the heat became oppressive. The day before, he had followed the tracks of the herd a short distance, seeing where they had crossed the Nile and noting their direction of travel. Now he chastised himself for not going on when he had the chance, because today, all trace of the herd was gone, obliterated by the rain and the wind.

Unable to think of anything else to do, he stayed the southwesterly course on which the herd had started. By midday, there seemed little hope that he would find his family anytime soon. The barren desert spread out in every direction, relieved only by low, sun-baked hills that dotted the flat landscape. For two days he rode on. When his water supply gave out, he found a small oasis where he and Faroan could slake their thirst. He remained at the oasis to let the stallion rest, but his own heart would not be still. He could not forgive himself the delay that might cost him the reunion he so desired.

Emotionally and physically spent, he waited for the fall of night and sought refuge in the embrace of the darkness. After a brief and fitful sleep, he awoke to the silence of an empty sky and land made violent by the heat. He fell to his knees beside the tiny spring, thinking to partake of the waters, but succumbing to his fear and his sorrow. "Where am I to go?" he called to the heavens. And then he waited. "Please help me," he whispered at last and in the wake of his prayer, a cool breeze drifted across his face.

From behind him, he felt a strong nudge. Turning, he saw Faroan, his head low, his muzzle still nearly touching Michael's back. The horseman stood and, understanding, he swung up onto the horse's back and gave the animal its head. Faroan would find the way. Michael knew only this, nothing more.

The stallion took off at a long trot, going first back over the ground they had covered the day before and then taking a winding trail up into an outcropping of hills that Michael had barely noticed when first he and Faroan passed by them. In a small basin marked by a dry spring, Faroan paused. Including the canyon they had come down to arrive at this place, four narrow draws spread like the fingers of an open hand. The stallion raised his head and breathed deeply. Again, Michael thought he felt a fresh wind pass by.

Michael waited until finally Faroan took one tentative step and then another toward the ravine that cut through the hills to the west. Once committed to this route, the stallion's steps gained certainty, and soon he extended himself through the long trot into an easy gallop. Dun colored slopes that rose away on either side of the trail soon became red-brown rock walls that towered ever higher toward the narrowing sliver of sky far above. Though the ground beneath Faroan's feet didn't seem to be descending, there was a great sense of traveling downward. As they trekked on in this way, Michael's physical power was drained and his hope was exhausted. More than once, he wanted to pull Faroan to a stop, but something prevented him. It was almost as though that which he most feared was the very thing that drew him on.

Abruptly the stallion stopped and Michael was nearly pitched over his head. All around them, the silence was absolute and penetrating. Only the horseman's breathing and that of the big stallion echoed down the canyon. After a split second's hesitation, Faroan moved on, his ears tight forward as if he could hear something just ahead. Then, as suddenly as he had stopped moments earlier, Faroan made a sharp turn. It seemed to Michael as though the horse had become disoriented, perhaps confused by the sound of his own hoof beats as their sound bounced from wall to wall. But just when the horseman was about to take control and turn back, he realized that they were traveling toward a light that grew stronger with every step.

At the end of the short passage, an enormous valley spread out and went on farther than Michael's eye could see. Nearby, tall grasses lay over as though something heavy had weighed them down. And Michael began to smile. "You've found them," Michael all but shouted, joyfully slapping Faroan on the neck. The stallion nickered low, bumped out his nose and pawed at the ground. There was not a horse or a human in sight, but there were signs everywhere. Michael urged Faroan forward and the big animal jumped into a lope, following the broad swath across the meadow cut by the moving herd.

It seemed to Michael that they had traveled at this pace for nearly half a day before they saw at last the place they were seeking. The trail made by the herd had led them to a high mountain that split the grassy plain. At the foot of that mountain, ran a shallow river and beside the running water, the trail went on. A lower hill climbed out of the valley floor on Michael's right, creating a wide passageway to another vast meadow where the waters of a lake glistened in the late afternoon sun. Beside the lake was the herd. Atop a foothill overlooking his domain stood Zabbai, his brilliant white coat shining, his head high. And beside him was Adrianna.

Michael watched his wife slip up onto the stallion's back. He held his breath as they charged down off of their hilltop and ran toward him. Faroan stood stock still, every muscle in his great body tensed. He did not call to the herd, as lone horses are wont to do. Michael's heart roared in his chest, but like the stallion he sat on, he could only wait.

Seconds later the waiting was over. Still aboard their horses, Michael and Adrianna fell into each other's arms. Tears and laughter mingled and conversation began mid-sentence. Soon they were surrounded by their children; then Phillip came, and the horsemen gathered, and joy overflowed all around them.

For days on end the very air was exultant. It was in this atmosphere that life began anew for this people who had been saved by the angels of God from so much danger, against such terrible odds.

⬥

The years passed peacefully. The herd increased in number and in quality. The horsemen's families grew and thrived. Soon after they settled into this vast land of mysterious abundance, they packed away their tents and built log houses. Now and then they reminisced about the old days of wandering. But rarely did anyone complain of missing that life.

There was no need to ever leave this remote outpost. Everything the people and their horses needed was right here. And the danger was minimal. It was so far outside Roman jurisdiction, and such a great distance off any regularly traveled highway that no one was ever likely to find them. Sometimes there was talk of taking a few horses to market, but this idea soon dissipated when the logistics were considered. It was many days ride to the nearest settlement, and it was a part of the Roman Empire. Besides, no one had any desire to venture out across the awful desert away from this paradise.

Phillip remained in the mystical valley with his adopted family for three years. Then one morning he announced to Michael and Adrianna that he had dreamt of his father, and that he felt he must go to the old soldier, if indeed he was still alive. There was great sadness at this parting. But also there was hope.

"Perhaps I'll return with news of both of our fathers," Phillip said. "We'll all meet again, one day. Of this I am certain." And then he rode away.

Archanus

When Zadoc was well enough to travel, Joel took him home to the estate that had been his since his sons were children and his beautiful wife was still with him. On leave from the Roman Army, he began to heal in earnest. And from his tired face, the years began to melt away. He had only one great regret. With all his heart, he wished he had done away with Marvelius on one of the many occasions the man had committed a military infraction for which he could have been executed.

In nearby Rome, Archanus and Luke, protected by their dear friend, Simon, continued their healing ministry among the poor and the ill and the dying.

As the years went by, Joel fulfilled his promise to keep his father and Archanus apprised of anything he heard in regard to Michael and Marvelius. It was clear that Michael had escaped since his wicked enemy—from time to time—still went into rages because he had not been able to exact the revenge he desired. Hearing of these tirades, Archanus gained a strange sort of peace, knowing that his son lived on, somewhere beyond the realm of the monster who still sought to destroy him.

PART
Three

33 A.D.

For God so loved the world,
that He gave His only begotten Son,
that whosoever believeth in Him
should not perish,
but have everlasting life.

John 3:16 KJV

CHAPTER
Thirteen

ADRIANNA

Silver threads mingled with strands of old gold in the silken tresses that fell like a veil toward the pond. A small, confused frown knit the brow of the aging woman who looked up in the reflection. Then from somewhere within the observer, a small laugh escaped, and the watery face creased in a smile.

Adrianna touched the apparition and watched the ripples carry it away. She straightened her aching back and looked up. She had ridden out alone that morning, into the high country where snowmelt made streams of every crevice, and glistening pools of every little bowl carved out of the rocks and the earth by the hands of God.

She sat back against a tall pine and held out toward the sun the hand that had brushed aside her hair and touched her face in the shining water. It was a well-worn hand, wrinkled and scarred, painful like her back. She filled her lungs with fine, cool mountain air. And, in defiance of those things that troubled her, she thanked the One God for the life He had given her and for the agelessness she felt aboard a horse, where she would be fifteen forever—on earth and in the Heavens beyond.

Ashamed to have succumbed to the temptations of self-pity and misplaced nostalgia, she willed her mind to follow other thoughts, not of herself, but of the ones she loved. One's own pain, no matter its origin, could be borne. It was the suffering of her children that a mother could not endure. And even in paradise, one's children could suffer.

She thought of her sons in the order of their birth. Junias, the golden child named for his grandmother, the long dead woman with whom Adrianna would always share her beloved Michael. She saw Junias today—at eighteen a young man grown taller than his father—a horseman of rare talent who could scarcely have cared less about his gifts. She wondered at the yearning she saw in him for something he seemed unable to name, if not to hide.

Then she thought of Matthias, the one who had never been a child, the young man who grieved the death of a love he seemed to think had never even been born. At seventeen, her second son was the exact image of his father, in appearance, in manner, in depth, and apparently in the belief that he didn't deserve to be loved. He too was a horseman beyond repute, and yet he was always trying to be better, to improve on his best, perhaps on the best of his father. She considered the way Matthias looked at Michael when he believed that no one was paying attention, in his eyes, a painful longing for approval. Matthias, the one who always tried so hard.

She thought about how Matthias had never left her side throughout the journey that brought her family to this place. She wondered why that had not bothered Junias—as it would have his brother if the situation had been reversed. Her boys were so different. Junias needed nothing from any human, but appeared to seek something beyond his mother's understanding; while Matthias so desperately sought the small gift of human approval that would satisfy only if it came from his father.

And then there was Neeka. Had any girl of sixteen ever been this beautiful, this bright, this assured of her place in the hearts of her parents and the world? If Neeka longed for anything or anyone, it was Jesus. But her yearning was not the kind normal to a teenaged girl. Instead it was something of an otherworldly extreme, so intense that it could neither be grasped nor described.

"Oh my daughter," Adrianna said to the bright day and the breeze that caressed her face. "What lies ahead for you? Will you find the fullness of life that I have known with your father? Or is there another path that you must follow? And will your heart break, as mine wants to do now, when one day your youthful beauty is behind you?"

A nearby stream danced down the hill toward the valley below where Adrianna could see ribbons of smoke rising from morning fires. The chill of winter was almost over and with the early spring came the first foals . . . and the flowers . . . and the hope. Every year there was rebirth, a resurrection of that which had fallen asleep in the past autumn.

Adrianna had always understood that all things must die to make room for new life. She realized now that until it is time for the body to pass on, the heart must remain open to welcome the changing of the seasons. "But in this season of change, what happens to the mother?" she asked of the wakening sky. "Is she destined only to watch from a distance as her grown children make their way along the path over which she can no longer guide them?"

So far within herself had she withdrawn that Adrianna did not distinguish the sound of hooves making their careful way over the rocks, from that of the noisy stream that paid the rocks no mind at all.

"Mother? Are you all right?" Matthias asked softly in the voice that belonged to his father. He stepped down from his horse as he spoke, dropping the reins even as the animal lowered its lovely head to partake of sweet water from the stream and the new grasses that grew beside it.

"Oh . . . well . . . yes," Adrianna said, rising painfully.

"Is it your back?" Matthias asked, gently taking his mother's arm, bearing as much of her insubstantial weight as he could. "Can I help you?"

"You have helped me just by coming here and interrupting an old woman's thoughts."

"You are not an old woman. You are as beautiful as you were when I was a little boy."

"And you are kind, if not entirely honest. Now, what brings you to this quiet place?"

"We missed you when we all came back from morning chores . . ."

"I'm sorry. Did you eat?"

"Yes." Matthias laughed. "Neeka did her worst imitation of you. But she managed to fill us up somehow."

"Is your father all right this morning?" She regretted the question before it was fully asked.

"I think something has been bothering him. I saw him ride away on Zabbai before the dawn. When I didn't see you at breakfast, I thought one of you might have gone in search of the other. But when I followed the trails of your two horses away from the herd, they went in different directions. Your mare's gait and the lightness of her rider are obvious in her tracks. I chose to follow you."

"Thank you, son." Adrianna smiled. Then her brow knit in a frown. "I'm worried about your father. He was restless before he fell asleep last night, then he thrashed around in his dreams. He woke me up before first light calling out to Jesus. I tried to wake him, but he wouldn't be roused. So I got up and rode to this place. I don't know what drew me."

"It's peaceful here," Matthias offered.

"Yes, perhaps that's it." Adrianna reached up and with an open hand, caressed her son's cheek and looked into his blue eyes.

"What is it, Mother?" he asked.

"I just want you to know how much I love you. No matter what happens—ever—in your life. Always know that my heart is with you."

"There's change coming, isn't there?" Matthias' words were calm, but in his eyes, there was fear. He leaned his face into the palm of his mother's loving hand, as if for support.

Adrianna didn't answer at once. She looked again toward the distant valley. The horses were barely specks and the cabins that were tucked up into the hillsides were invisible except for the smoke winding up out of their chimneys. "Yes," she said, looking back at her son. "I think your father may have heard last night from one of Neeka's angels—or his own." She tried to smile.

"That's what Neeka said."

As Adrianna watched and listened to her son, she could only see her husband, and she could think only of her long ago parting with Michael in another Egyptian meadow far to the North. Terror overtook her then, as it had at that previous parting, and she knew a sense of equal helplessness. "We should go back," she said after a while. "Perhaps there will be some news today."

Matthias didn't ask what she meant but just helped her up onto her horse and rode with her down the hill.

MICHAEL

Zabbai crossed the valley at a gait somewhere between a lope and an easy, but purposeful gallop. Michael made no effort to control the stallion's speed, and he wondered only briefly at the youthful stamina of this horse that showed no signs of his nearly three and thirty years. It was rare for a horse to live beyond twenty, and when one did, there were always the infirmities of old age and the fading of beauty. But as he had been in all things, Zabbai was different. He still had the appearance and the vigor of a ten-year-old. Michael was sure this was an effect of the Blessing that he never mentioned to anyone—and, by the grace of God—it was a mystery about which no one ever commented.

Michael too enjoyed unique stamina for a man of his age. At fifty, his general physique and countenance were those of a much younger man. But this did not occur to him. He only thought about aging and mortality when he wondered if his father was still alive—and if they would ever meet again.

As the galloping Zabbai created a breeze and cut through it, Michael tried to shake off the foreboding that gripped his heart in the wake of the previous night's angelic dream.

"A change is coming," the angel had said.

As he rode, Michael brought to mind his own anxious questions, spoken in a state of coherence that drifted between wakefulness and dreams. "What is it? Jesus, are You there? Do You need me?" He had called out over and over again. Vaguely, now, he remembered Adrianna's efforts to awaken him and he recalled fully his inability to respond. Even now, he knew the attendant fear he had not been able to escape.

"You must ride to the passageway between this land and the next," the angel had answered at last. "Your mission is not yet over."

That was all. There were no other instructions and no hints as to the reason Michael must make this short journey. The angel disappeared as he had arrived. As always, in the aftermath of such visitations, Michael felt a gaping hole in his heart and an aloneness that was all consuming.

In the bright morning light these emotions rode with him and his heart cried out to Jesus.

The horse and his man had departed just ahead of the dawn. Now, as they arrived at their destination, the sun was halfway to its zenith. From a low hill tucked into the trees, Michael looked toward the well-hidden corridor that led to the world he and his family had left behind nearly a decade earlier.

All morning, half-formed pictures of Jesus had filled the landscape of Michael's mind then dissolved without resolution. In one vision his brother knelt amidst an angry looking crowd, drawing something in the dirt. In another, Jesus stood atop a hill that Michael thought must be Mount Tabor, enveloped in a cloud. In some images, Jesus spoke. In others, He was silent. No matter how hard he tried, Michael could not hold on to the portraits, nor could he follow their messages to any sort of conclusion.

Trying to wait patiently and to supplant the mysterious images of the grown-up Jesus, the horseman called to mind a long ago day and a similar vigil. In that memory, the young Michael and the Child Jesus rode to a promontory high above the Nile River delta and waited for Mary and Joseph to arrive at another paradise not unlike this one.

Interrupting Michael's recollections, Zabbai raised his head and snorted softly. The horseman followed the stallion's gaze to the cleft in the rock wall from which a bay horse carrying a soldier was just emerging. In the shelter of the trees, Michael waited. The bay jogged steadily into the meadow, unhurried, unafraid. When the animal drew near, Michael saw the quick joy that suffused the rider's face and lit his eyes. It was as though the book of his life had fallen open to a page from a yesterday beyond remembering, and the great soldier Zadoc rode toward him. Then the pages fluttered, the bridges of time fell away, and Phillip appeared, in every aspect the perfect likeness of his father.

For just a moment, the joy of reunion overshadowed the ominous portent of this unexpected visit. But Michael could not hold back his fear for long.

"I am glad to see you," he said, unable to smile in greeting. "But I must know, why have you come? Is there trouble?"

"Not yet," Phillip said. "But I fear there will be. Can we go to the camp? This fine horse and I are all but spent. We have traveled nearly one full cycle of the moon as fast as we could go."

"Yes, of course." Michael shook his head, aggravated with himself. "I am sorry."

"Don't be. You're right to be concerned. It is about your brother, Jesus, that I have come," the soldier began. "This may be a fool's errand. There is surely nothing either of us can do to turn the tide. But I could not live with myself if you had no chance to at least say goodbye to this One you love so dearly."

"Is He ill? Has He been injured? Is anyone with Him?" Terror rushed through Michael like a violent mistral, devastating all that lay in its path.

"Physically, He appears fine. But the Jewish leaders are saying that He has gone mad and that He is a danger to their society. And the Romans are beginning to listen."

"I don't understand."

"Nor do I, entirely," Phillip said. "But let me tell you what I know."

Throughout the rest of their journey toward the horsemen's encampment, Phillip summarized everything he had heard in regard to Jesus for the past three years.

"In the beginning, Jesus was thought to be just another itinerant teacher who went around telling stories about the God of the Jews. He gathered a diverse band of misfits, from fishermen to tax collectors and prostitutes, who followed Him from town to town causing no real disturbance. Then, when His followers referred to Him as the Messiah, the chief priests of the Sanhedrin and the Pharisees denied this claim with such vehemence that many suspected its truth.

"Since the Jews are always talking about the Messiah they expect to save them, and because dozens of men have claimed to be such a redeemer, the Romans generally ignore assertions of this nature. That's how they handled the Jesus rumors in the beginning. Even when the early talk of miracles and healings began, the Roman authorities paid little attention to the complaints that increased among those in power within the Jewish hierarchy.

"When many people began to publicly express their belief in Jesus as the Messiah, the Christ, the Jewish leaders went wild.

One of the first stories I heard was that of an adulterous woman who was about to be stoned by an angry crowd of Jewish elders when Jesus showed up. They say that He bent down and drew something in the dirt then told the men, 'whichever of you has not sinned should cast the first stone.' The crowd soon disbursed, but someone heard Jesus say to the woman, 'Go now, and sin no more.' For some reason, this further incensed His accusers."

Phillip paused. The companions continued to pass almost silently through the tall grasses with the horses walking stride for stride. Birds sang the songs of spring. Pale clouds scudded across the sky. And Michael waited for his friend to go on.

"I didn't know who everyone was talking about at first," Phillip began again. "Then a centurion of my acquaintance told me how his paralyzed servant had been saved by a healer named Jesus and I began to wonder if this could be your Brother. So I started looking for the mysterious healer. I kept hearing one fantastic story after another about how He expelled demons, healed the sick, gave sight to the blind, opened deaf ears, caused the lame to walk, and even raised people from the dead. I wondered always if these tales were being made up, or if they were true. But I couldn't get the centurion's story out of my mind, so I kept searching.

"The strangest thing happened. For too long, I had heard nothing from my father. Then all at once, I received word that he and three friends were headed toward Jerusalem from Rome, also in search of this man called Jesus."

"Did you see him, then? Your father?"

"No, he had not arrived when I received permission to take leave of Herod's army. I said that I was going to meet him and that satisfied my superiors. In truth, I made the decision to come to you right after I finally found Jesus near a town called Capernaum on a hill that overlooked the Sea of Galilee . . ."

"Describe the place," Michael said, interrupting for the first time.

"There were thousands of people gathered . . ."

"No, not the people, the place. What did it look like? How far was it from the shore?"

"Not that far, and high enough so that one standing upon it could see a great distance in all directions. It was on the north shore. But why do you ask this?"

"What did He speak of there?" Michael asked, ignoring Phillip's question.

"Well, He said many confusing things, things I could not understand."

"Can you recall His words?" Michael prodded. "Anything?"

"How strange that you should ask this and that I should remember. Until this moment all that He said has been beyond my comprehension, contradictory to all that makes sense—at least to me."

"And now?"

"What He said changed me, somehow—despite my inability to understand," Phillip said with a puzzled frown. "It was as though He was speaking straight into my heart, as if He knew what I needed and gave it to me, and me alone."

"He has always been able to do this," Michael said, his voice husky. "Even when He was just a little boy, each person who heard His words had the strange sense that He was speaking to them alone." He looked at Phillip and beseeched him, "Please tell me more. Allow me to hear Him through you."

"Jesus taught from the hillside where He could be seen and heard by the multitudes. His every word is engraved forever on my heart and in my mind, perhaps so that I can share them with you—perhaps even come to understand the full meaning myself."

Phillip began then to recite the words of Jesus, speaking in a voice and a rhythm that seemed not his own. He said:

"'Rejoice and be glad because great is your reward in heaven . . .'" Michael interrupted his friend, adding the final words of this discourse.

"Blessed are the poor in spirit,
for theirs is the kingdom of heaven.

'Blessed are those who mourn,
for they will be comforted.

'Blessed are the meek,
for they will inherit the earth.

'Blessed are those who hunger and thirst for
righteousness, for they will be filled.

'Blessed are the merciful,
for they will be shown mercy.

'Blessed are the pure in heart,
for they will see God.

'Blessed are the peacemakers,
for they will be called sons of God.

'Blessed are those who are persecuted because of
righteousness, for theirs is the kingdom of heaven.

'Blessed are you when people insult you, persecute you
and falsely say all kinds of evil against you
because of me . . ."

"How do you know what He said?" Phillip asked.

"My Brother shared these truths with me on the day of our last goodbye," Michael said. "We were on a hillside that must surely have been the same one you have just described." The horseman paused. "And again last night I saw and heard many of the events about which you have just told me, including this teaching."

"I cannot understand this," Phillip said softly. "But neither can I deny its truth . . ."

"So now my Brother is in danger," Michael said. It was not a question.

"Yes. I fear that He is." The joy in Phillip's eyes was now supplanted by obvious concern. "He has gained too many followers, performed too many miracles, angered too many Pharisees and powerful men of the Sanhedrin. Now those leaders are determined to be rid of Him."

"How do they propose to do this?" Michael asked.

"By convincing the Romans who govern their land that Jesus is a criminal who deserves to be executed."

"Can they do this?"

"Perhaps," Phillip said. "And perhaps not. The trouble is that the ones consumed by their jealousy of Jesus are determined to see Him dead and they will not let the Roman authorities rest. Sometimes, those in power acquiesce simply to avoid having to listen to the complainers any longer."

"Do you have a plan for how we can help my Brother?" Michael asked.

"Would that I did." Phillip shook his head sadly. "I see no way to save Him. But as I said before, I could not watch His life come to an end without giving you a chance to say one more goodbye. I also fear for His mother. Perhaps you can convince her that she should depart before her life too is endangered."

"Why do you say this?"

"She is with Him wherever He goes, always leading people to Him." Phillip paused. "The twelve men Jesus calls His disciples may also be in peril. But I know of your devotion to His mother . . ."

"Mary will do what her God calls her to do," Michael said. "I can only see her being a comfort to others. But I will go to her."

When they arrived at the camp, Phillip was met with a hero's welcome. Great sadness followed the telling of his tale, and the warriors among the people began to discuss how they could go and save the One who meant so much to them all.

In the end, Phillip convinced these brave men that they must remain with the herd, promising that he would do all he could for Jesus.

"You must rest," Michael said to Phillip when the debate ended. "You and I will leave for Jerusalem in the morning."

"You know the danger you still face," Phillip reminded him

"This does not matter. I must go to my Brother and do whatever I can. There is no other choice."

ARCHANUS

In Rome, rumor reached Luke and Archanus that there was a young teacher in Jerusalem whom some were claiming was the long-awaited Messiah. Soon after the physician and his companions heard of this, Zadoc called them to his home and told them of the danger faced by this teacher.

"I think it is time for you and I, Archanus, to go again in search of Michael," Zadoc said as they sat in conversation on the veranda that overlooked his vineyard.

"I am grateful," said Archanus. "But may I ask why this is?"

"I believe the claims of Jesus' followers to be true," Zadoc said. "I believe that He is the Christ of God. If so, there is no doubt that word of this trouble will reach your son."

"I don't understand." Archanus' brow knit in a puzzled frown.

"Do you recall some three decades ago when I told you that Michael had been seen in Egypt in the company of a husband and wife and their baby child?"

"I do." Archanus nodded.

"It is said among the Jewish people that this man called Jesus whom they seek to destroy was sought by King Herod thirty years ago because that wicked King feared the boy's ascension to Herod's throne."

"This must have been when all the male children in Bethlehem were slaughtered," Luke interjected.

"That's right," said Zadoc. "Legend has it that the family of the child then heralded as the savior of the world was spirited out of the country by a handsome young man and his two beautiful horses."

"Michael . . ." Archanus breathed the name. "The timing is perfect! That was exactly when you told me that my son had left the horsemen!"

"Yes, my friend. It was."

"And the love he must have for this teacher is bound to put him once more in harm's way," said Archanus. "We must go at once."

"I don't know if we can avert disaster," Zadoc said. "But you are right. We must prepare to depart."

CHAPTER *Fourteen*

MICHAEL & ADRIANNA

In their tent that night, Adrianna wept. She had never before begged Michael to change his plans, to stay with her, to seek peace within his family. Over the years, when her husband had gone in search of his father, she had always understood and somehow known that he would return. But a part of her heart had been lost during her journey to Egypt, separate from her beloved husband, and on this night, she could not be consoled.

"Even Phillip says that you can do nothing," she pleaded at one point. "Why must you go if it is only to say yet another goodbye? I fear not only the loss of you to us—but even more the loss of Jesus to you. How will you survive, my husband, when again you are left behind by the One you love beyond all others?"

"I must go to Him," Michael said, his head low, his voice tender. "If I do not at least try to help Him, there will be nothing left of my heart for loving you or our children, or anything that is left of this life."

When Michael paused, his wife did not try to fill the silence. Knowing him as she did, she understood that he had more to say.

"My dear wife," he whispered. "I know that you believe in the One God and in His Son. Believe then, as I do, what Jesus told us when we saw Him last . . ."

"He told us many things," Adrianna said, "and I shall believe them all forever. Of which truth do you speak?"

"With God all things are possible . . . And from this truth, we must take hope."

Adrianna could not argue. She was silent for a time, thoughtful. Finally she made one final entreaty. "I want you to take Matthias with you. Please," she said.

"But why?" Michael was astonished at the suggestion. "If you fear I will not return, how can you ask me to take our son along and endanger him as well?"

"I cannot tell you how I know this," Adrianna said, "but I am certain that if you can be brought home to us, Matthias will be the one to bring you. And I know I will see him again in this land of the living."

"Still, I do not understand. I will be with Phillip. Do you not trust him to protect me?"

"I trust Phillip as we have always trusted his father. But my heart tells me you must also take Matthias. This is the son of our love who has the heart of a warrior. I learned so much about him when you were last away. He was born, like you, a man grown. You will see yourself in his eyes, and with him at your side, you will take greater care to return."

Michael cupped Adrianna's face in his hands. For long moments he said nothing, but met her tears with his own. When he spoke at last, he could only whisper. "In Matthias, I have always seen my father, not myself. For this reason, I have guarded my heart where the boy is concerned. Not a day has passed since he was born that I haven't feared the loss of him."

"And not a day has gone by without his longing for your love, my husband. As your heart will perish if you do not go to your Brother, so your son's heart will wither and his life force fade away if he is left, once more, behind."

"And what of Junias?" Michael asked, unable to dispute Adrianna's point, yet not ready to concede.

"Our eldest son longs only for something beyond us, something he will one day seek in earnest on his own. Meanwhile, he has the heart of a leader and the courage to hold our people together in your absence. Junias loves his brother and he will understand why Matthias must accompany you."

"And the headstrong Neeka?" Michael asked, a smile faintly lighting his eyes.

"Neeka will care for this old woman who is her mother." Adrianna smiled, then turned away, trying not to show him the tears that again filled her eyes.

Gently caressing her cheek and turning her to face him, Michael said, "You are not an old woman. You are the most beautiful creature I have ever known. You are the heart of my heart, and we will ride together forever, you and I. You must believe in my love for you—it is my reason for living through all the dark nights of my soul. You are a gift to me from the One God, blessed by His Son. Never forget this. Hold my love in your heart, as I will hold your love in mine."

Adrianna buried her face in her husband's chest, and she wept.

⟡

Before dawn the next morning, Adrianna and Michael summoned their children. Together, the family walked through the herd to Zabbai's hill. There, the parents spoke of the journey ahead, the peril, and the hope. Uncharacteristically, Neeka was as silent as were her brothers. Listening, the three moved closer together. They seemed to exchange some unspoken communication, perhaps gaining strength from one another. None questioned the wisdom of their parents' choice, at least not out loud.

By the time they returned to the camp, Phillip had gathered all of the horsemen and their families so that Michael could explain his plans.

"Though you face no danger here," Michael began, "you will need a leader. In my absence, Junias will have this responsibility." He waited for some grumbling about his son's youth or inexperience, or some other perceived unfairness. But none came. A deep sadness hovered in the air and no one broke its hold with words or with movement.

Finally, Michael asked his sons to go and pick out six strong horses. "Phillip's horse is still weary from the long journey so he will stay with the herd. Choose a gelding that is similar in appearance to replace him. All must be animals of great endurance and some speed," Michael said. "You'll know which ones to choose."

Neeka followed her brothers into the herd. Wordlessly the other families went back to their morning chores. Even the children were unusually subdued.

In a short time, Neeka rode up on Zabbai, followed by her brothers riding two young stallions and leading the three best geldings the herd had to offer.

"We need one more," Michael said, looking at his sons.

"Zabbai is the one," said Neeka.

"No, he is far too old," Adrianna scolded. "He never carries your father on journeys such as this."

"He will not be left behind this time," Michael said, surprised by his own words.

"But my husband . . ."

"Just as I must go," Michael said with assurance, "so must Zabbai."

"Yes, of course." Understanding touched Adrianna's eyes. "How foolish of me to have thought otherwise. He will carry you with valor. Of this, there can be no doubt."

Michael leaned down and touched his wife's cheek with his own. "I will return," he said. "As were you when you insisted I take Matthias with me, I am uncertain of the origin of this knowledge, but sure of its truth."

Neeka had slipped down from Zabbai's back and moved to stand in front of the stallion. Now, she bent her head and breathed into his nostrils, allowing her tears to fall without shame. "We will see you again," she whispered to the stallion. "Until then, do not forget us . . ."

Michael went to his daughter, pulled her into his arms and held her there. "I want you to care for your mother when Junias is busy with the herd," he said. Then the horseman turned to his wife. Once more, he held Adrianna in a long embrace, kissing her shining hair and her cheeks and her eyes. Finally, forcing himself to let go, he swung up onto Zabbai.

Phillip sat astride the horse that had been chosen for him and waited in silence. Before mounting the giant bay stallion he would ride, Matthias went to his mother, wrapped his arms around her and whispered something into her hair that no one else could hear. Then he turned and vaulted up onto the big horse.

As the three moved to depart, Junias went to his brother. "You will come back to us," the older boy said, placing a hand on Matthias's leg. "If there is trouble, get word to Zadoc or one of his sons, and then to us. And bring our father home when this mission is over."

Matthias nodded solemnly and the companions rode away.

Michael & Matthias & Phillip

For days, they moved with urgency to the North, covering ground as rapidly as possible without endangering the horses. Each day the riders changed horses at midday so that no animal was ridden from dawn until dusk. Conversation was rare and sparse as they ate and slept beneath the waxing moon.

Traveling beside the Nile there was no shortage of grass and water. But the meager provisions the men had brought for themselves were gone by the time they approached Thebes, so Phillip went into the city and procured enough dried fruits and meats to sustain them until they reached the Great Sea some ten to twelve days hence.

While they dined on an unusually sumptuous meal that night, Matthias asked about the rest of their journey.

"I am expected to rejoin my battalion at our hill camp near Lydda by the next full moon," Phillip said.

"Can we make it to this place in time?" Matthias asked.

"It will be close, and we will not go there together."

"Of course we won't." Matthias shook his head. "How stupid of me. You cannot take a chance on being seen with us in case my father is recognized."

"No, I cannot. If our association is suspected, I will not be able to help, should you meet danger. It will be safest if we take separate paths before we enter Judea."

"Where will we part?" Michael asked.

"A short distance south of Gaza, you will head into the mountains. I'll stay beside the Great Sea. At this time of year there will still be plenty of water in the mountain streams and grass for the horses."

"What will we do with the horses when we get to the city of Jerusalem?" Matthias wanted to know.

"There is good grassland in the hills between that city and the Sea," said Phillip. "With your father's ingenuity I'm sure you'll find the perfect place to leave them in safety."

For ten more days, they traveled North along the banks of the Nile. They avoided the heavily trafficked city of Memphis and soon thereafter moved away from the river, heading in a northeasterly route along the eastern edge of the Nile Delta toward the old city of Sin, known lately as Pelusium. There again, Michael and Matthias camped in the hills while Phillip went into town to replenish their supplies.

Three days later they parted company, Phillip taking the Way of the Sea, Michael and Matthias moving toward the hills of Judea.

"We will meet again," Phillip said as his friends prepared to leave on this twenty-seventh morning of their long journey. "I will know if you are in danger."

"Take care, good friend," Michael said. "Keep yourself from harm's way." He paused. "And Phillip, if there is a choice to be made, you must make it in favor of my son. I will ask nothing of you again, only this. See to it that Matthias is reunited with his mother." The horseman turned then and rode away before Phillip could answer.

"Take care of your father," Phillip said to Matthias. "And remember, I will know if there is trouble and I will find you."

Adrianna & Neeka

Night fell without warning behind clouds heavy with rain. The day of her father and brother's departure had been long, and the pain in Neeka's heart unbearable. From a distance she had watched her mother throughout the day while the still beautiful woman walked among the horses or sat beside the stream. About Adrianna there was a malaise that could not be breached. It was a contagious sorrow that enveloped Neeka as well as her mother, and the girl felt a helplessness she had never known before.

Now, sitting atop Zabbai's hill, Neeka began to work out a plan. She would wait until everyone was sleeping, then she would slip away, riding silently out of the herd at a place between the night watchmen. She knew well every contour and pathway within this valley and throughout the hills around it. And she knew the schedules of the men who kept watch over the herd at night.

Alone, on the right horse, she thought she could travel a little faster than could her father and his companions. She would catch up to them in less than a day and tell her father that he could not go without Adrianna because her dear heart would not survive another parting. Of this, Neeka was certain and, loving her mother as she did, she could not sit by and wait. She must do something.

She began to think about the horse she would ride. It must be fleet of foot and have great endurance, and it must be willing as only the sons and daughters of Zabbai were willing. She walked down the hill and started to make her way through the herd. In the face of the coming storm, the horses were restless. But she knew them and felt no fear. Talking softly, she touched here a long mane, there a sweet face. Her strides were long as she headed through the sea of mares toward the field where the young stallions were set apart. As she walked, she felt something behind her. She turned to look just as a beautiful little chestnut mare nudged her and issued a small snort.

"What is it, girl?" Neeka asked. "Do you want to go along with me to choose the horse I'll ride tonight?"

The mare bobbed her head and bumped her nose against Neeka's arm. "I hope you're not telling me that you want to be the one." The girl laughed. "You're too pretty and small and, well, it's just not possible." Neeka turned away then, meaning to continue her walk through the herd.

Again, the mare nudged her, then moved closer and rubbed her face up and down on Neeka's back.

"What?" Neeka said in a voice too loud for the stealthy mission she had undertaken.

"She has chosen you, just as her grandmother chose your father."

"Mother," Neeka gasped. "What are you doing here?"

"Looking for the horse I'll ride," Adrianna said firmly. "I'm going with you."

"What do you mean?" Neeka tried to sound innocent.

"I've been watching you all day, as you were watching me. I know what you're planning and I'm going along."

"I don't understand," Neeka said, feigning innocence.

"Oh yes you do." Adrianna smiled. "We're going to follow your father and Matthias. Neither one of us can stay behind, so we might as well go together."

"Have you told anyone about this?" Neeka asked, afraid that someone would try to stop them.

"I told Junias and he agreed. He'll explain everything to the others, who will also understand."

Neeka threw her arms around her mother, feeling a great weight lift from her shoulders as they laughed together.

"You don't really think I should ride little Alexandria, do you?" Neeka asked when their laughter had settled into conspiratorial smiles.

"Yes, I do. She is the most like Lalaynia of any mare I have ever known." She paused and the tone of her voice softened. "Do you remember how she followed Jesus everywhere all those years ago when He came to visit?"

"I do." Neeka nodded. "And that's one of the reasons I'm so concerned about riding her such a great distance now. She was a young mare when we left the north-country nearly a decade ago. She is no longer as young and powerful as she once was."

"Nor am I, my daughter, nor am I."

"I didn't mean that," Neeka said, reaching out to touch her mother's arm. "I am sorry. My terrible tongue is always causing me to say things I shouldn't."

"Never mind." Adrianna smiled and patted her daughter's hand. "We will be the best of partners, you and I. And somehow this tired old woman and her beautiful daughter will help divert the disaster I fear we will soon face."

They hugged again, then made preparations for their journey. Junias met them at the edge of the herd leading his mother's favorite gold colored mare and two tall, strong geldings. Packed on the geldings were provisions that would last the travelers for many days.

"If any other pair of women were planning such an expedition, I would fear desperately for their lives," Junias said with a laugh. "But in the case of you two, I fear more for anyone who is fool enough to accost you."

The handsome Junias took his mother and then his sister into his arms and held each of them as Michael had done before he left. "May the One God be with you," he said. "And may you return with my father and my brother very soon. Until then, we will pray—all of us—just as Jesus taught us to do."

Moments later, as the mother and daughter rode away, Neeka turned back to her brother. "The angels will travel with us," she said. "And we will return."

⌘

Following the same route taken by Michael and Matthias and Phillip, Adrianna and Neeka covered ground as rapidly as had the men. But they took care not to be seen by the ones they followed, at first fearful of being sent back, and later sensing somehow that they needed to remain separate and apart.

As Neeka had predicted, they traveled in the company of a great band of angels. Beneath the same moon that guided the ones they loved, Adrianna and Neeka journeyed in hope—carried forth on the faith that Jesus had given them in a time that seemed to both so long ago.

ARCHANUS

A virulent epidemic was sweeping through Rome, killing hundreds of people every day. Luke felt that he must stay behind to help the suffering masses. Zadoc insisted on remaining to protect the physician in this city gone mad with fear and anguish. So Archanus and Simon were forced to embark upon the long journey to Jerusalem without their dearest friends.

"I cannot leave you," Archanus told his friends on the night before he and Simon were to depart. "I cannot."

"But you must," said Zadoc softly. "Or forfeit what may be the last opportunity you will ever have to reunite with your son."

"We will follow you when we can," Luke promised. "Meanwhile, go with God."

Dawn ACROSS THE *Mountains* 189

CHAPTER *Fifteen*

MICHAEL & MATTHIAS

For more than half of the day after they bid Phillip farewell, the father and son traversed grassy steppes. As the sun began to lower, they passed through a small forest and into the green Judean hills. They camped that night on a high knoll overlooking the road that ran between Ascalon, on the Great Sea, and Hebron, on the trade route known as The Way of Shur.

Once they had cared for the horses and eaten their own small meal, Matthias fell into the deep sleep of the fearless and the innocent. But for Michael, there was no rest. Throughout the long journey the horseman's heart had beaten with a dull ache while, in his mind, he concentrated on arriving safely in the land where his Brother was in danger.

Since Michael had no idea of the situation, there was no way for him to plan what he might do to help Jesus. Thus it remained on this warm night as a pall of impending doom settled over him. A cloud of unknowing and fear dimmed his vision, and the weight of an agony he could not name crushed him.

He tried to think through his dilemma. But every thought led to an unknown. He tried not to fear for those he loved. But every such effort failed and the burning anguish of a love too deep engulfed him. He was a man who had always valued control, choosing the pathways he would follow, banishing or containing matters of his heart, planning each day as though he could avoid the pain that sought always to consume him.

But on this night, all control was gone. He could not envision his destination. He did not know what he would meet when he arrived. He had no idea how he would find Jesus or how he would help this One he knew did not want to be helped.

Beside him, Matthias stirred in his sleep. Michael's heart reached out toward this boy he loved too well and this time, his loving would neither be denied nor limited. He tried to ignore the emotion. He tried not to think of what might happen to Matthias in the days ahead. He almost woke the boy to insist that he turn back, or go in search of Phillip. But, so often had he already made this request that he knew without doubt its futility.

Finally, somewhere in the deep of the night, Michael succumbed to the oblivion of sleep, hoping with his last waking thought for a visit from his angel, receiving none.

TUESDAY

After a short respite, Michael awoke to find Matthias preparing the morning meal. The horses grazed beside a narrow stream. The familiar, hopeful sounds of morning contradicted the desperate apprehension with which he had lived these many days.

"Will we leave the horses here?" Matthias asked. "It seems a good place with plenty of water and food."

"No, we'll ride on a little farther. There is a place I recall near the town of Bethlehem where Jesus was born. Shepherds keeping watch that long ago night were told of the miracle and came to pay homage to the Holy Child." A frown wrinkled his brow. "I believe we'll find this family . . ." Surprised at his own words, Michael paused.

"We'll be able to entrust the horses to these people," Matthias said, not questioning his father.

"Yes . . . yes, we will . . ."

They rode for another half day with only the sound of the horses' hooves and their breathing to break the silence. Michael's thoughts were scattered and conflicting. Again he tried to map out a strategy, again to no avail. The dear faces of Jesus and Mary and Adrianna, Neeka and Junias and Matthias presented themselves to him; and love reached out toward these dear ones from the very depths of his heart. As always, the emotion confused him, believing as he did that he must be strong and courageous, and that love made him weak. In the wake of this conflict, feelings collided with faith, and the battle overshadowed a truth that lingered just around the corners of his mind.

Sometimes, he would notice his son watching him. But whenever he looked toward the boy, Matthias would turn his eyes to the trail ahead. Michael was at once confused by and grateful for this silent acceptance.

As the sun arrived at the summit on its journey across the sky, the two horsemen crested a range of gentle hills and saw in the valley below a vast herd of sheep. A tall shepherd and a boy that looked to be perhaps ten years old met them on their way down the hill.

"Greetings," said the man. "I am Jonah. This is my son, Zachariah. We have been expecting you."

"How can this be?" Michael asked.

"An angel came to Zachariah last night," said the older man, as he stroked the neck of the big bay. "The angel told my son that two horseman would soon bring four fine horses that we are to protect until the horsemen's return."

"That is all?" Michael said. "The angel told him no more?"

"He said that we're to tell you where you must go from here," said the boy.

"Come now and share our midday meal." Jonah looked from his son to the riders. "We'll explain what you need to know while we dine."

In the shepherds' camp a feast had been prepared, attesting to the belief these people had in the messages of their angels. The horsemen were welcomed and invited to sit. While they enjoyed the fine meal, Michael looked around at the people gathered and listened to bits of their conversation. Across the ring where these people's night fire must burn, the horseman's eye fell on one old shepherd who returned his gaze and held it.

"I *am* the one," said the shepherd as if in answer to an unspoken question. "My name is Petras. We met, you and I, one long ago night in the little town of Bethlehem."

"Yes," Michael said, nodding. Then he waited.

When the meal was finished, everyone except the familiar shepherd, Petras, and the boy, Zechariah, moved quietly away. "We'll go to the north hill," said the man. "From there we can show you the way."

The horses—even Zabbai—grazed peacefully beside the sheep. Jonah stood with them, stroking Zabbai's neck. Michael raised one hand in salute then followed the old shepherd and the boy.

"If you follow this path," said the shepherd when they arrived at the top of the hill, "you'll reach Bethlehem before nightfall."

"And then?" asked Michael. "Do you have some message for us?"

"You seek the One who was born to us on that night long ago," said the shepherd.

"Yes. Do you know where we will find Him?"

Now the boy spoke. "I am to tell you that in two days' time He will share a very important supper with His disciples somewhere in Jerusalem."

"That is all?"

"He is in danger now," said the old shepherd. "He arrived in Jerusalem amidst great joy two days ago. Because the people have honored Him too much—especially as the solemn commemoration of the Jewish Passover approaches—He is in grave danger."

"We heard that He has been in peril for some time," Michael said. "Is it worse now?"

"Yes," said the shepherd. "The chief priests and the elders have been looking for reasons to be rid of Him. Now their jealousy and hatred are so inflamed that there is little hope for Him to continue escaping."

"But what of the people who welcomed and revered Him just two days ago?" Michael asked. "Where are they now?"

"Some are moving away from Him in doubt, some in fear," said Zachariah. "This is what I was told by the angel."

"Did the angel tell you what we are to do?"

"He said that you too would be in danger, but that we would not be able to persuade you to stay away. He said we are to care for the horses until at least one of you returns. That is all."

There was nothing that Michael could say. He looked back down into the valley where Zabbai stood surrounded by sheep, attended by the shepherd called Jonah. A part of the horseman wanted to turn around, to take his son and his horses home to safety. But the stronger part would not allow this.

"We will go now," said Matthias, breaking the silence. "We are grateful to you, and we will return."

WEDNESDAY

It was early the next morning when Michael and Matthias arrived on the outskirts of Jerusalem. The shepherds had provided them with robes of the type worn by city dwellers so that they might look more like those people from whom they were so different.

"This is not a good place for us," said Matthias as they walked through the streets, listening and watching, hoping for some word of Jesus. "We do not belong here."

Michael said nothing in reply, only nodded his assent. As always, the closeness of the city was unbearable to this man of the wilderness whose heart could not abide confinement. In places such as this his breathing became shallow and his heart raced as though the walls would close in on him and hold him captive.

"The man is mad!" The sharp words pulled Michael out of the abyss into which his thoughts had descended.

"It was not enough that He angered the scribes and the Pharisees by making the common people love Him. Now, He is accusing those same leaders of sin and faithlessness." The voice was harsh.

A group of men stood near a small well where women filled earthen vessels with water. The men talked loudly and gestured with their hands while the women worked in silence. Michael and Matthias paused in an alley, moving into the shadows where they could listen without being noticed.

"I wonder what He will do today," said one man.

"He should be hiding after what He did in the temple on Monday and what He said there yesterday." Another man spoke.

"I wasn't in the city. What happened on Monday?"

"He went into the temple and began driving out those who were selling. He said to them, 'My house will be a house of prayer; but you have made it a den of robbers.' This was a terribly dangerous act."

"And yesterday He went back into the temple and began preaching again," a third man said. "He told the people to beware of the teachers of the law. He spoke of their arrogance and their pride. But worse, He said that such men will be punished most severely."

"Does He not know that these teachers and their cohorts are looking for a way to arrest Him and have Him killed?" asked the first man.

"How could He not have heard this? Everyone knows!" Another voice joined the conversation. "I thought of following this Jesus of Nazareth when He came into the city on Sunday. Everyone was praising Him and trying to be near Him that day. But He has taken things too far. Now everyone who stays with Him is in danger. The priests will surely see Him dead, and His followers as well."

"We have to find Him," Michael whispered.

"But where?" asked Matthias. "How will we know where to go?"

Michael said nothing, just motioned for his son to follow him down the alley.

For all of that day and part of the night, they searched. Several times, they asked if anyone knew where Jesus could be found only to be told that He had been there recently, but had left ahead of their arrival. In the third watch of the night, when neither the father nor the son could go on, they went to an olive garden just outside the city and slept for a few hours, intending to resume their search for Jesus the next morning. But alas, this was not meant to be.

THURSDAY

At dawn, a small cadre of Roman soldiers searching for Jesus came upon Michael and Matthias. Among these was Marvelius, the man whose hatred had driven the horsemen into hiding. The now politically powerful soldier had not forgotten the face of his most despised enemy.

Michael and Matthias were arrested forthwith. They were beaten and dragged off to jail where Marvelius himself locked the tiny, dark cell into which they were thrown. "When we have finished with the insurrectionist known as Jesus, I'll return for you," he said, glaring fiercely at Michael. "I haven't decided if I'll watch you wither and die in this place beneath the streets, or if

I'll tear you apart with my own hands. But you can be sure your death will not be easy."

"Let my son go," Michael said to the retreating figure. "He has done nothing to you."

"Perhaps not," said Marvelius with an evil grin. "But watching him die will make your torture that much more exquisite."

ADRIANNA & NEEKA

In an effort to close the gap between themselves and the men, Adrianna and Neeka pushed their horses too hard and, in their own exhaustion, missed some of the signs that marked the trail of the men they followed. Because of this, they continued on the Way of the Sea until they reached the port town of Ascalon where they heard tales of a man called Jesus who was said to be in some danger in Jerusalem. They were told that this man was a teacher and healer who had angered Jewish leaders. In the town bazaar, Adrianna asked a merchant about the shortest route to the city of Jerusalem. He directed her to the small village of Marisa where they would find a path that would take them to Bethlehem, then the main road to Jerusalem. He explained that they would pass through a great herd of sheep and perhaps the shepherds could give them more directions and information.

As the merchant promised, the mother and daughter found the village and, late that same afternoon, the vast herd of sheep. Adrianna's heart leapt with joy, then descended immediately into fear when she saw Zabbai and the other horses grazing in the midst of the sheep. Beside Zabbai a tall shepherd, an old man and a boy stood watch. The tall man nodded as the boy moved toward them through the herd.

"Welcome," said the boy when he reached them. "Do not fear. Your men left these fine horses with us."

Adrianna sighed deeply and the tense muscles in her neck and shoulders relaxed. "Thank you," she said softly.

"I am Zachariah," said the smiling boy. "And you must be the wife and daughter of the great horseman, Michael."

"Yes," the beautiful girl said as she jumped down from her horse. "I am Neeka. This is my mother who is also a great horseman. She is called Adrianna."

"My father will be glad to meet you," said Zachariah. "He and the elder, Petras, have not left the white stallion's side since your father and brother departed two days ago."

"It seems as though you knew we were coming," said Neeka, walking now with the boy toward the place where Zabbai stood patiently waiting.

"Yes, we had word from the angels."

"Did my father know?"

Unafraid, the sheep moved aside as the boy spoke to them and to Neeka, touching a lamb or a ewe now and then. He didn't respond to Neeka's question at once and Adrianna, riding behind them, held her breath waiting for the answer.

Finally the boy spoke. "Your father may have known that you were coming."

"But you're not sure?" Neeka said.

"They both spoke of you and your father kept looking back across the hills as though he might be watching for someone."

"My father always senses my mother's presence," Neeka said. "They are never truly absent one from the other."

Before anything more could be said, Zabbai nickered in greeting and Neeka ran to him. Adrianna slipped down from her horse and went to her daughter who had thrown her arms around Zabbai's neck and buried her face in his mane. Adrianna took the great stallion's head in her arms, rested her face on his, and wept into his tangled forelock. For several moments no one spoke. Finally, Adrianna looked up, wiped her eyes and turned to the tall shepherd and the old man. "Forgive me," she said, "I am Adrianna and this is Neeka. We must thank you."

The men introduced themselves and then Jonah asked, "Will you take the horses now?"

"No!" Zachariah said. "They cannot."

"What is this impudence?" asked Jonah sternly. But before he could admonish his son further, Adrianna spoke again. "We will be grateful if you'll keep these that have brought us here as well. We must go in search of Michael and Matthias and it is dangerous for any of us to be seen with the horses."

"That is what the angel has told me, my father," said Zachariah. "This is why I said what I did." He turned then to Adrianna. "Please forgive me."

Adrianna reached for the boy's hand. "You owe us no apology. We heard from a merchant that we might find Jesus in Jerusalem, and we have worried about where we could leave the horses when we go to that city. Tell me," she said to the old shepherd, "is it to Jerusalem that my husband and son have gone?"

"It is." Petras nodded.

"But you must not go tonight," said Jonah. "It is plain that you are exhausted. You must refresh yourselves here with us. Tomorrow we'll send two of our men with you into the city. The walk will take only a few hours if you are rested."

"We cannot . . ." Adrianna began.

"The angel told me you need to stay with us this night," Zachariah interrupted before Adrianna could say any more. "He said you will be in danger if you go tonight."

"Please stay," said Petras. "If not for yourself nor for your husband, then at least for your daughter."

Adrianna could not disagree with this. "All right then," she said. "Neeka, will you see to the horses? Be sure they drink their fill and settle in with the others."

"Yes, my mother." Neeka answered obediently then turned to the boy. "Come with me, won't you Zachariah?"

Adrianna watched as her daughter walked away with the boy, then she followed Jonah to the camp where the night fire was just being set and the evening meal prepared. The women greeted her warmly and one showed her to the tent where she and Neeka would rest that night.

"Was there a soldier with my husband?" Adrianna asked the woman, realizing suddenly that no one had mentioned Phillip.

"No," the woman answered. "It was only the two handsome horsemen who came to us."

After a sumptuous meal, the mother and daughter curled up in the warm tent and slept, as do those who are deeply weary in both body and spirit. Dreams of Michael and of Jesus, of near reunions and of danger, haunted Adrianna. But, too exhausted to escape her torment, she did not awaken.

FRIDAY

"My dreams last night were brutal and terrifying," said Neeka as they walked along eating the morning meal that Jonah had insisted they take with them. "But no matter how hard I tried, I could not wake up and run away."

"I too had awful dreams," said Adrianna. "Now we must shake them off and keep going."

With two big herdsmen, the women had left the shepherds' camp at dawn. In silence they covered ground as quickly as their feet would carry them. Adrianna felt none of her usual enjoyment of the day's resurrection in the sunrise and the small sounds of morning that normally enchanted her.

The little company arrived at the city of Jerusalem near the second hour of this ominous day. "Thank you for coming this far," Adrianna said to the herdsmen. "You must go back to your people now."

"Are you certain?" asked one of the men. "We can stay with you. You do not need to go on alone."

"No, no," Adrianna said. "You have already been too kind. We will be fine. Do not fear for us."

"Tell Zachariah that our angels are with us," Neeka added. "None of you must worry. Please take care of our horses. We will see you soon."

As they walked down a narrow lane with no idea where they should begin their search for Michael and Matthias, Adrianna wondered if her daughter's words were prophetic, or only hopeful.

ARCHANUS

While they traveled, Archanus and Simon made plans to seek an old friend who had a home in Jerusalem. This man, Joseph of Arimathea, had fallen ill some years earlier and sought care in Luke's Roman clinic. During his protracted illness, Joseph had exchanged ideas and philosophies and matters of faith with Archanus, and the two had formed a lasting bond. Among the beliefs shared by these two great thinkers was that the Jews' Messiah and the Greeks' Christ were one and the same Savior. They were also certain that this One had been born some years earlier to a peasant girl in the town of Bethlehem.

Arriving in Jerusalem on the day when the Jewish people began the celebration of Passover, Archanus and Simon went at once in search of Joseph. But no one they asked was interested in talking to them. The entire town was caught up in a mad frenzy. There would be that day an execution. Three men would be crucified, and one of those was the teacher that was believed by many to be the Messiah.

Following the crowd, Archanus and Simon soon found themselves on the Way of Sorrows, the path to Golgotha where the crucifixion would soon take place.

CHAPTER *Sixteen*

MICHAEL & MATTHIAS

In the dim recesses of the jail beneath the streets of Jerusalem, there was little sense of night or day, but rather an agony of time that seemed never to pass. Occasionally there were cries from new prisoners being cast into the foul cells nearby. But for the most part, the stagnant silence was broken only by the low moans of those who had been too long in the dark.

Several hours after their incarceration, Michael and Matthias were aroused by a commotion.

"The One they call Jesus is being taken to Golgotha!" someone shouted.

"Is He here? In the jail?" someone else called out.

"If He is the One He claims to be, He can get us all out of here!" The voice of another.

"If He is the Messiah, He can open our cells!"

"I'm innocent!" someone screamed.

"If I die, my blood is on His hands!"

The calls and pleas and accusations went on. But to them, there was no answer.

"Could He be here among us?" Matthias asked.

"No . . . no." Michael shook his head in an anguish beyond any pain he had ever known.

"We're going to get out of here!" Matthias roared like a young lion. "I will destroy Marvelius. Then we'll find Jesus and save Him."

Michael wanted to respond, but he could not. He had tasted nothing but his own blood since the beating and the arrest. His mouth was dry and the damaged skin on his lips tore open with the least movement. His right eye was swollen shut and his hands were bruised from efforts to protect his son, and himself. In his weakness, he could do nothing but lean against the dank prison wall and wait.

Adrianna & Neeka

"I think we should go this way," Neeka said, nodding to a narrow path that forked away from what appeared to be one of the city's main thoroughfares.

Adrianna did not ask why. She just followed her daughter in silence. Something within her had broken during these last hours. She had felt some small measure of hope when they arrived in Jerusalem, but as they passed through one street after another, with every one looking the same as the last, and no sign of Michael or Matthias, her hope had begun to fade, and her strength had ebbed away. Had it not been for her daughter, Adrianna might have given up, sat down in the harsh sunlight and waited for the dust of this awful place to consume her. If it were not for Neeka . . .

As the women approached a small open square, they saw a group of soldiers gathered beside a well. Neeka held her arm out in front of her mother and motioned for silence.

"Marvelius is a mad man!" one of the soldiers said.

"If Pilate finds out what he's planning, that fool will be the one executed," a second soldier said.

"I've never heard of Pilate being so undone," another said.

"He doesn't want to crucify the Prophet. That's plain. And those priests are driving him crazy with their demands." A fourth man's voice entered the conversation.

"Maybe that's why Pilate assigned Marvelius to guard the Jewish leaders. Everyone knows our leader has a hideous temper and no heart. Maybe Pilate hopes the most wicked of his centurions will lose that temper on the equally wicked elders," said the first speaker.

"What do you think Pilate will do if Marvelius leaves his post to go back to the jail and torture the horseman?"

"I think Pilate will have the head of this beast we all hate, and we'll be shed of him at last." At that, they all laughed.

Against her will, Adrianna gasped. She had been holding her breath, and now her lungs rebelled. The laughter covered the sound, and Neeka pushed her mother further back into the shadows. Just then, several soldiers on horseback arrived in the square.

"Where is Marvelius?" The sharp words came from a familiar voice.

"He's away, but not for long." The soldier who had spoken first answered with a snicker.

"What is that supposed to mean?" Again, that voice.

"It's Phillip!" Neeka whispered. Adrianna started to step forward, but her daughter held her back. "NO! We can't endanger him." She spoke directly into her mother's ear. "He'll know what to do."

PHILLIP

Phillip had arrived in the city on Thursday, summoned from Lydda by his eldest brother, Marcus, who was the Tribune presently in command of the forces that controlled Jerusalem.

Troops from all over Judea were being called to the city to stand by in case of a rebellion. The chief priests and teachers of Jewish law were insisting that the prophet known as Jesus of Nazareth must be arrested. It was feared that should such an arrest occur, the followers of this alleged Messiah would take up arms against the Roman army. On the other hand, it was almost a certainty that if the Romans did not comply with the Jewish Council's demands, a revolt would come from this quarter.

From Marcus, Phillip had heard that morning how reluctant Pilate was to carry out the crucifixion being insisted upon by the Jews. And he had heard of the chief priests' threats against Pilate if he did not agree to their treachery. Jerusalem was a tinderbox ready to ignite—a volcano set to erupt at any moment. Still, despite the chaos that reigned in the city, Phillip could think of nothing except Michael.

Over and over the cavalryman berated himself for telling his friend and mentor of this trouble that had been pending, and was now all too real. Over and over, he castigated himself for bringing Michael back to Judea where his own life was in mortal danger.

"Answer me," he said to the foot soldiers lounging beside the well. "Why do you expect Marvelius to leave his post? And why are you not with him?"

"We are to guard the road that leads to Golgotha—to the place of the skull," said one of the soldiers.

"The criminals will soon be walking that last mile to their crucifixions. Many of us will line the street to hold back the crowds," another offered.

"What of Marvelius?" Phillip shouted, his small degree of patience exhausted.

"When everyone is engaged during the crucifixions, he will return to the jail."

"Why?" Phillip demanded.

"At dawn yesterday, while we were looking for the One called Jesus near the Mount of Olives, we came across the horseman Marvelius has sworn to kill. We beat him and threw him in the jail along with his son."

It took every ounce of control that Phillip possessed to keep from ripping his sword from its scabbard and slashing to pieces every one of these monsters. The only thing that enabled him to hold his tongue and his weapon in check was the knowledge that if he revealed his connection to Michael, he would not be able to help this dearest friend of his heart.

"Get on with your assignment!" He barked out the order. Then he turned to the cavalrymen who followed him. "Ride back to our post at the edge of town," he said. "I'll meet you there shortly." He urged his horse into a gallop and raced down the alley where Adrianna and Neeka were hiding. So close was he to them that the horse's tail brushed the women's faces. But Phillip was too intent on his objective to notice a pair of women huddled together in the shadows.

MICHAEL & MATTHIAS

Metal clanked against metal. Resolute footfalls marched along the corridor. The scuttling sound of tiny rat feet mingled with the rustle of bodies shrinking back into the deepest darkness.

"Come. Now," a low voice commanded as a key turned in the lock and the door to Michael and Matthias' cell opened. Matthias stood up and reached for his father. When Michael was unable to rise, even with his son's help, Matthias turned to the giant of a soldier who stood in the doorway, blocking what little light there was in the catacomb.

"My father is badly hurt," Matthias said.

Gently, the big man moved Matthias aside and knelt beside Michael. "Come," he said. "Do not fear. It is I, Marcus, the son of Zadoc."

Michael drew a painful breath as Marcus helped him to his feet. He looked up into the face of the man and knew that his words were true. Even in the dimness, he could see that the

Tribune's eyes were those of his father, as were his voice and the kind touch of his powerful hands.

"Come," Marcus said again, this time to Matthias. "There is little time. You must escape now. Take your father's other arm."

Between his son and his old friend, Michael shuffled on legs and feet gone numb from pain and immobility. None of the usually noisome prisoners spoke as the three passed by. When they emerged from the long tunnel, both Michael and Matthias squinted against the light of day that shocked and stung eyes grown accustomed to darkness.

"How did you find us?" Matthias asked when they stopped to let Michael rest in an alley near the jail entrance.

"My brother Phillip learned of your plight and entreated me to come to your aid. Now I must leave you to escape on your own. There is great trouble in Jerusalem and I cannot stay with you."

"Thank you," Michael whispered. "Thank you."

A tall horse was tied to a rail just a few feet from where the men stood. Marcus took a skin filled with water and a pouch of dried fruit from their places on the saddle and handed it to Matthias. "Give your father small drafts of water and little bits of the fruit. Drink and eat slowly yourself. Too much, too fast will make you ill. I wish I could give you this horse for your escape. But I cannot. I must return with all haste."

"Which way should we go?" Matthias asked.

"Away from the city," said Marcus, climbing into the saddle and pointing to the east. "That street will take you to the outskirts. Stay low and do not let yourselves be seen. You should not chance upon any soldiers because all are assigned to the Way of Sorrow and the hill called Golgotha and to the main exits from this town, the places where we expect the most trouble. Still, some may have wandered away, so be on your guard. Head back to Egypt. Keep away from anything that looks like a trafficked thoroughfare. Phillip will come for you if ever it is safe for you to return to this miserable land."

They drank sparingly of the water as Marcus had told them to do and each took a few bites of the fruit. Michael leaned against the wall until his strength and his resolve began to return. Then he straightened up and began to go the way Marcus had gone.

"That's the wrong way, my father," Matthias said, touching Michael's arm and looking in the direction the Tribune had indicated they should go.

"We . . . must go . . . to Jesus . . ." His words were halting and cost him great pain.

Matthias nodded and followed his father without argument.

Soon they could hear a loud hubbub, people shouting, whips cracking, hooves striking hard packed ground. At an intersection near the noise, Michael stopped and turned to Matthias.

"If . . . we are . . . recognized again . . ." He struggled to speak. "You . . . escape."

Sorrow filled Matthias' eyes and he shook his head.

"Promise . . ." a cut in Michael's lower lip opened and he winced. "Your mother . . ." he managed. But then he could not go on.

"Yes," Matthias said, taking a deep breath. "I promise, I will obey. I will not let my mother lose us both."

Adrianna & Neeka

When the sound of retreating hoof beats and men's voices died away, Adrianna took Neeka's hand and the two ran in the direction Phillip had taken. They did not speak as they moved resolutely toward the center of the city and the road Adrianna thought the foot soldiers had referred to in their conversation with Phillip.

They soon arrived on that street amidst catcalls, screams and crying, the shrieks of metal swords being torn from scabbards, the cracking of whips and hooves crashing against the ground in confusion.

A wall of bodies separated the mother and daughter from the street. But Neeka would not be held back. Once more, she assumed control, taking her mother's hand and pulling her through the crowd.

Only when the women broke through did they realize the horror of what lay ahead. Three men struggling to carry heavy wooden crosses were being herded up the road. The incline was not steep, but these sufferers might as well have been trying to climb a sheer rock wall. Beside and behind and before them cruel soldiers on foot and on horseback held away the crowd and lashed and shouted at the men to move on.

The last man in line, who was torn and bloodied almost beyond recognition, staggered and fell before he reached the place where Adrianna and Neeka stood. Beside them an old man was held back from going to the fallen One by his tall, dark companion.

"Please, let me help Him," the old man begged.

The tall man shook his head sadly. "I cannot let them kill you too," he said.

The sound of the old voice was strangely familiar. But something drew Adrianna's thoughts away from this mystery and compelled her to look across the road. There, in the dusty sunlight, was her beloved Michael, bruised and bleeding, held up by their son. She fell to her knees and a horrible keening wail escaped the very depths of her being.

ARCHANUS

With Simon holding him back, Archanus tore his eyes away from the besieged One and looked around for a break in the line of soldiers. He could not stop himself from hoping against hope for the torture to stop, so that he could comfort this poor stranger he did not know but somehow adored, with a fervor beyond his understanding.

And then his old eyes fell upon another—a handsome youth whose face he knew in a way he had never known any other. In disbelief, Archanus shook his head and wiped his eyes with the sleeve of his robe. But the countenance did not change. An injured man of middle age strained against the youth who held him back from the street when he, like Archanus, would have run to the fallen One.

The older of these two had evidently been beaten. One eye was swollen shut. There were cuts around his mouth and on his chin. Blood was caked on the front of his dirty tunic and he held one hand gingerly near his chest as though it caused him great pain. To Archanus, the wounded man was slightly familiar, but it was the younger one that held his eyes and made his heart feel as though it must cease.

"My son," he whispered. "My son . . . it cannot be . . ."

Now, directly in front of Archanus and Simon, the One who suffered fell again; and in a swift succession of events the old Wise Man's world was torn apart. He felt himself escape Simon's hold and bolt into the street at the same moment that he saw the man with the bloody face tear himself away from the youth he thought to be his dear son, grown so little older in all these long years.

Archanus tried to breach the small mob of soldiers on foot and horseback that had descended on the two bloodied men. A pulsating light engulfed the fallen ones as they continued to strain toward each other, their eyes touching if not their hands. That was the old man's last sight before he too was brutally struck down.

MATTHIAS

Matthias dragged himself out from beneath a sea of sandal-shod feet that were trampling him. Had he been knocked out? He didn't think so, but he was disoriented and dizzy, unsure of where he was. Then all at once he remembered. In a sudden, unbelievable burst of strength, his father had jerked away and thrust himself into the street where the torn and bloodied prisoner had fallen beneath His cross.

Weakened and confused, he moved back from the street and sat down, hoping to regain his bearings and to gather enough energy to go in search of his father.

Neeka

In the street, a new ruckus erupted. A man had lunged from the crowd as if in an effort to reach the fallen One. Foot and horse soldiers rushed forward, trying to keep the men apart. Horses reared and whinnied fearfully beneath the assault of their riders. But the animals would not be forced to step on either of the bruised and bleeding men reaching toward one another in the street.

Finally one soldier leapt from his horse, seized the man who had come out of the crowd and hauled him away. At that moment, Neeka's attention was diverted when two foot soldiers grabbed the old man's companion and thrust him toward the place where the wounded One lay beneath His cross.

The big man protested. "My friend is hurt," he said. "Let someone else help!"

One of the soldiers kicked the unconscious man and shouted to his friend, "Get out there or we'll make sure this worthless old fool is as dead as he looks!"

With that, the one the old man had called Simon went to the fallen victim and bent to shoulder His cross. Then, with the heavy burden on his own back, the dark giant leaned down and helped the fallen One to His feet. Something drew Neeka to follow, to try to stay near. And then the suffering Jesus turned to look at her and the girl's heart was ripped from within her.

"NO!" she heard herself cry out. "It cannot be." Hot tears sprung from her eyes. Her lungs expanded as if to burst, and her mind screamed at her to move, to do something, to act. She started toward the street, but a soldier shoved her back. Then Simon lost his hold on Jesus and the Beloved One fell again. Neeka dashed to Jesus, not caring, indeed not even thinking, what might happen to her.

She knelt beside Him, weeping and saying His Name over and over again, touching His face and His broken body, trying at once to hold Him down and to pick Him up. She felt nothing but the love of Him. She heard nothing but His breathing, at first a labored sound that, as she listened, became the song of a great wave washing over a waiting shore. As though they were alone, the roar of the crowd and the suffocating heat fell away.

To Neeka, it seemed as though a gale force wind whirled around them creating a world apart, then leaving behind a gentle breeze that whispered into the sphere of their private silence. And the only light in this separate world emanated from the eyes of Jesus.

Tenderly, she lifted His head. With her tears falling on His bloody face, she took from her waist the blue sash He had given her so long ago, the only garment that never left her. With the wide cloth, she covered His face and His eyes and the crown of thorns He wore, and the drops of blood made by that crown.

His lips moved, and with great care she took the cloth away.

"Veronica . . ." He reached for her, and with fingers gnarled in pain, He traced the outline of her cheek. "Thank you . . ."

Then He was gone, snatched roughly away and thrust once more to the ground.

"Jesus . . . Oh my Jesus," Neeka cried, rising to go to Him once more. But one of the soldiers who had yanked Him from her arms struck her in the face and knocked her to the ground. She fought the weakness that overcame her as some mysterious force sought to extinguish the light of Jesus from within her.

MATTHIAS

As though emerging from a horrendous dream, Matthias rubbed his eyes and tried to moisten his lips with a tongue too dry to be of any aid. He did not know how long his mind had swirled between wakefulness and the oblivion of sleep. Too many hours with neither food nor rest had robbed him of clarity. Now he leaned against a building a few yards away from an almost empty road that climbed toward a rock outcropping. The noise and the crowd and the confusion had moved away, following the three who were to be crucified. Further up the incline, on the Way of Sorrow, ten soldiers on horseback traveled five abreast behind a procession he could barely make out.

Shaking his head sadly, the weary young horseman turned away from the disappearing crowd and looked across the street. There, to his great amazement and joy, he saw his mother moving between an old man and a girl, both of whom lay prostrate in the shadow of an extended portico.

NEEKA

Neeka awoke in utter bewilderment with no idea of how long she had remained unconscious. The crowd was gone. Matthias was holding her in his arms, rocking her gently and singing to her a soft song of their childhood.

She reached up and touched his cheek and he lifted her to him. "Oh Neeka, sweet Neeka," he crooned, "I thought they had killed you." Then he called out, "Mother, she is alive! Our Neeka is with us!"

Following his gaze, Neeka saw her mother ministering to the old man who had been hurt before she was. Like her own, the old man's eyes were now open. Like her own and those of her brothers, those eyes were as clear and blue as a crystalline pool in sunlight.

Memory flooded over her in a torrent too horrible to endure. She tried to sit up. "We must go to Him," she cried. "We must hurry . . ."

But Matthias held her. "It is too late, my sister," he whispered, brushing a damp tendril of hair away from her face. "It is too late."

MICHAEL

In the dark confines of the jail, his hands tied in front of him, his head once again swimming with faintness and pain, Michael tried to make sense of the episode just passed. He wanted to understand why, this time, there had been no angelic help. He wanted to know why Jesus had to suffer in such a terrible way—why He could not save Himself, if the angels would not attend. Had he been wrong all these years? Was this not the One his father had told him of so very long ago. Could he believe—still—what he thought he had always known in the face of what he had just seen? Could he ever again find hope?

He willed himself to stop questioning and tried to relive the events of the horrible day he had somehow managed to survive. Everything had happened so fast. First, his eyes had met those of his beloved wife who stood with their daughter across the Way of Sorrow. Then Jesus had fallen in front of him and, unable to contain himself, he had pulled away from Matthias, knocking the boy to the ground beneath the feet of the maniacs in the crowd. He had wanted to help his son, but that was not possible. He could not turn away from Jesus.

Before he could get to his brother, Michael had fallen under the assault of three soldiers. The brothers had reached toward one another and Jesus' outstretched hand had grazed Michael's straining fingers. There were foot and horse soldiers all around them as they continued to strain toward one another. The men kicked them and lashed them with whips, but the horses could not be forced to step on any part of their prone figures. The animals reared and screamed in terror and pain as their riders beat them. But they would not let their hooves fall upon Jesus nor upon Michael.

With dust billowing up around them, in spirit, the brothers escaped, their hearts touching as their hands could not. When their eyes met, a strange amber light illuminated them in its embrace. The roar of the crowd became like the crashing of waves against a sea wall, and the wall around them became impenetrable. With every fiber of his being, Michael sought Jesus—begging, beseeching, he knew not what. Fear and failure, hopelessness and confusion vied for position in the horseman's raging heart. In answer Jesus spoke with only a look. Absolute love emanated from His silence. And, if only for a moment, there was peace.

Then a sharp kick to his ribs from a foot soldier's heavy boot curled Michael around the pain and knocked the breath of life from within him. He rolled toward the feet of a horse that shied away, knocking down two other soldiers. The horse would not hurt him, but he could not be saved from the blows of the men. And soon, the light faded from his eyes.

Unconsciousness gave him brief respite from the dreadful storm that had engulfed him since Phillip's arrival weeks earlier at the horsemen's camp. But neither that oblivion, nor the peace that had come with a look from his Brother, were gifts he could keep.

Now, he sat alone in the darkness wondering how soon he would die, though it didn't really matter. He did not care to live in a world without Jesus. And surely that godless mob must have murdered Him by now.

From Michael's heart, all hope was gone. He could not even bring himself to desire life for his family. In a world without Jesus, why would anyone who had known Him care to go on?

CHAPTER Seventeen

ARCHANUS

The old Wise Man's eyes opened to the vision of his wife, a woman of beauty at once young and old, whose golden hair fell across his face, shading him from the relentless sun. But the image, and the moment, swirled away. The darkness returned, and then the light came back. Like waves of the sea, consciousness collected him then dropped him back into a dark abyss, brought him forth and sent him away. He was alone and he was surrounded. There was silence and there was sound—amorphous, then clear.

The footfalls of horses and humans had receded. Archanus recalled the echo of motion, but not the reason for its existence. He felt something cool and damp on his closed eyes, but he couldn't force them to open again. He tried to raise his head and his shoulders, but weakness and a gentle touch held him down.

"Be still, my friend." Archanus heard the voice and knew it.

"Simon . . ." His lips parted and the sound of his own voice crashed from one side of his aching head to the other.

"Is he coming back?" This was a woman's voice, melodious, unfamiliar. He strained to hear more, but again, he drifted away.

"I'm going to give you some water," Simon said. "Try to drink."

He felt the cool liquid seeking his throat and running from the sides of his mouth into his beard. He wanted to speak, to reach for his friend, but he could not.

"Can you stay with him while I go in search of my children?" he heard the woman ask.

"I can care for him." Simon's tone was tender. "But you should not go."

"I must find them."

"They'll come back to you. They know where you are." Simon paused. "You should not go to the top of that hill, and they should not stay there."

"Did you see them?" the woman asked.

"When the soldiers released me, I started back here at once. I saw your daughter and a handsome young man who must be your son. They were trying to stay away from the soldiers, but they were headed up the hill."

"I must go to them," Archanus heard the woman say.

"What is happening up there is too awful for you to see." Simon shook his head and in his dark eyes there was depth of sorrow beyond enduring. "Please don't go."

Archanus slipped away again. When he awoke at last, he and Simon were alone. Above them the sky was filled with ominous black clouds slashed by lightening. Thunder roared and the earth trembled.

ADRIANNA

"Please don't," Adrianna had begged her son and daughter when Neeka insisted that they go to Jesus after she regained full consciousness under the tender ministrations of her brother. But Neeka would not be deterred. Jesus was the only goal of her heart, and she would not forsake Him.

Now, as Adrianna made her way up the long incline toward the top of the hill, she prayed that she would find her children. The crowd and the soldiers were out of sight and the mother was not accosted. Between the enormous cracks of lightening and thunder she could hear shouting. But she couldn't make out what was being said and she could see nothing over the rim of the bluff.

Enormous green-black clouds rolled across the sky like a fearsome herd of wild horses gone mad with terror and unable to keep from destroying everything in its path. Adrianna bent low against the wind, anticipating waves of rain. As the storm approached, people fleeing the hilltop began to rush down the road, a smaller but still dangerous herd, careening out of control. And then she crested the hill and staggered, undone by the sight that met her.

Three men hung in the throes of death on the wooden crosses they had been forced to drag up the hill. She could neither imagine nor bear to think of the suffering they had endured in the hours since her children had left to follow Jesus while she stayed to care for the injured old man.

Wildly, she began to run through what was left of the crowd that surged against her. She could think of nothing but finding her children and getting them away from this brutal scene. "Neeka!" she called out in a voice so frantic she scarcely recognized it as her own. "Neeka! Matthias! Where are you?" Sobs swelled in her chest and tears filled her eyes, but neither would overflow. Like the rain, her crying awaited something yet to come.

They found her just as she was falling to her knees. There was a great roaring in her ears but it had nothing to do with the wind or the thunder. Her heart was beating with such ferocity that she knew it must leap from her chest or shatter into a million pieces. She needed to be sick and to scream, to attack and to retreat.

Matthias gathered her into his arms, lifted her up and carried her away from the terrified mob. When Adrianna opened her eyes, Neeka was beside her, touching her hair and whispering to her as she might to a frightened horse. Some distance from the place where the Way of Sorrow met the hill, Matthias sat down on a small knoll, still holding his mother in his arms. People continued to spill over the edges of the road as they tried to escape the hilltop and the storm and perhaps the horror of what they had done.

The tempest within Adrianna subsided momentarily. She forced herself to breathe, to be thankful that her children were with her. Together they could surely escape, since the soldiers didn't seem to be paying attention to any of the people running away.

"We must go," she said. "We must go . . ."

"We will," Matthias promised, his voice soothing. "The soldiers don't care about us. Catch your breath, then we'll go."

She nodded and drew in a great draft of air. Then something drew her attention to the center cross, the one from which she had tried hardest to look away. The figure that hung there was beaten and bloodied almost beyond recognition. And yet, He was a light in the gathering darkness. A woman, beautiful even in the extremis of her own pain, clung to His cross, kissing His feet, her lips moving in a prayer that no one could hear. Beside her, two other women knelt, and just behind her stood a young man with tears running unchecked down his cheeks.

The black clouds seemed to be converging at a point behind this cross. But around it, there was a subtle glow that held away the sound and the thunder and all of the other grim desolation of this horrible place in time.

"She is His mother," Neeka gasped. "The one at His feet . . ."

"How can you know this?" Matthias said, touching his sister's cheek.

"She is, she is . . ." Neeka's eyes were wide with wonder.

Adrianna held her breath, straining to hear what the woman at the foot of the cross was saying. Then, by some strange miracle, the two mothers' hearts touched; and for Adrianna there would never again be any question about the identity of the woman who knelt at her Son's feet in an agony of pure love.

Wrenching her concentration away from the woman, Adrianna looked up to Jesus. She saw His eyes flutter open, then followed His gaze to the face of His mother—a face wherein resided all of the pain in the world—and all of the love. Jesus lips parted and again Adrianna strained to hear.

"Dear woman . . ." the words were so low and ragged as to be almost unintelligible. " . . . Behold . . . your son." His words came between tortured breaths, broken by pauses that seemed to Adrianna to stop the passage of time. "Son," Jesus moved His eyes to the young man standing below Him with the women. "Behold . . . your mother."

"No . . ." Adrianna's heart moaned within her. "There can be no surrogate for our own sons. No healing in the wake of their loss." She thought she must be screaming. But when she looked at her children, whose eyes had not wavered from the woman at the foot of the cross, she knew her words, like her tears, remained trapped within her.

Matthias turned to her then and drew her closer. Gently stroking her hair, he pressed her face against him. At last, her emotions released by her son's loving-kindness, she wept inconsolably into his chest.

"Do not fear," Neeka said, putting an arm around her mother and resting her face on Adrianna's shoulder. "He has given her to us, and us to her."

"What are you saying, my daughter?"

"It is His bequest. I know it is," Neeka whispered. "He has not left His mother alone. Nor has He abandoned us. She is our mother now and we are her children, all of us, forever and ever."

"But Neeka . . ."

"It is true." Neeka's eyes were steady, but her voice beseeched Adrianna to believe her. "He said He would leave none of us alone. He promised—and I trust Him."

Before Adrianna could question Neeka any further, a great veil of darkness fell across the land. So absolute was the end of the light that even the gray-black clouds that had surged across the sky like a terrible army were obscured. Within the void, the rains were at last released. Sheets of stinging water fell in torrents and thunder raged, but the lightning that must have come before its echo could not be seen.

To Adrianna it seemed as though the mystifying onslaught of water and darkness had engulfed them for hours when she heard Jesus call out in a loud voice, "Father, into Your hands I commend My Spirit."

At those words, the veil of darkness ripped apart. A fearsome light escaped and the air pulsed with portent and foreboding. Adrianna's eyes had been fixed on Jesus when the darkness descended, and to Him her attention returned now. His chest heaved and He allowed His head to fall forward as He said in a tone that was clear and firm and filled with peace, "It is finished."

And then the earth began to shake with a mighty force. Rocks split apart. Boulders dislodged and rumbled down hills, crushing everything that lay in their paths. The walls of long standing structures broke apart and fell in upon themselves. All around Adrianna, the quaking of the earth wreaked havoc and devastation; and the wailing of the wounded and the lost cried toward a Heaven whose heart, for a time, would remain unopened.

It was near the ninth hour of the day when the sound and the fury began to subside and a dull, exhausted light returned. Adrianna and her children had huddled against the hillock, waiting for what seemed the inevitable end. When their eyes adjusted to the awakening world, they saw that only one centurion and a few soldiers remained on guard near the mother of Jesus and her companions, who had stayed through it all at the foot of His cross.

Adrianna had noticed the centurion when he rode up on a handsome bay horse shortly before the cataclysm. But she had not seen the man's face. Now he stood near the cross of Jesus and called out for all the world to hear, "Surely this was the Son of God."

Recognizing Phillip's voice, Adrianna realized that he was the centurion standing at the foot of the cross. She started to run to her family's dear friend, but Matthias held her back. "Not now," her son whispered. "We could all be in danger if we go to him now. We'll find him later."

"Yes, yes, you're right," Adrianna said. "We need to find your father. And we must see to the old man, if he is still alive. Phillip will find us when it is safe."

PHILLIP

The blood rushed away from Phillip's head and he swayed as he stood up. Never had he been so overcome by emotion. Never had he felt such utter love and pain, guilt and sorrow, outrage and devastation all tearing through him, one sensation overpowering another, gripping his heart and his mind with a force he could neither resist nor understand.

How had he ended up here, at this, of all crucifixions? Knowing his aversion to this custom, Marcus had seen to it that Phillip and his men were assigned to one of the city portals. But when Marvelius deserted his post on Golgotha, Phillip had been ordered to take the evil one's place. Phillip was sure this was done without his brother's permission. But he could not refuse. In this tense climate, the least insubordination could lead to death.

Like his brothers and their father, Phillip despised every kind of Roman violence, especially this barbaric form of execution. He had joined the army to protect the horses. But soon, he had learned that he was powerless. He could defend neither horses nor ill-fated humans from the brutality that seemed the very nature of too many of those with whom he served.

Now, in the wake of this tragic crucifixion, he knew what he must do. He must leave the Roman Army at once to join the followers of the One they had murdered this awful day. Nothing would deter him.

All at once he realized that he had taken a warrior's stance beneath the cross, his fists clenched, his feet wide apart, his countenance fierce. He looked around at the few people who remained on the hilltop. The mother of Jesus and a young man still stood at the foot of His cross, clinging to His feet. Nor had the other two women gone away.

Now, a man of some dignity approached him. "Pilate has given me permission to take the body to a tomb nearby," the man said.

For some reason unable to respond, Phillip just looked at the man.

The man waited patiently, but when there was no response, he spoke again. "May we take the body now?"

"Yes, yes," Phillip said at last. "I will help you . . ."

He would never clearly recall the events that transpired over the next few minutes. Taking the ruined body from the cross was too horrible a task—a memory that had to be obliterated if Phillip was to live on. He would not be spared, however, the remembrance of Mary, the Blessed Mother, in whose arms he laid the Son she had borne and nursed and loved. The look on her face would travel with him all the days of his life, seared indelibly into his memory.

When he was satisfied that Mary could hold her Son alone, he had stepped back from the grieving mother and looked up at the sign on the top of the cross. In three languages it announced that the One who had hung there was *The King of the Jews.* He thought about how many had claimed to be the Messiah over the years. He pondered the fact that, up to now, this had been a great joke within the Roman forces—a repeated illustration of the characteristic foolishness of these people they governed and held in such low esteem.

And yet, this time, Phillip was sure the claim had been justified. And again, softly now, he said, "Surely this was the Son of God."

"Come, my brother."

Startled by the voice, Phillip whirled around. Joel placed a comforting hand on his shoulder and spoke again. "Marcus found out that you had been reassigned to this place and sent me here to see if you were all right."

"I will never be all right again," Phillip said, looking levelly into his brother's eyes.

"But you are alive," Joel said. He turned then and shouted to one of the men who had ridden up with him, "Go to Marcus. Tell him our brother is safe. Tell him we will remain with the body as he commanded."

The soldier spun his horse around and dashed away.

"It is over," Joel said. "We can do nothing more than accompany these grieving people to the grave and stand guard there."

"We must wait until they are ready," Phillip said, nodding toward the foot of the cross where Mary still sat holding the lifeless body of her Son. "We cannot rush them."

Joel said nothing as he stepped back with his brother and waited.

MICHAEL

The horseman was alone, bereft, as he had not been since the day his father rode away so long ago. Dazed and confused, he struggled to recall what had happened, what had caused him to be left by himself in the suffocating dust and the semi-darkness that now surrounded him. Then, gradually, memory began to wash over him and with it came an agony of heart beyond enduring.

The jail had gone dark as though this basement's few, small windows huddled beneath a stormy sky. Soon afterward, Marvelius had come to Michael's cell, promising to kill him slowly. There had been no guards in evidence, no one to call for help, no way to escape. When Marvelius began to savagely beat him, he had tried to protect himself. But he was too weak to fend off the blows, let alone to fight back.

He was losing consciousness when he heard in the depths of his heart the voice of Jesus saying, "It is finished . . ." The words were clear and firm and filled with peace. Before he could wonder at their meaning or their source, the earth had begun to shake and the walls of the prison had tumbled down around him.

Now a sliver of light came through the broken ceiling and in the dim illumination Michael could see Marvelius lying crushed beneath a wall and a pillar. His eyes, open wide in the shock of death, were devoid of their wicked gleam. A small stream of blood was drying beside the cruel mouth that gaped open as though in a long and silent scream. Michael could not see Marvelius' legs, but the soldier's torso was twisted in a way that said his back had been broken.

So why, Michael asked himself, when he was at last free of the danger that had stalked him for so long in the person of this evil adversary, was he gripped by such abject sorrow? Shouldn't he be exulting? And then, he was bombarded by the memory of what had brought him back to this jail a second time.

"Jesus . . . oh my Jesus," he shouted and he raged and he wept. Again, he saw his Brother falling, beaten and bloodied almost beyond recognition. He saw their hands outstretched, as he reached for Jesus and Jesus for him. He felt the rush of love that had washed over him when, with a look from His tortured eyes, Jesus spoke to his heart as they lay in the street, at once a breath and a day's ride apart. He felt the excruciating pain written in every lash mark on Jesus' back; and he felt once more the horror of being helpless, unable to save his Brother.

Like great waves of the sea, the agony threw him on the rocks then washed him back to the depths, ebbing and flowing without pity. The unrelenting misery surged through him until he wished that he could die from it.

When his emotion at last seemed spent, Michael tried to stand up. His legs trembled. His clothing was torn and soaked with blood. He could not raise his right arm, nor could he close the hand that hung limp at its end. With his left hand, he touched a tender spot on the back of his neck at the base of his skull. In his mouth, he felt loosened teeth and tasted blood. But he was breathing. He was alive. For some reason, he had been spared. All around his cell, the roof of the jail had fallen in, the walls had come down, and the other captives had been crushed.

He listened for sounds of life, but heard none. Mounds of crumbled walls surrounded him. Of the entire jail, it appeared that the only thing left was this small tomb he shared with the dead Marvelius. Above him, a slab of rock hung at a precarious angle into an opening that appeared too small for him to pass through. But there was no other way out, so he climbed up onto a pile of dirt and broken bits of rock and reached for the slab. At first it seemed as though the heavy barrier would not be moved. But the light beckoned and, with painful effort, he struggled toward it. Finally, the massive shard broke apart and Michael escaped.

He lay panting in the faded light, coughing up dust, unable to think or to plan, momentarily grateful to be alive, despite his sorrow. He lay still, again listening for sounds of life, once more hearing none. He thought surely some must have escaped the earthquake. But it was so quiet. Perhaps everyone was hiding from whatever danger might still be lurking in this city of the great betrayal.

Then he heard the careful footfalls of a horse making its way across the rubble-strewn road. Too exhausted to move, he waited for whatever cataclysm must now befall him. Then he felt the warm breath of a horse and the animal's soft muzzle exploring the back of his neck, and finally he found the strength to roll over. A long, rolling snort and the bump of a nose against his blood-caked cheek urged him to look at something he could not believe. He shook his head and blinked his eyes.

"It cannot be," he said in a voice he scarcely recognized. "It cannot be . . ."

But it was. There, standing above him, was Zabbai. There was no one else around, no sign to explain how the horse might have found him. But he was there. Michael touched the stallion's face, then reached for his leg and holding on, pulled himself into a sitting position. Zabbai snorted again and nudged him. Then the great creature lay down beside his man and Michael found the strength to throw his right leg over the broad, white back and to hold on while the stallion stood up.

The horseman didn't even think about trying to control where they were going. He just slumped over, resting his head and shoulders on Zabbai's neck, allowing the stallion to choose his path. With every step Michael felt his strength returning in that mysterious gift of energy he had always received from the horse.

Soon they were climbing the Way of Sorrow where he had last seen Jesus and toward the place of the skull where Michael could see three crosses jutting upward into an angry sky. Distant thunder grumbled in a rolling echo that met the steady beat of Zabbai's footfalls on the hard packed ground. And the brokenhearted wind wailed across the Heavens above.

As if torn away from the stronger gale, a forlorn breeze wafted down the deserted street. Behind curtained windows, there was neither sound, nor light. Random destruction marked the path of the earthquake. Here and there undamaged buildings stood right beside piles of debris where other structures had fallen. Zabbai jumped across the deep fissures that cut across the road, carefully avoiding the small cracks that spread out from the secondary faults.

Apprehension rode with Michael along this last path trod by his beloved Brother. But the shock of the seriously wounded protected him from the unbearable pain and emotion he should have felt.

So, when they crested the hill and his heart did not stop beating as he had too often wished it would, he was not astonished; and he did not cry out. Almost soundlessly, Zabbai walked toward a small tableau at the foot of the middle cross.

There, within a sphere of mystifying amber light, sat Mary, the mother of Jesus, holding in her arms the body of her Son. As Michael had seen her do when Jesus was a little boy, she rocked Him, and she crooned to Him, a sweet and soothing song. And her tears fell into His eyes.

The air was motionless, neither hot nor cold. Two women and a young man knelt close to Mary and Jesus. An older man stood just behind them. At a respectful distance, a pair of centurions stood with their backs to him beside their horses. Behind these men, a small cadre of soldiers watched in silence.

Time stood still, and it moved on, and in its fullness, Mary looked up. When her eyes met Michael's, a wave of something unexplainable washed over him. At once consoling and powerful, a comfort and an awakening, the mother's gaze held within it an end and a beginning.

After a while, Mary released Michael's eyes and turned her attention to the young man who stood nearby. As though he understood her wordless summons, the sorrowful youth went to her at once. For a long and tender moment, everyone watched as Mary whispered to Jesus words that could only have been farewell. When she spoke no more, the young man knelt and lifted Jesus from His mother's arms. He turned then and carried the body to Michael, who bent low and lifted his slain Brother onto Zabbai's waiting back.

Michael did not weep as he took Jesus into his arms. Cradling his Brother's bloody head in the crook of the arm he had not, until then, been able to use, Michael held the body as he had once held his own children. By the grace of a merciful God, the horseman saw in his arms not the lifeless form of a tortured man, but the face of the laughing boy who had saved

Michael from his sorrow and taught him of joy once upon a very long ago.

He looked to Mary, wanting to share with her this revelation, to rescue and carry her beyond the end to the beginning he had seen in her eyes. But with those eyes, she told him she understood and bid him to go on.

No words were exchanged by anyone present. With a brief nod, the older man motioned for Michael to follow him as he walked down a narrow path that descended the hill in the direction opposite the Way of Sorrow.

They moved at a slow and somber pace the short distance to the base of a high, rock wall where a massive boulder sat beside the opening to a tomb. A verdant garden spread out from the wall. From the branches of silvery olive trees birds looked on, strangely silent and still.

They were met by another man, dressed in the robes of a Jewish nobleman, carrying jars of oil and unguents. With her eyes, Mary beckoned Michael. Still holding Jesus in his arms, he slipped down from Zabbai's back and followed the Blessed Mother into the tomb. There, he laid the body down on a ledge and stepped back. Mary did not ask him to leave, so he stayed and watched her prepare Jesus for burial, anointing Him with the oils the man had brought and wrapping His face and body in separate cloths.

When she was finished, she knelt and Michael bent gingerly to his knees behind her.

After they emerged, four soldiers came forward and rolled the massive stone across the entrance and secured and sealed it.

"You will take the first watch and I will remain with you," said one of the centurions. "The priests fear that the body will be stolen, so Pilate has assigned us to stand guard. No one of less strength than you four together will be able to move aside the stone."

Until then, Michael had barely glanced at the centurions and their men ignoring even the two fine horses ridden by the officers. But when he heard the familiar voice giving commands, he looked at the speaker and shook his head in wonder.

"Yes, it is I," the speaker said, looking at Michael. Then Joel, the brother of Phillip and Marcus, the sons of Zadoc stepped forward. "Come," he said, taking Michael by the arm and leading him away from the tomb. "We must talk."

Michael's breath caught in his throat. Surprise and fear mingled in his thoughts. He watched as the other centurion whose back was still to him began to lead Mary and her companions away.

"Do not fear," said Joel when they were well away from the other soldiers. "Nothing has changed between us. But my brother and I have been assigned to keep everyone away from the tomb and to see that there is no uprising. There is still terrible unrest in this city and everyone who was a disciple of Jesus, including you, might still be in danger."

"I don't understand," Michael said. "They have killed Him. How can they go on being afraid and angry?"

"The people loved Him once and they will love Him again," Joel said with firm assurance. "The chief priests are right in thinking that when His many followers recover from the shock of His death, they may take up arms in rebellion against the injustice."

"And what of His mother? Is she safe?"

"My brother escorts her and the others to the home of the disciple called John. Neither the Romans nor the Jews will know of this place."

"Is that Phillip of whom you speak?" Michael started forward as if to go after his friend.

"Yes, but you cannot follow him. You must ride away from here. Go back to Egypt and wait until we come for you. It is the only way we can be assured of your well-being."

"I cannot leave until I find my family," Michael said. "I saw my wife and daughter before I was last arrested. And my son remains somewhere in these mean streets."

"They are together," Joel said.

"How do you know this?"

"We have seen them."

"Did you talk to them? Did you also tell them to beware?"

"No," said Joel, "I am sorry. Phillip saw them on the hill just before the storm and the earthquake struck. By the time the sky began to clear, they had disappeared . . ." Again, he gripped Michael's arm. "Wait," he said. "Let me finish."

"I'm sorry." Michael shook his head. "Go on."

"Phillip told me that they are dressed like peasants. And they have no horses, so it's unlikely that they'll be accosted. You know your family. What do you think they'll do?"

"They'll be looking for me . . ."

"Perhaps not." Joel looked down at his feet.

"Again the fool, I don't understand." Michael frowned.

"The jail was completely destroyed." Joel looked squarely at Michael. "You are the only survivor . . . something your family cannot know."

"So they'll hear of the devastation and think I too am dead."

"I'm afraid so."

"Joel, can you find them?"

"In three days time we will begin a search. Until then, we are assigned to this post. If we desert it, we will be arrested and face execution."

"Why three days? And why such extreme punishment?"

"The One inside," Joel said, nodding toward the tomb, "promised that He would arise in three days. We must stay for that time to be sure no one steals the body and claims that He has risen."

"And the severity of punishment?"

"This place remains volatile and dangerous. It doesn't matter that this part of the drama is over. From all quarters there is the threat of revolution, and Pilate has gone a little mad with guilt over this Man's crucifixion and the sure knowledge that Rome will hold him responsible for any further chaos in this place that he so hates."

"But why must I not stay and seek Adrianna and the children on my own?"

"Some of those who followed Marvelius are still here. They are a ruthless lot who kill for sport. Until Phillip and I can find them, they are a threat to you."

"What will you do then?"

"That is not for you to worry about. Know only that they will be rendered helpless and no longer a menace to you. This you must simply trust."

"So what now?" Michael asked, sadness beginning to well up within him once more.

"Ride away while there is enough confusion within our ranks that one lone man on a horse will not raise suspicion. Allow Zabbai to take you home."

CHAPTER *Eighteen*

MICHAEL

The city was behind them, as was the day. Night had fallen beneath a sea of clouds, pregnant with the tears of heaven. Neither moon nor stars relieved the darkness. No night bird called. No human ventured out into the fearful unknown. No hope touched Michael's grieving heart.

Zabbai walked on as though he knew and could see where he was going. And the night passed and the sun rose somewhere behind the mournful clouds that did not move across the wakening sky, but hovered suspended and waiting.

Michael gave no thought to this day, to their route of travel, to tomorrow. It mattered not at all where they were going. His heart did not even yearn toward his family. There was a stillness within him, a final sense of loss that continued to rob him of the will to live. Like the clouds, his very being was suspended in time, awaiting something he did not try to name.

But Zabbai walked on. He took water when he came upon it and waited until Michael climbed down and knelt to drink. During the first night, the stallion had stopped in a meadow beside a running stream and lay down. It was not the usual way of the horse to make itself so vulnerable, lying prone in an unknown place. But Zabbai was not the usual horse.

Finally, Michael reclined beside Zabbai and fell into a deep and merciful sleep. When the man awoke, the horse was grazing in the sweet grass beside the stream. There was a fig tree and wild grape vines in the crook of the small river's curving arm, and from this bounty, Michael ate his fill.

Now they traveled on, the motive and physical power belonging alone to Zabbai while Michael remained imprisoned by his sorrow.

If the horseman had paid the least attention to his surroundings, he would have seen that the landscape was not as it should have been were they enroute to Egypt. If he had noticed the faint coming and going of the sun behind the deep wall of clouds, he would have realized that they moved on a northerly course instead of traveling south. But along with his will to live, his awareness slumbered.

For two nights and one long day, Michael remained in this state of vague oblivion, alone and separate from all he held most dear. On the morning of the third day since his world ended with the crucifixion of his Brother, the clouds parted for the rising sun and the chill in the horseman's heart began to thaw.

At midday, Zabbai stopped at the base of a mountain and Michael let his eyes follow the shadows along the ridges and valleys that led toward the summit. The beginning of an emotion stirred within him when a memory glanced across his mind, drawing him up out of the abyss in which he had lingered too long.

Near day's end, Zabbai and Michael arrived at a place where placid waters lapped against the shore on the Sea of Galilee. A gentle breeze drifted across this familiar lake and caressed Michael's face on its way to his broken heart.

The companions rested awhile beside the Sea. Then, by the light of a still brilliant, if waning moon, they journeyed on until they reached the hill of the last goodbye, where Michael and Jesus had parted company one spring day long ago.

A great sea change had somehow taken place and they were partners again—this horse and his man—heading into a future that beckoned Michael toward a hope that was both mystifying and desired. Neither the stallion nor the man slept that night, waiting instead, alert and expectant. And then the morning came.

In the East, dawn spread across the mountains. Nudging aside the subtle effulgence that implied the end of night, brilliant rays of light soared toward the heavens in a golden fan above the emergent sun. And, within the arched portal of that glory, a man appeared. The song of the earth swelled in harmony with the splendor above it, as all that had been at rest awakened. Together, Michael and Zabbai breathed deeply of the power that hung in the air. Time stood still—and it raced forward, as the figure drew near.

And then, at last He stood before them, a man, and yet, a God. In the stark angles of His face, there shown infinite kindness and unfathomable love. In the depth of His eyes, lay the world's joys, and its sorrows. From Him emanated the life force of the earth and all that resided upon it.

"It can't be You." Michael whispered into the pregnant silence. "No, no." He shook his head. "This time it really can't be You . . ."

"It is I."

The voice was clear and strong, the dearest melody Michael had ever heard. Yet still, he could not believe.

"No, I want this so much that I have dreamed it. You cannot be . . . We carried Your lifeless body to the tomb. And a heavy stone sealed the place where You lay."

"Peace be with you, My brother. It is I. Touch Me and know."

Michael could not move, but Zabbai stepped forward and rested the flat of his great head on Jesus' chest. Jesus raised His arms and placed an open hand on each side of the stallion's neck. Then He looked to the Heavens and whispered words that Michael could not hear.

From the spot where he stood paralyzed, Michael could see an awful wound in Jesus' hand, surrounded by blood that did not fall from it. On Jesus' forehead, drops of blood marked the path of the thorny crown He had worn to His death; and each of His sandal-shod feet was pierced and marked, as were His hands.

Michael fell to his knees and wept as the truth came to him.

"No more sorrow, My brother," Jesus said, turning away from Zabbai, drawing Michael up and embracing him. "Now is the time for joy."

The arms that held Michael were strong, the body solid. And when he looked into the eyes of the One he loved, the bonds of lingering doubt at last fell away.

They sat down then, on the hillside where so much had passed between them, and into the stillness of Michael's heart, Jesus spoke. In the aftermath, Michael would recall no words. But he would know much, and he would understand that the knowing had come to him in silence.

In time a warm wind came and swathed the horseman in its mighty embrace. He was at once alone and utterly surrounded as a thousand angels sang to him and carried him forth beyond all that had been toward all that could be. In moments that might have been days, Michael's shattered heart was fully healed and he was ushered forward into the life that would forevermore be his.

"What happens now, my Brother?" Michael asked, as though there had been no break in their conversation.

"I'll walk this earth for a little longer. My disciples need to see Me and touch Me as you have done—to know and believe that I have risen."

"And then?"

"And then I will return to the Father."

Again, Michael fell silent, fearing that it would be impossible for him to absorb all that he had learned and experienced this day.

"You are right, My brother," Jesus said, responding to Michael's thoughts. "On your own, you can neither accept nor recall all that you have just heard and felt. But the Holy Spirit who came upon you with the wind will feed you gently like a baby child. He will fill your own spirit little by little until it overflows with the graces of faith and love and forgiveness that you'll share because you'll not be able to keep them to yourself."

"I don't want to stay on this earth without You," Michael said.

"You cannot go with Me, My brother. Like the others I leave behind, I need you to stay and testify to what you have seen and to the Truth of the One you have known."

"But how can I face this life without You?"

"You see Me now and you know the safety of My love for you. When you can look no longer upon Me, My Holy Spirit will live within you. He will be your guide and your consoler, and He will show you that I am with you always, until the end of the earth."

Michael knew, then, the grace of peace. And the horseman's aging heart beat with the strength of his youth.

"There is more," Jesus said. "I place upon you a great responsibility. Will you accept this and obey My Father's call?"

"Yes," Michael said. "Yes . . ."

You must know and ever recall, My brother, that I am the Bread of Life," Jesus said. "Those who come to Me shall not hunger. To this you will be My witness. You will carry to your people the Truth of Me and of My Father's merciful love expressed to the world through Me. And from generation to generation, down through the ages, they will pass it on. Even when doubt reigns supreme in the world, My Truth will be held safe in the hearts of your descendants and a multitude of others who choose Me over the world."

Jesus paused and looked to the wild horizon.

"Carry Me now, My brother," He went on, turning back to Michael, looking deeply into the horseman's eyes, "Carry me across the miles and beyond time as you know it. With your heart, dear Michael, I ask you to do this in memory of Me," Jesus said softly.

"And so I must stay." Michael's voice was husky and his eyes bright with tears. "I have never been able to deny You anything, and now You have charged me with a mission from which I cannot turn away . . . not even to follow You."

"By accepting My call, you *will* follow Me," Jesus said. "And you will lead others to do the same."

"But will I ever see You again?"

"Not as you see Me now, walking this earth. But you will sense My presence in every sunrise, feel Me in every breeze, hear the beating of My heart in the pounding of hooves as the horses that I love carry you across this land we have ridden together. When your travels through the earth are over, we will meet again in the hills and the meadows of Heaven where we'll ride like the wind, and face no more parting."

Jesus paused and gazed out across the Sea of Galilee. Then He turned and once more, looked deeply into His brother's eyes. "I must ask one last thing of you . . ."

"Anything," Michael said, "Anything at all . . ."

"There is one more truth that I want you to accept and remember and teach," Jesus said. "Of all that I have told you over the years, this is the most important message." Again He stopped speaking. Holding Michael with His eyes, He seemed to be waiting.

When the horseman settled at last into the stillness, the Lord spoke. "My brother," He said, "know in the very depths of your being that *Love is stronger than death*. Never forget this. Repeat it to yourself over and over, every time your heart yearns toward Me, in moments of silence, in fearful times, and when you are at peace. I write this certainty upon your dear heart . . . *Love is stronger than death* and we will meet again.

With that, Jesus stood up and Michael stood with Him.

"I must go now," Jesus said. "And Zabbai must go with Me. His journey here is over. This part of his mission is completed."

Michael's breath caught in his throat, and, he could not respond. Only when his Brother's heart reached out and filled him once more with peace, could he speak.

"And he could not live without You," Michael said finally. He rested his head for one last time on the neck of the great white stallion. And then he went on, not moving, but looking into his Brother's eyes. "All the years of Zabbai's life, when You were away from us, he waited. If You went without him now, he would know You did not mean to return, and he would die of a broken heart."

"But your own heart will not break again, My brother," Jesus said. "You have the Holy Spirit and My promise of reunion. And you will go on."

Michael nodded his head, unable to speak for the emotion that swept through him. He wrapped his arms around Zabbai's neck and buried his face in the great horse's mane. And one last time the horseman inhaled the scent of his beloved friend. Jesus placed a hand on Michael's shoulder and spoke softly.

"You will see him again, just as you will see Me. Upon Zabbai's back I'll lead a glorious army when I return. And you'll ride beside Me on one of his sons when we come to claim the earth and victory in the final battle."

The brothers embraced once more, neither willing to let the other go. Then finally, Jesus swung up onto Zabbai's back.

Michael rested his hand on the stallion's neck. "I *will* go on," he said, looking up into the face of his Lord, "just as You have called me to do. I'll share You with my people, and they'll share You with the ones who follow. And through us, YOU will go on, living always in the hearts of the greatest horseman."

"Yes," Jesus said, reaching down to touch Michael's face. "You will do this, and more. Now, you must not leave this place just yet. Stay the night. I have for you one more gift. But you must wait here for it to come."

And then, as mysteriously as Jesus had appeared, the Lord and His horse were gone.

Michael watched the departing figures until he could see them no more. He tried to think of days gone by and to look toward days that were yet to come. But only this moment belonged to him, and so he lived it as he had lived no moment ever before. His heart and his mind swelled with love and, to his surprise, with the most complete and absolute joy he had ever known.

He thought he should have felt utter sorrow, but of that emotion, he was thoroughly devoid. As the truth rose within him, he knew that the Holy Spirit, the Paraclete promised by Jesus had taken him over, emptying him of all that he had been, making room for all that he would become.

So he sat down once more on that hill of the last goodbye. And he waited for something he believed would come even though he could not yet see it.

CHAPTER Nineteen

ADRIANNA

Adrianna sat alone in the courtyard of the house where she and her children and their companions had stayed for the past two days. The others were inside talking and planning and conjecturing about what they had heard earlier that morning. But in her grief, Adrianna could think of nothing other than her beloved Michael. She could not even bear the company of her children, both of whom refused to believe that their father had perished.

"No one knows for sure," Neeka said firmly whenever anyone mentioned the death of her father. "I won't believe he's gone until I see and touch his body. I don't feel an emptiness in my heart where a part of him always lives. He cannot be dead."

Nor did Adrianna feel such a void within her. So one more time, she forced herself to recall in detail everything that had happened that terrible day, and since. She saw again her dear husband lying in the street, reaching for Jesus who had fallen beneath His cross. Then she jumped forward to the earthquake, unwilling to torture herself further with the vision of Michael being dragged away by the soldiers, and Jesus being murdered.

She thought about the intensity of the cataclysm that had surely shaken the earth to its very core; and then, in her memory, the events began again to unfold.

❧

When the ground stopped shaking and a grim cloud-cover replaced the total absence of light, Adrianna, Neeka and Matthias fled the horrible hill called Golgotha. The Way of Sorrow was deserted, and as they descended toward the place where they had left the old man and his friend, no one accosted them.

The two had not moved. The old man still drifted in and out of consciousness and his friend still ministered to him. "We must take him to a place where we can better care for him," Adrianna said, bending low to touch the old one's cheek and look into his eyes.

"We know a man who lives in this town," Simon said. "He is a merchant called Joseph who hails from Arimathea. We'll go to him."

"If you are not from here, how do you know this man?" Matthias asked.

"Some years ago he fell ill in Rome. He came to the hospital where we labored with another friend trying to alleviate suffering. We met again on this journey and traveled together for some distance."

"Where is his house?" Adrianna asked.

"Not far from here. I wanted to take my friend to that place," said Simon, "but he would not leave until he knew you were safe. I have been praying that you would return."

"We're here now," Adrianna said. "He's a big man. Can you carry him?"

"Yes." A hint of a smile crossed Simon's face.

"All right, let us go," Adrianna said, standing up.

With one arm beneath Archanus' upper back and the other supporting his legs, Simon gently raised the old man from the ground and began walking. Adrianna and her children followed in silence. They started first down a nearby alley that bisected the Way of Sorrow and wound through the all but empty streets until they arrived at a grand house on the outskirts of the city.

Substantial white pillars supported the roof above a shaded colonnade that surrounded the home. A massive door opened before Simon could ring the bell beside it, and a mature woman, richly clad, stepped out.

"Simon!" she gasped. "Thank God you're safe! What has happened to the Wise Man?"

"My friend was knocked down by a soldier on the Way of Sorrow. He struck his head on a great block of marble."

"Is he alive?" the woman asked.

"Yes, yes," Simon nodded. "But he needs attention."

"Come in, all of you." She stepped back, opening the door as she moved. "Forgive my lack of hospitality. It is a fearful time."

"Forgive us for imposing on you," Adrianna broke in.

"This is no imposition. The good Archanus and his friends saved my husband's life. Anyone who travels with him or with Simon will always be welcome in our home."

"Archanus?" Adrianna said. "Did you call this man Archanus?"

"Yes?" the woman said with a puzzled frown.

Adrianna turned to the big, dark man, "Simon, you spoke of Rome. Was the other friend a Greek physician called Luke?"

"Well . . . yes. Yes he was." Now Simon looked confused.

"Did you know a man called Zadoc, a high official in the Roman army?"

"Yes," Simon said, excitement in his eyes and in his tone. "Zadoc is our dear friend. He would have traveled with us, but he remained in Rome to protect the great physician, Luke."

Adrianna turned to her children. "This is your grandfather," she said, her voice trembling. "This is your father's father." And then she wept. Matthias and Neeka went to their mother and put their arms around her. "We must find your father," she sobbed. "He cannot have missed this reunion. He cannot! The One God could not be so cruel."

"Come with me," said the lady of the house. "Come. Let us lay Archanus down and make him comfortable. Then we will talk about how to find your husband."

The woman led them to a big, shady room where a breeze lifted curtains that hung across the windows. At her bidding, Simon laid Archanus down on a cot piled high with blankets. Matthias and Neeka moved close to their grandfather. But Adrianna stayed behind.

"Michael . . ." the old man whispered, his voice weak as he reached for Matthias.

Simon looked at Matthias and shook his head. The boy took Archanus' outstretched hand. "Yes, my father," he said. "I am here."

"Junia . . ." another weak entreaty.

Simon beckoned Adrianna and she came forward. "I too am here, my husband," she said, kneeling beside Simon. "Now you must rest."

It was a small untruth, worth a great deal in comfort to a man who might be dying. But as it happened, Archanus did not die. Strengthened by the perceived presence of the two people he had loved most in this life, he began to mend. And throughout his friend's recovery, night and day, Simon remained with him, refusing to leave his side even when others were present.

When the old Wise Man fell into a deep sleep after greeting the ones he thought to be his wife and his son, the woman who at last introduced herself as Sarah, led Adrianna, her son and her daughter, into another large room where they were given a much needed and quite sumptuous meal. Near the end of that meal, Sarah's husband returned. He said nothing at first, just went to a chair in the corner of the room, sat down and dropped his head into his hands, ignoring his guests and his wife.

Sarah went to him and placed her hand gently on his back. "I know what has happened," she said. "The servants went out into the streets after the earthquake and returned to me with the news."

The man looked up, his face sad and haggard. "Thanks be to God that this house still stands. There has been random devastation all around us. The curtain in the Temple was torn in half, and all over the city there is damage. The jail beneath the square imploded upon itself and there is a great, gaping cavern where once it was . . ."

Adrianna jumped up. "The jail?" she said, her legs weak, her voice trembling.

The man frowned in consternation.

"Joseph, this is Adrianna." The woman paused. "Adrianna's husband is the son of our dear Archanus."

"Forgive me," he said. "I have just seen buried in my own tomb the greatest One who has ever lived, the One who was our hope. Forgive me . . ."

"But what about the jail?" Matthias had gone to his mother's side and slipped an arm around her. "You said the jail was gone?"

"Yes." Joseph nodded, his face a mirror of pain and sadness.

Gently, Matthias urged his mother to sit back down. Neeka moved closer, and Matthias turned back to Joseph. "Our father may have been in the jail. He was taken away by Roman soldiers when he tried to go to Jesus . . ."

"He is the One!" said Joseph. "Jesus is the One of whom I spoke, our hope. And now His is the Precious Body buried in my tomb."

Neeka looked at her brother. "We have to try to find our father," she said, tears welling up in her eyes and in her throat.

"No," Sarah said. "Night is falling and you must not go out into those streets. There is always danger when the sun is gone. Tonight there will be peril beyond anything we have faced before."

"But we have to find our father . . ." Neeka said again. Now the tears overflowed from her tired eyes and moved silently down her cheeks. She grasped the blue sash that hung around her waist. As she raised it to her face, she saw for the first time the image imprinted upon it—the beautiful, tortured face of her beloved Jesus.

"Oh, my mother," Neeka cried, holding up the sash, "Look, look at His face! Jesus is here! He is with us! He will lead us on. He will take us where we need to go . . ."

Believing that Neeka had gone mad, Adrianna pulled herself together. "My daughter," she said, beckoning the girl to sit down beside her. "We will find your father when it is safe. He is not dead. He is not . . ."

"Please . . . please look," Neeka begged, smoothing out the folds of the cloth, holding it up for all to see. "Please . . ."

Matthias was the first to recognize the truth of his sister's words and the unbearable beauty of the Face on the blue cloth. "HE IS!" was all the young man could say. "HE IS!"

Finally, the others gathered round trying to see what the young people were talking about. One after another, they gasped and fell to their knees as recognition dawned upon them.

"This is the face of our Lord," said Joseph, weeping. "This is the face I saw laid to rest and covered with a burial cloth in my tomb."

A new peace seemed to settle over the household even as everyone spoke at once about the miracle they were seeing.

"We must go now," Neeka said, when the talk began to die down. "We must go and find our father."

"The danger is too great in the darkness which will soon fall," Adrianna repeated Sarah's admonition.

"Our mother is right," said Matthias, turning to Sarah and Joseph. "May we rest here tonight then go in search of our father tomorrow?"

"You will stay with us until all danger has passed," said Sarah, her hand still resting on her husband's shoulder. "Tomorrow, we'll send out one of our men who knows the city. He can ask around and explore, then come back to us with word of your father. Meanwhile, you must rest."

Adrianna and her children shared a comfortable room that night. The following day, heavy storm clouds draped the sky, rumbling their discontent and hiding the sun. The servant who went out to search the city returned with word that all who were in the jail had been crushed beneath the pillars and the bricks of the city square. Only one body had been found and identified as a notoriously evil Roman soldier by the name of Marvelius. No other remains were accessible, nor would there be any effort to recover the bodies of the criminals consigned already to the bowels of the earth.

"My father is not dead," said Neeka when the man was finished presenting his information. "I would know if he had died."

"As would I," said Matthias, looking at his mother. But Adrianna could not speak and she could not be consoled.

The evening passed, and then the night. Adrianna— constantly attended by her children—neither ate nor drank, spoke nor slept. Sometime during the last watch, she stole quietly out of the room where Neeka and Matthias slumbered and went into the courtyard.

Before the dawn, she sensed, rather than saw, the warming of the sky. And something began to stir inside of her.

CHAPTER Twenty

ADRIANNA

As though the world could go on in the usual way, birds sang and people began to move about the house. In the street beyond the courtyard walls there was the sound of activity. And the sun returned.

Soon Matthias appeared. He knelt beside his mother, touched her hand and brushed back a lock of her still beautiful hair. "My mother," he said, "won't you come inside and have something to eat? We'll all need our strength today."

"I think I'll stay out here for a while longer," she said, looking into her son's blue eyes, caressing his cheek, seeing her beloved Michael in his son even more clearly than she had always seen him there.

Just then, they heard a commotion at the front of the house. "Stay here," Matthias said. "Let me be sure there is no danger."

Moments later he returned, "Come inside my mother," he said. "You must hear what they're saying."

In the room where the morning meal was being prepared, Joseph and Sarah stood listening to two men who gestured wildly as they spoke, shaking their heads as if unable to believe their own words.

"Calm down," Joseph said. "Listen to yourselves. Have you gone mad?"

"We saw what we saw," one said.

"The stone was rolled away," said his big companion. "Some women went into the tomb and came out saying there was no body inside."

"Then two men in clothes that gleamed like lightening came and stood beside the women." The small man's words came in a rush.

"Slow down," said Joseph, turning to the big man. "You tell the story."

"The women bowed down with their faces to the ground," he began, "and one of the shining ones said, 'Why do you look for the living among the dead? He is not here; he has risen!'"

"What else did he say?" Now Joseph was excited.

"Something about what the One in the tomb had said when He was still with them."

"The Son of Man must be delivered into the hands of sinful men, be crucified and on the third day be raised again . . ." the small man added. "That is what the shining one said."

"He is risen!" Joseph of Arimathea fell to his knees, clasped his hands, and threw his head back in ecstasy. "He is risen!"

"Come, my husband," Sarah said, touching Joseph's shoulder. "Come, this cannot be true. It cannot . . ."

"But I know it is," said Joseph. "This is what Jesus promised. This is what He told us, time and again. But we did not understand. We were confused by His words but afraid to ask what He meant. We did not understand . . ." He bowed his head and wept and laughed at once. Then he jumped to his feet. "We must go and tell the others. Come with me," he said to the men who had brought the news. "Come, there are many awaiting word of this triumph."

Neeka, who had come into the room while the men were telling their tale, stood in silence, listening. Now she moved to her mother's side. "He told me . . . he told me . . ." Her joy would not be contained. "A long time ago, when He came to us, He told me . . . He said that love is stronger than death. He said no matter what seemed to be, I must never despair. He said that He would rise from the dead to prove His love for us. He promised that I would understand one day." She paused, shaking her head, laughing and crying at once. "And now I do. I understand."

"When did He tell you all this?" Matthias wanted to know.

"When He was last with us," Neeka said, her voice still tremulous with excitement. "I must go to His Mother. I must follow her. She will lead me to Him."

"Why do you want to do this?" Matthias asked. "We don't even know where she is hiding. And we haven't looked for our father."

"No, no, you're right," said Neeka. "We'll find our father. Then I'll go to the Mother of Jesus."

"I don't understand, my daughter," Adrianna said, reaching for Neeka's hand.

"Oh mother, neither do I." Laughing again, Neeka flung her arms around Adrianna's neck. "I don't know why I am called to this. But I am."

"But you don't know this dear woman," Adrianna said, hugging her daughter to her. "How will you find her? And what of the danger you will face if you join her?"

"I will know her," Neeka stepped back and looked into Adrianna's eyes. "And she will know me. He told me, my mother . . . He told me that she would be with us when we could see Him no longer. This is what He meant. Remember, the cross? Remember how He gave her to us and us to her? Remember?"

"Yes, my daughter." Adrianna took Neeka's hands in hers. "I remember it all. I will never forget. But I cannot so easily let you go off into harm's way. I believe that you have been called to something none of us yet understands. Still, I fear the danger to you."

"I will be safe with her," Neeka said, caressing her mother's cheek. "She will not be harmed . . ."

Just then, Simon came into the room. "Archanus is asking for you," he said. "I am sorry to interrupt. But miraculously, he has regained his strength and he wants to go at once in search of his son."

"So he knows who we are?" said Matthias.

"Yes," Simon said. "When he awoke, he told me he had dreamed of Michael and of his mother, Junia. I explained that he had seen the two of you and been confused by your likenesses to those he so loved."

"But are you sure he is strong enough to travel?" Adrianna asked.

"I have known him for the better part of my life, and I have never seen him in more robust spirits or health." Simon looked down, his hand on the back of his neck, his head wagging from side to side. "There is no way to explain this except to see it as the miracle it is. Will you come with us?"

"Of course," Adrianna said. "But where will we begin?"

Before Simon could respond, the bell beside the front door clanged and Sarah went to answer the summons. Moments later she returned. Walking behind her was the old shepherd to whom the horses had been entrusted.

He inclined his white head toward Adrianna. "Greetings," he said. "I have brought the horses for your journey."

"But . . . how did you know?" Adrianna frowned. "How could you have known where to find us, much less that we were to take a journey this day?"

"It was the angel," said the shepherd known as Petras, beginning to smile. "The angel I have not seen since the night of the Star. He came to me once more and told me where I must go, what I must do . . ."

"Thank you!" Matthias stepped forward. "Please forgive our ingratitude. So much has happened—and all at once. Please forgive us for behaving badly."

"No, no," said the shepherd. "It is all right. I know of your fears and the torture that you have been through. But I come with glad tidings. Your father lives! You must ride to the far north, to a hill above the Sea of Galilee. There, he waits for you."

"The angel?" asked Neeka. "Did the angel tell you this?"

"Yes, my child," said Petras. "Now, you must make haste to leave this city while there is confusion amongst the Romans over the resurrection of the Christ. There could still be danger here. Come, the horses are just outside."

Archanus stood in the doorway, a broad smile filling his face and his eyes. To Adrianna he looked far younger than his nearly seventy years. In his eyes, she could see her husband and her son. She went to this man who was the father of her dear Michael and wrapped her arms around him as though they had always known one another, always loved.

"My daughter," Archanus said, holding Adrianna with one amazingly strong arm as he beckoned his grandchildren. Matthias and Neeka came to him and the four held each other in a long embrace. Finally, he released them and stepped back. "Come," he said. "Let us go and find your husband, your father, my son." He looked from one to the other as he spoke.

Just outside the door, two servants stood watch over seven glorious horses, five fitted out for riding, two packed with goods. Adrianna's golden mare nickered a greeting and the others followed suit, snorting, pawing at the ground, bobbing their heads and bumping out their noses. Neeka went to Alexandria, the chestnut mare that had come to her, insistent upon making the journey—so recently and yet, so long ago. Matthias went to a gray stallion and led the horse to Archanus. Then he took Simon to a tall, strong bay.

Suddenly, Adrianna looked around in alarm. "But where is Zabbai?" She turned to Petras.

"He has been gone these three days," said the shepherd. "On the morning of the great earthquake we awoke to find that he was no longer with us."

"Did you look for him?" she demanded. "Weren't you worried? He's not just some sheep." The words were barely out of her mouth before she regretted them. "Oh, I'm so sorry. It's just that . . ."

"It is all right," said Petras. "I understand. I was there, at the Blessing of this stallion's mother. I know who he is. But I did not fear when he had gone. I believe he went to your husband."

"But how?" Adrianna said.

"There are many mysteries that we are not meant to understand, but only to accept," said the old shepherd. "Now, you must go. You cannot delay. Allow the chestnut mare to lead the way. She will know how to escape the city and what paths to follow on the way to your reunion."

Goodbyes were said, and thanks. Sarah and Joseph stood with Petras watching the riders depart. Obeying the instructions she knew came from the angel, Neeka gave Alexandria her head, and sat calmly aboard the horse at the front of the procession. The mare chose a circuitous route through the city streets, and no one argued the wisdom of her course.

❧

The sound of hoof beats in the street below drew Mary to the window. From the upper room where she had spent most of her time since her Son's crucifixion trying to comfort His disciples, she watched the horsemen pass by. In her heart, although she had never met them, she knew this family so dearly loved by her Son. Praying for the safety of these dear ones, the Mother of Jesus turned back to those who—even after the news of His Resurrection—would not be consoled.

❧

In Pilot's palace at the edge of the city where ranking officers in the Roman army met with the Procurator, Phillip looked down from a high window and watched the passage of his friends. Praying for their safety, he turned back to the men in the room who alternately laughed at the Jewish leaders and wondered what chaos they would create in the wake of this development.

"They're mad with envy and malice," said one official.

"As they have been for some time," said another. "But now they must face the awful thing they did. And they must realize that the One called Jesus was indeed their Messiah—and that His words were true."

When Phillip looked out the window again, the street was empty.

⌘

At the edge of the city, the chestnut mare paused for just a moment before choosing a well-worn, northerly path. Then she set the pace, galloping effortlessly, her hooves and those of the horses that followed barely glancing off of the hard packed ground.

Stopping only for water, resting not at all, the companions pressed on. Miraculously, no horse, no human felt exhaustion or hunger on this journey toward reunion. On the morning of their journey's third day, they passed by a high mountain and the chestnut mare turned to the east, making a trail of her own through the foothills. At midday the riders reached a great sea and the mare turned once more to the north, her speed increasing as she followed the shore.

⌘

Before he could see them, Michael sensed their approach. Within himself, he could feel the sound of hoof beats, like distant thunder. And he knew that the gift Jesus had promised would soon arrive. He did not know and he did not care how long he had waited. Though his body was still bruised, his

Hardesty ⟶ 254

broken ribs and hand not yet mended, he rose without pain to stand and watch for that which would soon fill his heart.

Seven horses, traveling in single file, wound across the valley below, like a river running swiftly and with great power. As they came closer, he could see his daughter in the lead, riding the chestnut mare Alexandria—a horse he loved too well for the resemblance she had to her grandmother, Lalaynia. Behind Neeka was Adrianna aboard her golden mare, appearing no older than her daughter. Then came Matthias, riding easy as always, but somehow showing new authority.

But what of the two men who rode behind Matthias? Each sat like a seasoned horseman. And there was something familiar about the one riding the gray. At first, Michael thought of Phillip. But no, this one had more years. And he was not dressed as a soldier.

Soon the riders arrived at the foot of the hill, slowed to a walk and began the gradual climb. Michael wanted to look into the faces of his wife and his daughter as they crested the low rise beneath him, but he could not take his eyes off of the tall old man on the gray horse.

❧

As they neared the summit, Adrianna rode past Neeka and motioned for her children to follow her lead. They moved aside together, so that Archanus could go to his son. Then they waited until Michael's father was there before him and the hope of a lifetime was at last fulfilled in reunion.

In its descent toward day's end, the sun had nearly breached the western horizon, but its light was still strong and sure. In the bold, amber dusk, Archanus stepped down from his horse and walked forward. Into one another's arms the father and the son settled, as nearly forty years of longing melted away. A gust of wind came out of the evening stillness and whirled around them. Particles of dust that sparkled like gold in the waning sun rose on the breeze and spun toward the heavens.

In the fullness of time, the two stepped back and surveyed one another. Then they began to talk and to laugh as though they had known not one moment apart. And love, too long suspended, reawakened in the evening of these lives that could now go on together in hope and gratitude.

After a while, Adrianna joined her husband and his father, then Neeka and Matthias moved together into the circle of their father's arms. Finally, at Archanus' insistence, came Simon.

"My friend," Archanus said looking to Simon and then to the others, "this is my family. This is the reason I have lived." Then, turning his eyes to Michael, he said, "My son, this is Simon, the friend of my heart who has consoled me and saved me and brought me home at last."

And so it was that the hill of the last goodbye became the mountain of the new beginning. From this headwater, the mighty river of life erupted and journeyed on. And the world was changed.

And—by the hand of the One who had lived and died and risen again that it might be so—all things were made new.

"... *And behold a white horse* ..."

Revelation 19:11-16

EPILOGUE
Epilogue

D rops of morning dew glistened on the spring-tender grass. Shining waters gurgled and flashed as they danced over the rocks on their way to the open meadow. Birdsong beckoned the day to begin as it bid the night farewell.

Beside the stream, a young stallion bent to taste the new grass. Beneath the gentle hand of the horseman who loved him, the animal's skin quivered. He raised his head, gave a little snort, and reached around to touch the man whose hand caressed his shoulder and moved down over his leg.

As he had done for all the years of his life, Michael examined the horse he would ride this day, checking for any soreness or injury, assuring himself of the animal's health and soundness. There was peace in the old routine, a sameness that bound the time long gone to the moment, and hinted at the sureness of the days yet to come.

His ministrations over, Michael straightened his back and stood up. He tried to stretch away from the pain that had found its way, of late, into every part of him. Not entirely successful in that effort, the aging horseman rested one hand on the stallion's withers and looked in the direction of the animal's gaze.

In the meadow, mares and their foals were stirring. Soon the young ones, having had their fill of mothers' milk, would begin the dance of the day. They would frolic together, as creatures of their kind had done since the beginning of time. And the horsemen who were their caretakers would speak once more of the resurrection—the blessing of new life—that came to them each spring.

"Corban . . ." Michael said softly, tasting the name on his tongue, inviting its meaning into his heart, allowing his spirit to remember—willing his mind to hope. Beside him now stood the last son of Zabbai, a testament to his sire's greatness, a memorial to what was past, the promise of all that lay ahead.

"Corban . . ." Michael said again, his tone now sure and strong. "Do you know what that means?" he asked as though the horse would answer. The stallion shook his head and snorted and the horseman patted his sleek and shining back.

On this bright morning, the stallion turned three-years-old. Never before had Michael waited so long to give one of his horses a name. He had always known what each animal should be called, even when the young ones were still at the sides of their mothers. But this horse was different. Perfect in every way from the day of his birth, this last-born son of Zabbai promised more, Michael thought, than he dared hope. But as the colt grew and became strong, the truth of him would not hide itself and could not be denied. He was the image of his father, and through him, Zabbai's great heart would go on.

Corban . . . the name had been Adrianna's idea. But it had taken Michael nearly a year to settle into the rightness of it. Now, at last, the horseman knew. Long, long ago, an angel had come to him with the name that must be given to another colt of matchless importance. "This colt you will name Zabbai, the angel had said, "because he is a gift from God."

Corban . . . in this moment, the horseman understood that the angel had come again, this time speaking to him through his dear wife. "His name is Corban," she had said, "because he must be, from us, a gift dedicated to God."

Hebrew words . . . names that would speak for all time of truths that would not fade, of the hope and the purpose for which these highly blessed animals were created by God. From Zabbai to Corban and beyond, to all of those who would come from this taproot bloodline—God's gift of the horse to humankind.

"Corban . . ." Michael whispered once more and the stallion turned to look at him as if in answer to the calling of his name. "You've known all along, haven't you?" Michael laughed, and the stallion bumped out his nose twice then three times, then nickered a soft call to the mares that all turned toward him in response.

❧

It had been three years since Jesus left him. And for the most part, Michael had accepted the rich blessing of peace that his Brother promised. Of course there were moments of uncertainty. Such is the human condition that even those whose faith in God is unshakeable cannot resist when the temptation to doubt themselves comes. But when the demons of distrust assailed Michael—as long as he remembered to ask—help would come. Sometimes the wind of the Spirit would embrace him as it had on the hill of the last goodbye. Often a word or a touch from Adrianna would remind him. In the best of times, he would recall the words of Jesus. Always, the Truth would return eventually and the horseman would know peace once more.

Following their reunion, Michael and his family had returned to Egypt where they remained for only a short while. With Marvelius gone, they could safely go back to the land of their forefathers and to the old routines of the horsemen's gypsy life. They might have remained in the peaceful valley that had sheltered them, but something in Michael's heart stirred him to take the horses and the hope they symbolized out into the greater world where his mission and that of the animals could begin.

Had it not been for his father, Michael might have ignored the gentle call. But Archanus could not stay apart from all that was happening now in the land from which he had fled so long ago. Much that he had hoped for had occurred, and this man of learning could not close life's door on all that he was sure must now transpire.

The old Wise Man knew beyond doubt that Jesus was, indeed, the Messiah, the Christ of God. And he understood that he must join those who had most closely followed the Savior. They would teach him of what Jesus had done, of who He had been. And Archanus would carry this Truth to the scholars, the ones who would surely have the most doubt, the ones with whom only the most erudite and learned could reason. For Archanus, believing that he was capable of this mission was not a matter of pride. It was simply obedience to God's call for him to use well the gifts he had been given.

If his father was going to go back to the Holy Land, Michael must follow. There could be no more parting while either resided on this earth. Michael's heart spoke to him, but it was his will that made him follow. For many of the other horsemen, there was no reason to leave behind the idyllic place they had long called home. There was no better place to raise fine horses, and they had long since found ways to market their good stock throughout the great cities of Egypt.

So it was that Michael and his family, with one-quarter of the herd and several other families, made the long journey back to the grassy steppes and the fertile valleys from whence they had long ago departed. There, they began life anew, embracing the reality that nothing—and everything—had changed, living each day as though it were the first—and the last.

Now, riding through the herd, grateful for the beauty and the promise that surrounded him, Michael prayed. So many of those he held dear had gone to follow a path different than his own. With his heart, he reached out to them across the miles.

As was often the case, Michael thought first of his beautiful daughter. Neeka was now a woman grown for whom there would be only One Love—her Lord, Jesus the Christ. From the moment she met Him, Neeka had been His and His alone. Never had she known the desire for a husband and children of her own. She had only wished to know Jesus, to hold Him deep in her heart, to share Him with the wives and children of others.

As soon as the horsemen arrived on the steppes where they would summer their small herd, Michael's beautiful daughter had announced that she was going in search of Mary, the Mother of Jesus. "I believe she will teach me of Him," Neeka said. "I believe she will lead me, along with all the others who choose to find her Son through her, to the door of His heart and beyond. This is the way for me," she had said, touching her father's cheek and holding him with her eyes. "This will be my life's journey."

Archanus had decided at once to accompany his granddaughter. Simon, of course, would stay with his friend. And Junias insisted that he must go along to protect these travelers, and to learn more of the One they sought. The sadness of this parting was tempered for Michael and for Adrianna because these loved ones would be in close enough proximity that they could go to them now and then. It would not be the same as keeping the family together, as the horsemen of their heritage had always done. But it would be better than losing them altogether. And for this, the husband and wife were grateful.

When he learned of Junias' and Neeka's plans, Michael took his middle son aside and asked him to stay. "For the sake of your mother," he had said, though this wasn't entirely true. Later, he learned that Adrianna had made the same entreaty, "For the sake of your father . . ." she had begged.

Matthias chose to stay with his parents and to one day carry on the mission he understood would be handed to him when his father's and his mother's sojourns on the earth were finished. Even now, this loyal and loving son had taken on most of the responsibility for the horses and the families that remained with them.

On their journey to Jesus, a new bond had been born between Michael and his second son. Now the father knew that just as the heart of Zabbai would go on through Corban, his own heart would live on through Matthias.

Having touched in love and memory the cheeks of his children and his father, Michael's thoughts turned to the others most dear. Old Zadoc, his protector and his friend, had not returned to the army. And from it, each of his sons had also managed to escape.

Of all the sons of Zadoc, Phillip had always been the least likely soldier. From the start, he had hated the brutality of the Romans, joining their forces only to protect the horses he loved. Too soon he came to understand the futility of this effort and began to seek a way to leave the bondage of the service he had mistakenly chosen. But it wasn't until the moment at the foot of the Cross—when he fully understood and proclaimed the Truth that Jesus was, indeed, the Son of God—that Phillip's desire became necessity.

In the aftermath of the Triumph of Resurrection that would change the world forever, Phillip saw in the Mother of Jesus the hope that her Son bequeathed to all of humankind. So it happened that Phillip ran away from the Roman army to join Mary and the disciples whom he would protect and serve for the remainder of his life. And so it was that this son of Zadoc would continue his earthly journey in the company of Junias and Veronica, son and daughter of Michael.

Marcus and Joel fled to distant lands to escape the treacherous Roman army. Adventurers and explorers to the end, each of these sons of Zadoc spent their lives carrying the

Truth of the Messiah to far off lands where fears were conquered and hopes ignited in the Name above all names.

Zadoc lived on for many years at his vineyard outside of Rome. In the absence of his wife and sons, the old soldier's greatest joy came from playing host to his dear friends, especially Archanus who was often accompanied by the great scholars of that time.

⚜

Michael and Adrianna too lived long, full lives, being blessed to know and love the children and grandchildren of Matthias. In the end, they drifted off to sleep one night and together, made their passage into Heaven.

Neither Junias nor Neeka ever returned to the lives they had known with the horses. Neeka, now called Veronica, remained with Mary and the other disciples of Jesus until the Lord called His Mother home. It is not known how long the daughter of Michael lived beyond that parting, but it is said that she did great good on this earth before her time here was over.

For his part, Junias followed the one whom many called the Great Lion of God—Paul, the passionate evangelist who traveled far and wide preaching and teaching the Gospel of Christ. It is believed that when Paul was martyred for his faith, Junias journeyed on with Luke, the physician and author who remained the dear friend of Archanus.

Archanus himself lived well beyond his hundredth year, becoming in the latter part of his life the sage to whom the great minds from Greece and Rome came to learn of the mystery that was the Christ.

Like his grandfather, Matthias became a teacher. Though he never left the horses, he gave to the world the gift of remembrance. As the first keeper of the Legend, Matthias carried out well this great commission. To his eldest son, Matthias bequeathed the responsibility of keeping alive this Legend about which you have just learned.

Just as Jesus promised, the Zabbai effect changed the entire course of civilization. Even now, the blood of Zabbai lives on, and in every modern breed of horse, his genetic gifts can be found. Two thousand years beyond the life of the great horse, the seeker just might be blessed with a glimpse of who Zabbai was—and of what the Creator conferred upon the world through him.

Now, thanks to the horsemen who have handed down this tale from generation to generation, you know the origin of the everlasting alliance between horses and humans. And from this day forward—through you—THE *Legend* will continue its endless journey . . .

And the hoof beats of horses,

with the heartbeats of humankind,

will remain the rhythm of the ages

beneath the passage of time.

A Note from the Author

Well, Dear Reader,

I hope you've enjoyed The Legend, a tale it has been my honor and my joy to tell.

Since I was a little girl, riding horses beside my Dad along the riverbeds of Southern California and through the mountains to the north, I've believed that these great and powerful creatures must have been a gift to us from a loving God. As I grew up and the exigencies of life turned me away from the faith of my childhood, I fell more in love with the horses, trusting them when I felt I could trust no human. For too long, I thought it was my destiny to journey through life alone. I didn't know, then, that I remained always in our Lord's loving arms—especially in the company of the horses He sent to be my guardian angels.

I was four years old when my Dad put me on my first horse. I was eleven when I started earning money for cleaning stalls and grooming rent horses at the Monterey Saddle Club on the San Gabriel River, south and east of Los Angeles. In the years that followed, I rode wild horses through auctions, exercised race horses, gave riding lessons to people of all ages and abilities, started colts under saddle, and even tried my hand at training show horses.

I've never met a horse I didn't care about and I've never run across a breed I didn't respect for its unique abilities. I was drawn to Arabians for their beauty and even more for their special affinity for people. As it happened, our Lord granted me a life's career that has kept me forever involved with these kind and beautiful creatures. Nonetheless, I still love them all.

When I was just eighteen, my first son was born and a new love affair began. Ultimately, my three beloved children, sons Rob and Russ and their sister, Riyan, did a grand job of raising me. Still, I remained true to the horses. For many years I've written magazine stories about horses and breeders and trainers. Over the course of time, I've had the honor of managing some of the world's most important Arabian horse ranches, as well as the careers of a few of that breed's greatest, most influential stallions.

In 1986, I began writing my first novel. Ten years and five major edits later I thought that book was complete. I may have been mistaken, however, since it remains to this day (2009) unpublished. Maybe someday.

In 1988, I married the soul mate sent to me by our Lord. A few years later, along came The Legend, a tale I know in my heart I was given the responsibility to tell.

As I look back over my own life's journey, it is impossible for me to disregard the role played by the horse. I am as certain as sunrise and sunset that God sent His horse to carry me ever toward Him across all the difficult days and nights and miles and years—most of all when I was least inclined to travel in His direction.

It is my fondest hope that some of you who read The Legend will allow yourselves to ride with the wind aboard God's beloved horse on your own journeys toward the Heaven He offers. May you hear His call and know His merciful love. And may we meet one day, you and I, somewhere along the road—if not in this life, perhaps we'll share a story and a memory as we ride the hills of Heaven.

With you in the arms of our Lord,

Jo

J.L. Hardesty

About the Author

J. L. (Jo) Hardesty has had a special bond with horses since she was a small child. In the *Lost Legend Trilogy*, she shares her passion for this gift from God, and speaks to the origin of the mystical bond between the horse and humankind.

Jo had her first child when she was 18, and became a grandmother at 35. The mother of three and grandmother of seven has been—since 1988—very happily married to Jim Lauter, her partner in life and love and creativity.

Today Jo and Jim live on a mountain twenty miles north of Steamboat Springs, Colorado. They share their little piece of paradise with grandson, Cole Pollard: a young Australian Shepherd, *Danny Boy* (pictured above with Jo), two giant house cats, *Smokey Lonesome* and *Tubby Tommy Tiger Toes Tucker*, a family of raccoons; and all manner of other wild creatures including deer, elk, foxes, porcupines and a variety of lovely birds. Soon *One Last Time*, a buckskin Half-Arabian colt that Jo's daughter, Riyan, presented to her on Mother's Day, 2007, will join the menagerie on the mountain.

Currently, Jo has three new books in the works, two in the final stages and one just beginning, as the adventure of life goes on.

One last note . . .

Through the horse, God gave to mankind a very special form of liberty, a bequest that altered not only the face of the earth, but the heart and spirit of its human inhabitants as well.

Still, for some reason, the Age of the Horse, and the miraculous changes brought about during this season in time, are most often overlooked. Largely thanks to humankind's partnership with the horse, territories were discovered, explored and civilized. Lands were cultivated and wars were won. In truth, the impact of this gallant creature on world progress is far more monumental than the changes brought about by any of the more heralded historic periods such as the Bronze Age, the Iron Age, and the Industrial Age.

The Lost Legend Trilogy aims to correct this injustice by revealing the origin of the mystical bond between horses and humans—and by reminding the world at large that without the horse, civilization as we know it today would quite simply not exist.

We hope you enjoyed this final installment of
The Lost Legend Trilogy

DAWN
Across the Mountains

Author signed editions of:

Book One
THE LOST LEGEND OF THE FIRST CHRISTMAS

Book Two
ESCAPE TO EGYPT

and Book Three
DAWN ACROSS THE MOUNTAINS
are available via our web site:
www.horselegend.com

For Christmas, 2009,
we plan to release a limited
casebound collector's edition of
Dawn Across the Mountains
You may reserve your copy
at *www.horselegend.com*

J-FORCE PUBLISHING COMPANY

51029 Smith Creek Road
Steamboat Springs, Colorado 80477
E-mail: info@horselegend.com